A Daddy Thing

A Daddy Thing

Kendra Reeves

www.urbanbooks.net

Urban Books, LLC
300 Farmingdale Road, N.Y.-Route 109
Farmingdale, NY 11735

ISBN 13: 978-1-64556-516-1
EBOOK ISBN: 978-1-64556-517-8

First Trade Paperback Printing August 2023
Printed in the United States of America

10 9 8 7 6 5 4 3 2 1

Distributed by Kensington Publishing Corp.
Submit Orders to:
Customer Service
400 Hahn Road
Westminster, MD 21157-4627
Phone: 1-800-733-3000
Fax: 1-800-659-2436

Chapter One

Rachel

After pulling in the drive, I put the car in park and looked up at the house. My head dropped back against the headrest. Closing my eyes, I let out a deep sigh. For a moment, I let the dread I felt run through my body.

Shaking it off, I opened my eyes and thought about how hard it was going to be to get out of the car, go up the walk, take the three steps leading to the porch, and open the door that led into the house I loved. For the first time since we bought this house, I didn't want to be home.

Another deep sigh escaped me. I didn't know how I was going to tell him. Hell, I didn't even know how it happened. Errick was determined to stick to our five-year plan, and my news would definitely be a shock.

I thought about our relationship. When we met three years ago, I never thought we would end up together.

On a beautiful summer day, the afternoon sun was streaming down from a clear blue sky with fat white clouds that drifted lazily across it. A light breeze blew, keeping the heat from being unbearable. Cane Ridge Park was busy with baseball and softball games, family and church picnics. Children's laughter rang out across the park from the play areas.

My best friend, Rosie, and I were at one of the ball fields watching Rosie's boyfriend play softball. The game was close, and we got into the spirit of the game, cheering, yelling, and rooting for his team to win.

After his team won the game, Pete met Rosie on the edge of the field, pulling her into his arms. Lifting her from her feet, he swung her around, making her squeal in delight. Another man stopped close to me, watching Pete and Rosie with a smile on his face. I looked him over while he was watching the couple. He was tall, taller than my five foot nine inches, with a smooth deep brown complexion, close-cut hair that was full of waves, a broad nose, big, dark eyes, and full lips that made naughty thoughts come to my mind.

Glancing away with a smirk on my lips, I couldn't help but find this man sexy. He had broad shoulders and a tapered waist, and he was slightly bowlegged. His jersey clung to his chest where he sweat, his pants showing off his thick thighs to perfection. This man oozed sex appeal.

"Hi, I'm Errick Stewart," he introduced himself, extending his hand.

"My bad, man." Pete laughed, setting Rosie back on her feet. "This is my girl, Rosie, and her friend Rachel."

"Rachel Hendricks." I slipped my hand into his. I admired the way his muscles flexed just under all that smooth brown skin. Errick smiled at me, a beautiful white flash of perfect teeth I was sure an orthodontist was able to vacation from.

Pete and the rest of the team wanted to celebrate, so they went to their favorite sports bar for a few beers. Rosie talked me into joining them. Errick and I talked for a little while over beers before I said my good-byes, leaving them to their celebration.

After our initial introduction, I was surprised when Errick called me one afternoon about a week later.

"I hope you don't mind. I got your number from Pete's girl. I was calling to invite you to dinner."

Oh, I did mind, and I would get with Rosie about giving my number out later. "That's very sweet of you, but I don't think so," *I declined politely.*

"What about lunch?" *he offered.*

"Really, I appreciate the offer, but I don't think that would be a good idea."

Errick turned out to be very persistent. He began calling me almost every evening. Our conversations started out as polite inquiries into each other's day. A little while later we became more comfortable with each other. We really got to know one another. I enjoyed talking to him, he made me laugh, and we talked about everything. Errick would often invite me to lunch, dinner, or drinks, but I always turned him down politely. I would be his friend, but I was looking for more than I thought he was willing to give.

Everything changed when Pete threw a birthday party for Rosie.

I arrived at the Inspiration of Life Center at Fountain Square, where the party was being held. Red balloons swayed in the breeze, indicating that this was the right place. All guests were asked to wear red—Rosie's favorite color. I wore a long red halter sundress that cupped my full breasts, brushed over my full hips, and hit me just below the ankle. My hair was pulled away from my face with a silver barrette. A silver cuff on my right upper arm and large silver hoops were my only jewelry other than the silver toe ring on my right middle toe.

Rosie spotted me as soon as I came in. She met me at the door, hugging me.

"You look great, girl," *I told her.*

"Uh-uh, chica. You trying to steal all my thunder up in here," *Rosie exclaimed, looking me over.* "You are hot in that red dress!"

"Yes, you are."

I heard the voice just before I felt the touch on my shoulder. Turning, I found Errick standing there smiling at me. That smile.

He handed Rosie a silver-wrapped package with a silver and red bow. "Hello, Rosie. Happy birthday."

"Hi." I blushed under his scrutinizing gaze.

From that moment on, Errick swept me off my feet. He kept me at his side all day, a perfect gentleman. We danced together, ate together, and talked late into the night, oblivious of the others at the party.

He didn't give up after we said our good-byes that night. He began to pursue me with a vengeance. We saw each other almost daily for two months before we finally slept together. He'd planned the perfect seduction. He prepared dinner at his place, and we ate while watching a movie. Plenty of laughs and wine later, we ended up on the floor in front of his fireplace. It was some of the best sex of my life.

The next day, the nerves turned me into a mess. Errick could sense something was wrong with me. I finally told him about my uncertainty about our relationship. He assured me that he wanted to be with me, only me. We became exclusive that day. To prove his point, he took me to meet his family that weekend. His family was wonderful from the beginning. They embraced me, making me feel like a part of their family. I was glad that they accepted me. I'd lost my mother two years before, and being an only child, I felt somewhat like an orphan after she was gone.

We dated for eighteen months, and things were good between us. That Thanksgiving we were having dinner at his parents' place. It was freezing cold outside, but the house was cozy. Errick's brother, Jamie, and his sister, Aimee, were there with their significant others, and the house felt full. We were in front of the television, full and satisfied, watching one of the football games. Errick sat on the floor, his back resting against my legs. I was absently running my hands over his shoulders when he looked up at me. My heart skipped when he smiled at me. I loved this man.

"Will you marry me?"

My hand stopped in mid-stroke. I didn't think I'd heard him correctly. "What?"

"Marry me?" Errick turned to face me.

This time there was no hesitation. "Yes!" I exclaimed.

That was one of the happiest times of my life. Six months after he proposed, we bought our first home and mapped out our five-year plan.

Opening my eyes, I looked at the house again. For the last four months, things had been going well. I taught at Blakemore Academy, where I'd been for the past five years. Errick had the opportunity for a promotion, a step in the right direction for his career. I didn't want to stress him out any more than he already was.

Another sigh escaped me. I shook my head, the dread hitting me again as I thought about Errick's anger after we had this conversation. *Mommy, I wish you were here with me. Tell me what to do.* Sending up a little prayer as I opened the door, I took a deep breath and tried to prepare myself for what was coming.

Chapter Two

Errick

Standing at the kitchen counter, I reached for the cold bottle of beer sitting on the counter beside me. Taking a long swallow, I glanced out the window overlooking the backyard. Three trees provided plenty of shade in the summer, but they would soon turn gold, red, and orange and lose their leaves once fall settled in. I could hear the neighbors' children laughing as they played behind the six-foot privacy fence that separated our yards.

After another long drink from the beer, I set it back down on the counter, then returned to chopping onions and bell peppers. I tossed them into the heated wok with freshly chopped garlic and sliced mushrooms, letting them sauté before I added thinly sliced beef. Stirring absently, I thought about my day.

After our usual Wednesday morning staff meeting, I was called in to the boss's office. I didn't know what to expect when the VP of design and development joined us. Taking the seat offered to me, I listened as they congratulated him on a job well done on the latest project. I was totally unprepared when they offered me a position in the Phoenix office—assistant director of design and development. This position and promotion were a dream come true and totally ahead of schedule of our five-year plan. This promotion included a substantial raise, a signing bonus, and moving expenses. At my hesitation, they threw in a company car to sweeten the deal. They urged me to think about it and let them know immediately as they wanted me in the Phoenix office within the month to learn the ropes from the retiring assistant director. After promising to think it over, I returned to my office, shut the door, and did a little victory dance. This promotion could mean everything to my career. Rachel and I could move to Phoenix, I could learn the ropes, Rachel could get a teaching position, and everything was falling into place.

I left the office early, too excited to get any work done. I decided to surprise Rachel with dinner tonight. I would fix her favorites: beef stir-fry with sides and a cherry cheesecake for dessert. After stops at the grocery store and Rachel's favorite bakery, I headed home floating on a cloud. If all stayed on track, Rachel and I would be married next year and start a family three years later. That would give her time to build up her teaching tenure, and she was talking about returning to school to get her master's degree. This would be the perfect opportunity for her to do that.

Dinner was finished, and I was just setting everything on the table in warming bowls when I heard Rachel come in the front door. The sound of her heels on the hardwood floor was loud in the silence of the house. Something about the sound sent a shiver of uneasiness through me. I shook it off and smiled as she came into sight from the hallway. The love I felt every time I saw her filled my heart. This woman was made for me. She was beautiful to me, full-figured and curvy with smooth caramel skin and bright root beer eyes surrounded by long lashes, with dark brown hair that she wore long, hanging in curls to where it brushed the bottom of her shoulder blades. She moved toward me with a sensual grace she didn't even seem to know she had.

"Hey, baby." I pulled her into my arms. I loved the way she felt against me. Her body fit mine perfectly. I kissed her until both our hearts were racing. I wanted to forget dinner and take her straight upstairs, but she broke the kiss and looked in my eyes.

She laughed. "Wow! What did I do to deserve that homecoming?" Her cheeks flushed. I loved it when she was bashful with me.

Letting her go, I laughed with her. I watched her as she went to the sink to wash her hands. Then she moved to the table, lifting lids to peek at what I'd made. She looked at me when she saw beef stir-fry, fried rice, spring rolls, and crab wontons.

"What is all this?" she asked.

"Sit down." I pulled out her chair for her.

Once she was settled, I crossed the room to the refrigerator to get her a glass of her favorite white wine and grab a beer for myself. I was going to wait until after we ate before telling her my news. After settling across from her at the table, I served us both. We made small talk while we ate. It was in the middle of me telling her my mom called and invited us to dinner later in the week that I realized she wasn't eating. She was just pushing the food around on her plate. She hadn't touched her wine either.

"Is everything okay with you?" I asked. I could tell she was bothered by something. It was obvious in her nervous gestures and bland answers.

When she looked up at me from her plate, she had tears swimming in her eyes. My heart lurched in my chest.

"What is it? What's wrong?" I was out of my seat and at her side, kneeling beside her. The tears she was trying to contain spilled over the rim of her eyes and down her cheeks. "What is it? Babe . . ." Fear unfurled in my stomach as I watched her try to get herself together. I wanted to scream because crazy thoughts were running through my head. Was she sick? Dying? Was someone else dying? *What the hell?*

"I'm pregnant."

Time stood still and sped up at the same time. I felt dizzy, like I was on the Whip ride at the fair, where you're slung back and forth as you spin in a circle. *Pregnant?* She was pregnant. I wondered if I'd heard her correctly, but looking at her face, I knew I had. My mind raced at the thought. This couldn't be happening. Not right now. I was just starting to move up in my career. The promotion? How could we relocate to Phoenix and start a family at the same time?

"What did you say?" I had to ask although I already knew.

"I'm pregnant." She looked at me, eyes wet and begging for comfort and understanding.

I knew she wanted me to reassure her, to tell her that it was okay, but I couldn't. I couldn't tell her that everything was going to work out. I was stunned just hearing her say the words.

"I found out this afternoon. That's why I was late coming in."

I stood and began to pace across the expanse of the large kitchen. Moving back and forth across the cream-colored tiles, I was restless. My mind was clicking in a hundred different directions at once. I was trying to think things through as I said, "How did this happen?"

The sharp look she gave me as she rolled her eyes let me know she was hurt and upset by my reaction.

"You know what I mean. We've been so careful. We're not ready for this. We can't have children right now. We're supposed to be concentrating on our careers. We want to travel. You want to go back to school. Having a baby will mess all that up." I was sure that she would agree with me. Having a baby would not be the best thing for us right now.

"It doesn't have to," Rachel said in a small voice, looking at me with sad eyes.

Turning to her, I said, "You're right. It doesn't have to."

Rachel smiled the first real smile she'd given me since our kiss when she came in.

"How far along are you?"

"Nine weeks."

I began to pace again, thinking. Nine weeks didn't give us much time. "Okay, tomorrow morning we'll call your doctor's office and make an appointment."

"Oh, Errick!" She smiled harder. "I've already made an appointment." She sounded relieved. This time her smile touched her red-rimmed, glassy eyes as she gazed at me.

"Okay, good." I nodded. "What day? I'll request a couple of days off so I can be here with you. I don't want you overdoing anything while you're recuperating."

When Rachel's gaze met mine this time, her eyes flashed with hurt and anger. "Recuperating?"

"Yes." I was confused by her expression. "I thought you made an appointment to take care of it." As soon as the words left my mouth and registered in her brain, I could see her expression change. We were definitely not thinking the same thing at all.

Jumping to her feet, she got in my face. Her anger was so intense I could feel the heat coming off of her. "Take care of it? You cannot be serious! Errick, this is our child!"

"No." I was trying to keep my cool because her screaming at me was pissing me off. We had our arguments, but we tried to keep them low-key even when we were at our most heated. "This is a mistake. An inconvenience. We can't have a baby right now, you know that. We agreed to wait. Having a baby right now will mess up all our plans."

Anger began to pump through me, making my stomach churn. Surely Rachel knew that having a baby right now was the wrong thing to do. We had so much more to accomplish. We both loved our careers and worked to get as far as we had. A baby would only be in the way. After all, we were only a year into our five-year plan, a plan we'd mapped out together.

"Errick." Her face and demeanor softened. She looked at me with big, sad eyes. Her voice was low. "You can't mean that. We are not some young, inexperienced kids who messed up. We were careful, but it still happened. We are going to have a baby."

Shaking my head, I refused to be swayed. Rachel had to understand I would not agree to this. Everything we'd been working toward would be thrown away by having a baby right now. "Rachel, how can you do this? You agreed we would wait. That it would be in our best interest not to have children yet! Now you want to change it up, change the game plan. How is that fair to me? To us? You know how strongly I feel about this. The only thing to do is take care of it."

Her tears had no effect on me, and the anger I felt was fanning higher and higher. The more she tried to talk to me, reason with me, and get me to see things her way, the more I knew that her having an abortion was the best thing for the both of us. There was no way I was ready to be a father.

Dinner, dessert, the promotion and move to Phoenix, a night of making love and making plans were all forgotten while we spent the better part of the night arguing about the situation.

"Errick, please don't be like this. We've talked about this. We talked about having children when we get married. Let's just go get married. We don't have to have a wedding. Your parents will understand once we explain it to them. This doesn't have to be the end of the world."

"But it is the end of the world!" I shouted at her. I was so tired of her trying to convince me to see this her way. "It's the end of the world as we know it. We were planning to go to Barbados for Christmas, remember? How are you going to travel if you're pregnant? What about the trip to Paris you want to take?"

"Oh, please! Pregnant women travel every day! If the doctor says it's okay, there shouldn't be any problems."

"What about all the other things we planned to do? Where does a child fit into all that?" I was pacing again because I felt like if I stood still, I would explode.

Rachel approached me. She stepped in front of me, stopping my back-and-forth movement. Laying a hand on my chest, she looked at me. "A baby can fit in any-where if you make the room. You know that. What is it that's scaring you?"

I stood there as anger coursed through my veins. I moved away from her because I was so mad I didn't want her close to me. "I am not scared. I just want you to live up to the agreement we made. We said we weren't going to have children soon. You were okay with that. Now you want to turn our lives upside down?"

I kept turning it over and over in my mind. Rachel had gotten pregnant even though we both agreed to wait. Now she was trying her best to talk me into something I couldn't agree with. How could she hurt me like this? I loved this woman. I loved her, but how could I trust her after this? It was totally selfish of her not to take what I wanted into consideration. It wasn't like she was asking for my input on the situation. She seemed to have made up her mind.

Needing to get away, to think about all this, I turned and left her standing in the middle of the kitchen floor. I needed to put some space between us so I could calm down. I went upstairs, and I threw a few things in a bag and stormed out of the house. Rachel watched as I walked out, but neither of us said anything. I got into my truck and sat behind the wheel for a long time. *How could she do this to us?*

I exhaled. Maybe if I gave her some time to realize I was right, she would do the right thing. Maybe then I could get over feeling like she betrayed me. Because that was what it felt like—betrayal. It was a few days of discomfort, and our lives could go back to normal. I didn't understand what was wrong with waiting until we were ready to be parents emotionally and financially.

I started the car and backed out of the drive, not looking back. This was supposed to be one of the best days of my career so far, and Rachel had ruined it. I just wanted to come home, surprise her with my news, love her, and plan our future after the move. Now Rachel was trying to foist an unwanted pregnancy on me. Shaking my head as the radio started playing her favorite Jaheim song, I knew I could forgive her for trying to convince me to agree to this, but she would have to take care of the situation. When she decided to do that, I would be there for her. Right now, I was going to give her time to realize I wasn't going to be giving in to this.

Chapter Three

Rachel

Shutting off the engine, I laid my head against the headrest, closed my eyes, and exhaled. The beautiful day outside did not match my mood. The sun was shining brightly, and fat white clouds drifted lazily across the sky. A lingering summer kept the temperature in the high seventies, and kids in the neighborhood were taking advantage of the weather, playing basketball, skating and riding bikes in the cul-de-sac down the street from our place. For a moment, I wished for the blissful ignorance of childhood again. Instead, I now dreaded coming home to the strained silences that were a part of my daily life.

Gone were the content evenings Errick and I shared. He was a totally different person since I'd told him about the baby, someone I didn't know or like very much. When he stormed out of the house the night I told him I was pregnant, he stayed gone for two days. I was frantic with worry that in his anger something had happened to him. The worry turned to sadness, then anger that he would treat me like this. When he returned to the house, there was nothing but stress. He referred to the baby as "it" or "the problem," not even acknowledging that it was his child I was carrying.

The last two weeks were terrible with Errick and me. I was nauseated, my ankles were starting to swell, and

I was tired all the time. I wanted nothing more than to sleep twelve hours a day, but every time Errick saw me napping, he had something slick to say. I practically begged Errick to come to my first doctor's appointment with me, but he wouldn't even answer. He just looked at me as if I were crazy and he was disgusted by my presence. He never said a word to me unless it was to tell me to "take care of the problem."

The day of my appointment, I was a nervous wreck. Dr. John Charles was a pleasant older man with dark mocha skin and salt-and-pepper hair. He'd put me right at ease as soon as he walked in the room. He talked to me as he did his examination, and I cried hard, heaving sobs when I heard my baby's heartbeat for the first time.

I wanted to share with Errick what the doctor said and how it felt to hear the baby's heartbeat, but he walked through the house totally ignoring me. It hurt that he wouldn't take part in this with me. I never thought things between us would be like this.

Rosie could tell something was wrong, but I couldn't talk to her right now. How the hell was I going to tell her that Errick didn't want our child?

It took a minute before I realized that Errick's car wasn't in his usual parking spot. I was actually glad he wasn't home. I could breathe for a little while.

Climbing from the car, I waved at Mrs. Stanley, our next-door neighbor. She was a friendly elderly woman who kept up with everyone on our block.

"Busy day for you, huh?" she called from where she was weeding in her flowerbed.

"Yes, ma'am." I smiled and waved at her once again as I headed up the walk. It had been a busy day. My students were rowdy, ready for the weekend. I was too.

Making my way up the walk, I looked up at the house that I loved. The wide front porch had a swing I'd found and refurbished, and several ferns hanging along the eaves surrounded the porch. They swayed in the light breeze. Tulips would bloom along the edges of the walk in the spring. I planted new colors every fall. The house was small and cozy.

At least it had been.

Opening the heavy front door, I dropped my keys in the bowl on the table beside it. I kicked off my shoes at the bottom of the staircase that ran up the left side of the foyer. Heading toward the kitchen I got a strange, empty feeling. My steps faltered as I moved by the living room. I took a step back and then stopped, my mouth dropping open.

The living room was empty. My heart slammed in my chest. The TV and all the movies and CDs were gone from the small shelf beside where the stereo system used to sit. Pictures were gone from the wall. The sofa and chair, along with the end tables, were gone.

Rushing through the rest of the first floor, I was stunned to see that the rooms were empty except for the small, round table in the eat-in kitchen.

I raced back through the house, then stopped long enough to step into my shoes, grab my purse and keys, and get out of the house. We'd been robbed. I couldn't believe it. I pulled my phone from my purse and hit the number for Errick. I almost tripped over my own feet when I got the message that the number had been disconnected. Stopping in my tracks, I knew this couldn't be right.

I redialed. "C'mon, Errick. C'mon," I muttered under my breath, breath that was knocked out of me when the same message saying that the number was disconnected played in my ear again.

I dialed his office number, but a generic voicemail picked up, telling me to press zero if I needed immediate assistance. Following directions, I did just that. When a pleasant voice on the other end answered, I asked to speak with Errick. I was informed that Errick no longer worked in that office, but I was offered the person who'd replaced him.

"What? That can't be possible," I exclaimed, but it was more to myself than in response to her.

"I'm sorry, ma'am, but Mr. Martin has transferred. I can take a message if you'd like. He will be picking up messages as he travels."

"Oh. No, no," I said, declining her offer. My heart was racing so fast I was beginning to feel faint. "Thank you for your help." I hung up with a trembling hand.

Transferred? What the hell did that mean? Tears burned my eyes and throat as I dialed Anna's cell phone.

"Are you all right, young lady?"

I jumped, startled. Looking up, I saw Mrs. Stanley heading my way. "No. I think we've been robbed." I tried to keep the tears under control. Anna's voicemail picked up in my ear, so I hung up. My heart pounded as Mrs. Stanley continued.

"Now I've been home all day taking care of my plants before the bad weather comes. It's coming, too. I can feel it in my bones. My 'thritis is acting up. Anyway," she said, shaking her head, mentally getting herself back on track, I guessed, "I saw your young man and a couple of other fellas loading up a truck. I thought maybe you were moving."

"What?" This could not be happening. I was feeling lightheaded with all the emotions running through me. Was this real?

My cell phone rang. It was Anna calling me back. Trying not to panic, I answered. "Anna, have you heard from Errick? I came home and most of our furniture is missing. I thought maybe we'd been robbed, but Mrs.

Stanley said she saw Errick and some guys packing up a truck."

I felt the hysteria settling in, but I couldn't do anything to contain it. I felt out of control. My heart was twisting painfully in my chest. The truth was slowly squeezing past the confusion and denial. Errick left me. I knew it. I was certain of it. I was pregnant with his child, and he'd left me.

"Rachel," Anna snapped in my ear, bringing me back from the brink of snapping, "take a breath. I haven't heard from Errick. Paul and I will be there shortly. Did you call him?"

"I tried," I managed to whisper past the lump that settled in my throat.

"You stay with Mrs. Stanley until we get there. We are on our way," Anna said before disconnecting the call.

I tried not to cry but didn't succeed. Tears rolled down my face as I tried to wrap my heart around what my mind was telling me. Mrs. Stanley took my arm, leading me to her front porch. She sat me there, then headed inside. My mind and heart were racing uncontrollably. *Did Errick do this? Did he really do this to me?*

Mrs. Stanley returned with a glass of sweet tea. She handed it to me, urging me to take a sip. I took several small sips, then set the glass on the small table between the chairs we were sitting in.

Shortly Anna's Honda CRV pulled up in the drive behind my car. She and Paul jumped out, Anna rushing over to where I sat on Mrs. Stanley's porch. When Anna wrapped her arms around me, I lost it. I cried hard, heavy sobs that racked my chest and made me take deep, heaving breaths.

Once I got myself under control, I filled Anna in on what I found when I had gone into the house. Mrs. Stanley told them about seeing Errick and the guys packing up the truck. Paul insisted that they stay on the porch while he go into the house. Once he was gone, Anna looked at me, running a hand over my hair. She was an attractive older woman with a smooth chocolate complexion. Laugh lines around her mouth and eyes gave her a jovial look all the time. She wore a short salt-and-pepper bob and was thin and athletic. She had accepted me as one of her own from the moment she met me. She mothered all her children's friends, cousins, nieces, and nephews.

Paul returned shortly. He thanked Mrs. Stanley for taking care of me, then led Anna and me back to the house. His face when we entered was stern and remote. His demeanor revealed his time in the military. Sitting me and Anna down on a couple of chairs he'd brought out of the kitchen, he handed me a note.

"I found this stuck to the bedroom door." He handed it to me. He paced in front of us.

I couldn't help but smile as I watched him. His demeanor was gruff, but I knew he was a teddy bear. Then I had to wipe tears from my eyes as his resemblance to Errick hit me. They had the same build, the same stance, the same deep, intense eyes.

Looking down at the note in my hands, I opened it with trembling fingers. I had to read it twice, and it still didn't sink in. I couldn't believe it. My worst fear was confirmed. I shook my head in denial. This couldn't be happening. *Errick cannot treat me like this. He wouldn't do this to me, to us.* Bolting to my feet, I raced down the hall to the bathroom, barely making it before getting violently ill.

"What is it? Paul? What did the note say?" I heard Anna ask.

As I came down the hall, my legs were shaking. I saw the fear on Anna's face. Settling back on the chair I'd left, I saw Paul's jaw flex as it clenched when he looked at me. For the first time since I'd known him, I was scared of

Paul. Was he angry at me? Did he blame me for Errick leaving? What was he thinking?

"The note says that our son left Rachel. It said that she broke her promise and that he couldn't trust her anymore," he informed her once he stopped pacing.

"Promise? What promise?" Anna asked, looking from Paul to me and back again before settling on me. "What promise is he talking about, honey?"

Wiping a tear from my eye, I guessed I took too long to answer because Anna bent and picked up the note, reading it for herself.

"What does this mean?" Anna looked at me again.

Looking from Anna to Paul, I didn't know if I should tell them. I didn't want to hurt either of them. This would devastate them. They looked so concerned. Taking a deep breath, I said, "It means that I'm pregnant."

Anna and Paul exchanged a glance. Anna gasped, her hand covering her mouth as tears filled her eyes. I saw hurt in her eyes, and I felt so bad that I had done this to her. To both of them.

"Errick and I have been fighting about it since I found out. He wanted me to get rid of it, and I refused. He told me that I had agreed to our five-year plan and that I was now going back on it."

Breaking down, I cried. The tears felt like they were coming from my soul. I cried for my unborn baby. I cried for the heartbreak I was feeling. I cried for the relationship I thought meant so much to both of us. I cried knowing that the man I loved and trusted walked away from me because I was pregnant with his child.

"I knew he was angry. I did, but I didn't think he would ever do anything like this. I thought he would get used to the idea of a baby. I guess he didn't love me enough."

Anna wrapped an arm around my shoulders, pulling me against her as she rocked me. I cried more. I missed my mother so much right now. I needed her. I needed her to help me through this pain. Unfortunately, my mother was in heaven, so I was thankful for Anna. Letting the tears flow, I rocked along with Anna, thankful for the comfort she was offering. I was just glad to be able to lean on someone for a while. This situation had been weighing on me so heavily I was exhausted. Finally, my tears tapered off, and I rose, wiping my face with the ball of tissues I clutched in my hand.

"How far along are you?" Paul asked.

"Almost three months," I told him.

Smiling like he'd won the lottery, he reached down, took my hands, and pulled me to my feet. He wrapped me in his arms and squeezed me in a hug. I held on to him for a long time. I needed that. When he released me, he looked in my eyes.

"Don't you worry about anything. Anna and I will be here for you. You are not alone. Thank you so much. Thank you for this gift."

Anna rose to join us, turning it into a group hug. The tears in her eyes and the smile on her face let me know she was happy with the news. "Thank you."

I tried to smile but failed miserably. I appreciated them for being there, but right at that moment, I felt alone. Very alone.

Chapter Four

Errick

I handed my boy David a cold beer before collapsing in the chair. The past two days had been long and hard. After packing all the stuff from the house before Rachel came home and then driving from Nashville to Phoenix, I was exhausted. The condo the company's Realtor found me was nice. It was a spacious two-bedroom, two-bath place with a gym, pool, and tennis courts on the property. I noticed a lot of BMWs, Volvos, and Lexus, and even a pretty yellow Porsche as we pulled in and were unloading the truck. I liked the feel of the place. The Realtor assured me that this area was mostly young up-and-coming businesspeople or couples who had no children. That was a definite bonus for me. With all that I was dealing with with Rachel, I was tired of hearing about children.

The thought of Rachel stayed with me. By now I knew she'd discovered I moved out. I was sure she and my parents had tried to reach me, but when I decided to end things with Rachel, I changed my number and instructed the receptionist and my assistant that I would only accept messages and not give out my information. Rachel made a choice, so I had to make mine. It hurt me though. As much as I didn't want to admit it because I was angry with her, I missed Rachel. Our relationship to this point was everything that I wanted it to be, but her insistence on not dealing with the problem was something I couldn't get over.

"Thanks, man," David said after taking a long swallow of his beer. He brought me from my thoughts. "I needed that. I'm beat."

I nodded in agreement. I was worn out, and I was glad I didn't have to report to work for another week so I could get unpacked and settled and familiarize myself with my new town. I was excited about the job and the new area. I really needed to get away from Nashville. Everything there was turning to shit, so this promotion was right on time.

David and I sat in companionable silence, an Arizona Diamondbacks baseball game on TV. I was glad he'd made the trip with me. David Chow and I had been friends since we were in elementary school. He was a handsome man with mixed heritage that gave him the best of both worlds—his mother's black heritage gave him his soft pecan complexion, his height, and his strong, chiseled jaw, while his father's Chinese heritage gave him his soft black hair and his slanted eyes. Each of our parents adopted the other like we were their own children. I was glad for David's company on the drive. It gave me a reason not to dwell on the situation with Rachel.

In the three weeks since Rachel had announced her pregnancy, I had tried over and over to convince her that the right thing to do was get rid of the problem. She refused to listen, so I stopped talking. When I packed up the house to move, I knew Rachel would be devastated. I never even told her about the promotion. She was going on and on about the problem, so I figured, why tell her? It was obvious she didn't want to be with me. She had given me no choice in the matter, and I refused to be held hostage because she wouldn't do what needed to be done.

Sadness hit me in a wave. Even as angry as I was with Rachel, the thought of her made my heart twist. Her laughter, her sparkling eyes, our late-night conversations and lovemaking, waking up beside her, I was missing all of that. I didn't think Rachel had any idea how much I loved her or what she'd put me through, and unfortunately, she didn't seem to care. I was heartbroken when I walked away from our house for the last time.

As if sensing my thoughts, David said, "Have you talked to Rachel?"

"No. Rachel and I have nothing else to say to each other. She's made it more than obvious that what I want doesn't matter, so it's best that things end now."

I tried keeping the anger from my voice, but I knew I hadn't succeeded. I heard it myself. I knew once I told David that Rachel and I were having problems and I was leaving, he wouldn't like how I was handling the situation, but he didn't ride me about it. My small circle knew that we were having problems, but they never expected me to up and move and leave Rachel in Nashville. He'd asked me a few times what had happened that would have me acting so rashly, but I just told him that Rachel felt like our five-year plan wasn't working for her. I still couldn't believe she'd fought so strongly about this. It would have been so easy to take care of it, and we could have gone back to our lives.

"Don't you think you should at least check on her? I mean, I know after three years it can't be easy just to walk away. I see the way you look when you think no one is paying attention."

"I never said it was easy. I love Rachel, but I can't trust her anymore."

"What happened between you guys? I mean, you just packed up without saying anything to her. You guys seemed so happy together. What happened in three weeks' time to make you leave her like this?"

Shaking my head, I reached for my iPad beside me on the end table. Logging in to my email, I replied, "Man, I really don't want to talk about it. Let's just say that Rachel's life plan became more important than our life plan."

David didn't press, and I was relieved. That was my boy. He knew if I wanted to talk about it, I would.

Turning my attention back to my email, I saw that I had several unread. Being unavailable while traveling and distancing myself from everyone without explanation over the last few weeks, I had really been out of touch. I hadn't talked to my parents much since Rachel had dropped her news on me because I knew what they would say. I had three emails from my father, five from my mother, one from my grandmother, and several from Rachel.

Opening the first from my dad, I wasn't surprised by it at all.

Son, your mother and I have talked with Rachel. We know that she is pregnant with your baby. Is this really the way you want to handle this? She is having your baby. How could you leave her because she's pregnant by you? Do you think she's been unfaithful? You need to face up to your responsibilities. Don't do something you will regret in the long run. Please contact your mother or me. Let us know that you're okay. But most of all, please call Rachel. She is sick with worry over you, and this situation isn't good for her or the baby. I love you.

I was going to have to call my parents soon. I didn't like to make them worry, but I just couldn't do it now. I wasn't ready to hear the lecture I knew was coming. I took a deep breath and exhaled, steeling myself to read the first email from Rachel.

Errick, I know that you're upset about the baby, but I cannot believe that you would walk away like I did this to hurt you. I didn't get pregnant alone, and I can't believe you blame me. You moved all our furniture out of the house. You walked away from me without even understanding what I'm going through or fighting for me. Did you ever really love me? Somehow, with it being so easy for you to walk away, I don't think so.

Those words hurt my heart. I had tried to get Rachel to understand. She wanted me to see things her way, but she never tried to see things my way. For her to question my love for her also hurt. She wouldn't believe how hard it was for me to walk away, but it was best for both of us. If she kept the baby and forced me to be a father, I would end up resenting her. If she got rid of it, she would resent me.

I opened the next and read on.

I know that you've transferred out of the Nashville office. I also know that this is over between us. I won't bother you again. I just wish you had been man enough to talk to me. I loved you with everything I have, Errick.

Tears burned my eyes, and guilt started to weigh me down. I shook it off. I couldn't let it make me regret my decision. I was tired of all the long, drawn-out arguments. If she had just taken care of the problem, we could be moving on with our lives.

I logged off my email. I sat back in my seat, closing my eyes and pinching the bridge of my nose between my fingertips. Looking over at David, I suggested we order something in for dinner. Finding several takeout menus in the kitchen, we decided on Mexican. I ordered, then let David know that I was gonna hit the shower while we waited for the food to be delivered.

Chapter Five

Rachel

I stepped into the empty house, closed the door, and leaned against it for a few minutes. I was exhausted, and coming home didn't make it any better. There were so many memories in this place that, no matter where I looked, I could see and hear Errick.

Heading down the hall to the kitchen, I decided to make something quick to eat because all I wanted to do was sleep for the next twelve hours. I tossed my bag on one of the chairs at the kitchen table, washed my hands, then looked into the fridge to see what I had. I needed to go to the store, but I settled for chicken and egg noodles since the baby had my stomach all messed up.

The past week had been an adjustment. I was still in shock with the way things happened, but I was slowly getting better. I cried almost nonstop the first three days, but then I had to get myself together and get back to work. Being with the kids kept me busy and kept me from dwelling on my situation. I was thankful for all the little smiles they gave me, even when they had me at my most frustrated.

The sound of my front door opening when I was sliding the chicken in the oven startled me.

"Rachel," Rosie yelled.

I washed my hands and then wiped them on a dish towel as I walked down the hall. I was surprised to find two men carrying two chairs into the living room. "What is this?"

Rosie walked over and hugged me. She rubbed my stomach even though there was nothing to rub. She waved in the direction of where the men placed the chairs like it was no big deal. "I saw these when I was shopping for a client."

"Rosie." I shook my head. She knew I would have told her no if she told me about this beforehand.

"Rachel," she mocked.

She thanked the guys and closed the door behind them when they left. She came into the kitchen where I was back at the stove. She washed her hands, then went to the fridge. She pulled out the bottle of wine she kept there and poured herself a glass.

I'd finally told her what happened between me and Errick two days after he left. I'd needed time to let it sink in a little. She was furious and had immediately come to be with me. I'd told her about the baby, and she was excited and making plans before I could get the words out of my mouth good. That was why I loved my best friend—she was always there for me.

She took a seat at the table when she finished.

"I talked to David today," I told her when I turned to face her. I leaned against the counter.

"What did he say?"

"He wouldn't tell me where Errick is, but he's okay. He sounded like he really hated to be in the middle. I don't want to put him there. I just can't understand how all this happened so fast." I wiped a few tears that ran down my face. I was tired of crying, but I couldn't seem to help it.

Rosie had a frown on her face as she watched me. "You can't upset yourself like this. I know it hurts, and I can't imagine how you feel, but this baby is a blessing, and you're going to be the best mom."

That made me feel better. I was nervous about being a mom, but I was determined to do my best.

While I finished dinner, I told her about my conversation with David. He didn't seem to know what was going on between Errick and me, and I wasn't going to tell him. I just wanted to know what he'd been told. It broke my heart all over again when he told me that Errick wouldn't even mention what happened other than to tell him I decided I didn't want to be with him. For him to make this my fault made me angry and hurt me at the same time.

When dinner was finished, I fixed our plates, and we sat in the kitchen talking about the future and what we needed to do to get ready for the baby. For the first time in days, I felt a little bit of excitement about my upcoming bundle. I had to focus on the good and leave Errick in my past. Easier said than done.

Chapter Six

Errick

I thanked the delivery guy, then closed the door and went to the kitchen to fix a plate. I was settling in my place and the office. I'd been in Phoenix a little over two weeks and was learning my way around the city. I had met a few colleagues and was introduced to my team that week. Everyone was cool, and they seemed to work well together.

I plated the Chinese food, grabbed a beer, then went to the living room to eat in front of the TV. I had just taken my first bite when my phone rang.

"What's up, man?" I answered my brother.

"Calling to check on you. How's it going?"

"Everything is good."

We talked a little longer before Jamie turned the conversation back to me.

"How you holding up, bruh, for real?"

"Man, I'm good."

"Nah, for real. How are you? I know this whole situation is crazy, so you can't be good," Jamie pressed. My brother loved Rachel.

"This shit is crazy," I admitted. I could talk to him about anything.

I told him about everything I'd been dealing with. I admitted that as angry as I was at Rachel, I missed her.

Being away from her felt like there was a hole in my life. Even though the decision to leave was right for me, I still had to deal with the pain of the end of my relationship.

I thought of her often at the oddest times. I still had the urge to call her, talk to her about my day, share news about the new position, make plans for the future. I'd shed plenty of tears over Rachel.

"Damn, bruh. I hate this for both of you. I don't know about anyone else, but I thought y'all were perfect for each other."

"Yeah, me too, and we see how that shit went."

We talked a few minutes longer before Jamie told me he'd pulled up at our parents'. With a promise to stay in touch, we ended the call.

I got up to take my empty plate into the kitchen. Talking to my brother made me feel homesick. I missed my parents, sister, the rest of my family, friends, and the life I had in Nashville. This was going to be hard, but I had to move on with my life.

Chapter Seven

Errick

Waking with a start, I lay in the darkness, my heart racing, as I listened to the quiet of the apartment around me intently, wondering what woke me. I didn't hear anything in the silence of my condo, but something brought me out of a dead sleep. Scrubbing a hand across my face, I rolled over on my side and exhaled.

I thought moving to Phoenix and accepting this promotion was going to make my life better. In a lot of ways it would, but leaving Rachel was harder than I ever imagined. I missed her every day. It had only been a couple of weeks since I'd been here. I tried my best not to think about her. I knew it was going to take some time to get over her and her betrayal, but the memory of her was with me always. Remembering the conversation with my mom a few days after I moved to Phoenix, I could hear the anger, disappointment, and sadness dripping from her words once I told her I'd moved.

"Hey, Ma, it's me," I greeted her when she answered the phone.

"Oh, Errick, thank God. Your father and I have been worried sick about you."

Feeling guilty when I heard the panic in her voice, I wanted her to know I was good. "No need to worry about me. I'm fine."

I could hear my father's voice in the background, but I couldn't hear the words he was saying.

"We're your parents. It's our job to worry. Son, what's going on? We've been frantic. Your brother and sister haven't heard from you. Rachel's sick with worry. You know the stress isn't good for her."

I knew at that moment they knew Rachel was pregnant. I felt cold, and my heart was hard. When would someone understand that it was hard for me too? I loved Rachel, and she hurt me. I was harsher than I intended when I said, "I don't know why Rachel would be worried about me. She made her choice."

"Made her choice? Son, she feels like she didn't have a choice." My mother's voice was sharp.

"I didn't have a choice either. We agreed we would wait, and Rachel made the decision to go back on that agreement. She made that decision by herself, so she can deal with it by herself."

"This is your child we're talking about. Your child. Why would you walk away from your own flesh and blood? I thought you loved Rachel."

"I do love Rachel, but how can I be with her when I can't trust her anymore? She lied to me, she hurt me, and she selfishly chose what she wanted over what we wanted. Look, Ma, Rachel will be okay."

"Have you at least talked to her?"

"No, I was going to tell her about my transfer the night she sprang her baby news on me but after all the arguing I never got around to it."

"Are you telling me you left that girl, moved across the country, and you haven't talked to her?"

Tired of the same old argument, I took a deep breath, then exhaled. "Ma, Rachel and I talked before I left. I begged her to reconsider. I love her, but she knows I'm not ready to be a dad. I don't want to be a dad right now. Rachel obviously didn't want to be with me, or she would have taken care of the problem. Look, I've gotta go. Love to everyone."

That was the last time I'd talked to either of my parents.

I thought about the dream I had that same night after the phone call to my mother. Rachel and I were on the beach sipping some kind of fruity concoction she'd made. We were kicked back in lounge chairs watching the waves roll in with the tide. A balmy breeze tickled the loose strands of hair framing Rachel's face. I took a sip of my drink but spit it out when Rachel's stomach began to protrude. It grew larger and larger until it looked like it was going to pop. My eyes widened with terror as I watched her stomach split open. Scorpions rushed from her belly in a never-ending flow, crawling over one another, their scaly bodies making a sickening clicking sound as they collided against each other. They raced toward me, their tails and claws lethal. I tried to move but was stuck in place, my heart racing to a sickening crescendo in my chest. The worst part of it was that Rachel kept sitting there sipping her drink like nothing was happening.

Was that what woke me? Was that dream haunting me? I didn't remember having it again, but maybe it was telling me that I was scared of this pregnancy, that I was scared of being a dad.

I climbed from the bed and went to the bathroom to splash water on my face. Looking at my reflection in the mirror, I saw the same man I saw every day, but for some reason I didn't feel like me right now.

After going back to bed, I lay there for a long time, trying to quiet my mind. Thoughts of Rachel bombarded me. Memories of our lives together flooded me—the day we met after our softball game at Cane Ridge Park, Rosie's birthday party where I took a chance on her, the day I proposed after Thanksgiving dinner at my parents' house, the day we moved into our home, any day waking up with her, going to sleep with her.

Dammit. I loved that woman. Three years of my life had come to an end.

I had to let Rachel go and move forward with my life.

Chapter Eight

Rachel

The bell over the door chimed when I walked in. I was meeting Anna to do some shopping for the house. I was taking my time to furnish the place since I didn't know if I wanted to stay there. My name and Errick's were on the deed, but since he disappeared, I hadn't thought about what to do with the place. I loved the house, but being there now made me sad. Memories were in every inch of the house, and right now the pain was fresh.

A saleswoman came over to assist, but I let her know I was just browsing and would tell her if I needed help. I took my time looking around the showroom. When the bell rang again, I glanced over to see Anna rushing through the door.

"Hello, sweetheart." She kissed my cheek and gave me a quick rub on my belly even though there was still nothing there.

Anna asked about the pregnancy as we looked around. I always got excited talking about it with her. It didn't matter what Errick thought about the baby. His parents were ecstatic to be grandparents. I shared how I'd been feeling, the morning sickness, the tiredness, but the excitement and fear of thinking about becoming a mom.

"Have you heard from Errick?"

Tears immediately filled my eyes, and the lump in my throat felt like it was going to choke me. I tried to brush the tears away, but there were too many.

"Oh, honey," Anna said sympathetically as she dug some tissues from her bag and pressed them into my hand.

My heart ached as I tried to get my tears under control. The sadness overwhelmed me at times. It had been a couple of weeks since Errick left, and the pain was still fresh. I tried to go about my life like it wasn't a big deal and I was strong, but I was struggling.

"I'm okay," I assured her as I wiped my face.

Once my emotions were under control, I told Anna I hadn't heard from her son and didn't expect to ever hear from him again. I was trying to get used to life without him, but it was hard.

"I don't know what's going on with my son. I know he loves you, but this baby situation seems to have set him off. I hate that this is even happening."

I had to remember that Anna didn't mean to hurt my feelings, because when she said that about the "baby situation" setting him off, it made me angry. *The only thing that set him off was selfishness.*

"I hate it too, but Errick did this to us. I know he's your son, but this is his baby. I didn't do this on my own." The anger in my voice was obvious.

Sensing that she'd upset me, she quickly apologized. "Oh, sweetie, I didn't mean anything. I just hate that both of you are hurting so bad."

That pissed me off even more. I didn't want to hear about Errick hurting when he'd caused all this. I hoped he was suffering because I definitely was.

Instead of reacting, I kept my mouth shut and moved off to browse some more. Anna must have realized I didn't want to talk about Errick anymore, because she changed the subject to my upcoming doctor's visit.

We spent the next hour shopping for the house. I found a sofa I liked, so I decided to get it along with two floor lamps. When I went to pay, the salesperson told me that it had already been taken care of. I was confused until Anna told me that she and Paul wanted to help, so they were taking care of this.

The tears returned with a vengeance. I tried to insist on paying, but Anna refused to hear it. I was thankful for my small tribe. Anna and Paul were truly a blessing in my life.

When we left the shop, I hugged the woman who should have been my mother-in-law, and I thanked her profusely. Even though I had savings and could handle replacing the things Errick took, I was grateful for those who wanted to help me. I promised to call Anna that evening, then left to finish my errands.

Chapter Nine

Rachel

Sitting in the chilly exam room, dressed only in the thin gown the nurse gave me, I waited for the doctor. Nervous and sad, I wished that I had invited Rosie or Anna to come with me because, now that I was here, I really didn't want to do this alone. I wanted to share this moment with someone—someone who would be excited with me.

Errick had been on my mind all day as I waited for the time for my appointment. It had been three weeks since Errick disappeared from my life. I emailed him for the last time when I found out he'd transferred out of the Nashville office. I hadn't tried to contact him since. Even if Errick returned tomorrow, I didn't think I could get over the way he had treated me. Never would I have imagined he would have behaved this way toward me. I never expected him to react the way he did. He seemed to forget his part in all this.

There was a knock on the door. Dr. Charles stuck his head in before coming in with his nurse. "Hello, mommy, how are you doing today?"

"I'm good. Still trying to pick up my appetite, but I think that's just stress," I told him honestly.

He checked my chart. "Well, whatever is stressing you out, you need to let it go."

Easier said than done. I lay back on the table while the doctor went about my checkup. Staring up at the ceiling, I wished again that Errick were here with me. Hearing the baby's heartbeat was a big deal.

"Are you ready?" the nurse asked once the doctor was done.

I nodded, and tears pooled in my eyes as soon as I heard the rapid-fire heartbeat of my baby. My own heart jumped when I heard it. Tears blurred my eyes. "Is everything okay?"

"The heartbeat is strong. Everything sounds the way it's supposed to," he assured me.

As I listened to the life force of my child, my heart filled with love and joy. Regardless of the bullshit with Errick, I knew having this baby was what I was supposed to do. I loved this baby already, regardless of my hesitation and indecision at first. I realized I loved this baby from the moment I found out I was pregnant.

Dressing a short time later, I tried to put aside all the anger and hurt that suddenly filled me. Errick really broke my heart. I still couldn't understand how, if he loved me so much, he could hurt me like this. There was always sadness when I thought about Errick and all that he was missing with this situation. What could our lives have been like if he had stepped up and been the man I needed?

Deciding to concentrate on the blessing this baby was, I wouldn't regret or pine over what could have been anymore. Errick made his decision, and I had to get over it. Anna and Paul had been a huge help already, helping me to furnish the house again. Although I would only accept a few necessary items, I appreciated they would want to do that for me. Anna assured me they would be here for me every step of the way. Regardless of how Errick felt about this pregnancy, Anna and Paul were thrilled. I also had Rosie. She was so excited to be an auntie that I couldn't help but be excited with her. All she could talk about was being *Tia* Rosie and spoiling her little princess. I laughed at her and asked what she was going to do if it was a boy. She just waved it off and told me she knew she was getting a girl.

Laying a hand over my belly, I felt a love I'd never felt before. "It's going to be okay, baby. You are loved."

I was searching in my bag for my car keys, not paying attention, when I collided with someone. A strong arm reached out to steady me, and I looked up into a man's beautiful green-blue eyes.

"Excuse me," I apologized. I couldn't help noticing how attractive he was. He had to be at least six foot two, with black hair and a tan. He was a sexy mixed man. I flashed him an absent smile when he released me. I stopped at the scheduling desk to make my next appointment and chatted with the lady behind the counter. When we finished, I wished her a good day, then left the office.

The weather was cold with fall settling in with a vengeance. I pulled my sweater closer around me as I crossed the parking lot to my car. I slid behind the steering wheel and pulled the copies of the ultrasound out of my bag. I smiled as I tried to decipher which way was up. For the first time since I'd told Errick about the baby, I was actually at peace about my decision. *I am going to have a baby.*

Storm clouds crossed the sky. Turning leaves on the trees twirled and fluttered as the October wind blew. By the time I got home, sprinkles dotted the windshield. I hurried up the walk and unlocked and opened the door.

I hated coming home to this empty house. I missed the nights we made dinner together, or watched movies cuddled up on the sofa, or when I sat at the dining room table grading papers while he moved around the kitchen. Shaking off the melancholy, I told myself I had to remember the baby would be here soon and the house would again be filled with love.

Upstairs, I kicked off my clothes right outside my bathroom door and walked across the spacious room to turn on the water. I needed a long, hot shower.

I dried off after I finished, then pulled on a long T-shirt before I went back downstairs. Settled on the sofa, I took papers from my satchel to go over. About an hour later, I stretched out on the new overstuffed sofa that had been delivered the day after my shopping trip with Anna, and I dozed off without eating dinner—again.

Chapter Ten

Saxon

Glancing at my watch, I hurried down the quiet hall, passing several empty rooms. I was late. I knew she was going to be upset with me. Finally, I found room 12. I stepped through the door and stopped, watching for a moment undetected. My niece Samarra and her teacher were sitting on a small square carpet as Samarra sounded out words from the book they were reading. The teacher's head was bent, her hair obscuring her face as her finger moved along the words. I stood there for a few moments before they realized they weren't alone. When Samarra saw me, she let out a little squeal, jumped to her feet, and ran across the room, throwing her arms around my legs.

"Uncle Sax. Uncle Sax," she sang in her little girl voice. "I was reading, Uncle Sax. Did you hear me?"

I beamed down at my niece. She was a beautiful, pudgy little girl with long brown pigtails and a gapped smile from where she lost her front tooth the week before. I loved this kid. "I did hear you. You were great. Maybe you'll read to me later?"

Samarra nodded, her eyes sparkling with excitement and happiness.

I looked up from Samarra to see the teacher stand. She placed the book they'd been reading back on the shelf, then turned to me. I was surprised when I recognized the woman who had bumped into me at the office a week or two before. Those same pretty brown eyes that held a hint of sadness touched me again as we made eye contact. I'd thought of her at odd times over the last couple of weeks. Something about this woman tugged at me. The attraction I felt for her was instant and intense. I didn't understand where it came from, but it ran deep. I'd watched her that day while she went to the scheduling desk, and I wondered who she'd been in the office to see. I was tempted to check, but one of my nurses stopped me before I had the chance. After that I got busy and forgot to ask.

"Hi, I'm Miss Hendricks." She extended her hand with a smile on her face.

A shiver ran over my skin when she spoke in her low, sultry, smoky voice. I noticed the smile she wore didn't quite touch her eyes, and I wondered about that. "Saxon Carmichael. I'm Samarra's uncle. I'm sorry I'm late."

As I took her hand, another shiver skated over me like an electric tingle. A closer look at the woman in front of me had me trying to figure out what it was about this woman that pulled at me. Why was she in my thoughts? She wasn't the type of woman I was usually attracted to. She was plus-sized, but I had to admit she carried her weight well. Normally I dated petite or willowy women, but she was sexy in just a denim dress.

A tug at my pants leg brought my attention back to my niece. She was all wide-eyed innocence when she asked, "Uncle Sax, can Miss Hendricks come to pizza with us?"

Miss Hendricks and I exchanged a glance. *I would very much like Miss Hendricks to join us for pizza.* Instead, I said, "I'm sure Miss Hendricks has other things to do tonight. She has been with you and the other kids all day. She may need to get home to her family."

I dropped in that last bit to see how she responded, but Samarra was a persistent 5-year-old. With a cute pout on her lips, she turned to her teacher and gave her puppy dog eyes. "Miss Hendricks, can you go to pizza with us? There won't be any kids but me."

Miss Hendricks smiled at Samarra. When she did that, the sadness left her eyes but only briefly. "Thank you for inviting me, but I'm having dinner with my friend."

Male friend? I wondered. There was a knock at the door. The three of us turned to see a beautiful Hispanic woman standing there. Relief hit me. I didn't know why. I didn't know this woman, but for some reason I wanted her to be unattached.

Taking Samarra's hand before she could get wound up, I tugged her toward the door. "Come on, Pooh. Let's leave Miss Hendricks with her friend. Say good night."

Tears swam in Samarra's eyes as she turned to her teacher, giving her a hug.

Miss Hendricks lifted the little girl's face. She smiled at her. "I will see you in the morning. I may even have a treat for the class, okay?"

Her tears dried up immediately, and Samarra smiled brightly. "Good night, Miss Hendricks. See you in the morning."

I was surprised by the way Samarra clung to her teacher. She was a friendly child, but there seemed to be something about Miss Hendricks that Samarra was attached to.

After a pizza dinner at Chuck E. Cheese and a bath, Samarra and I settled on the sofa with a bowl of ice cream to share. That was where Moira, my sister, found us when she and her husband came in a while later. Samarra fell asleep halfway through the movie. She tried to snuggle closer to me when Daniel picked her up. I smiled as she wrapped her arms around her dad's neck and immediately settled back into a deep sleep.

"You spoil her," Moira said as she moved toward the kitchen.

I followed her and took a seat on one of the barstools at the island while she put on the pot for tea. "That's what I'm supposed to do."

Moira and I were almost identical. Only ten months apart in age, we both had silky sandy brown hair, pale complexions, and hazel eyes that were a fierce green when we were angry and a soft honey when we were pleased. I was six two, and Moira was five eleven. You knew immediately that we were related.

"How was she for you?"

"Perfect, of course. Although I thought we were going to have a little trouble at school. I was a little late picking her up, and she invited the teacher to eat pizza with us. She almost threw a fit when Miss Hendricks declined."

Moira laughed. Moving efficiently around the kitchen, she took the kettle off the stove, grabbed mugs from the cabinet, poured the tea with milk we both loved, then slid me a mug. "That doesn't surprise me. She loves Miss Hendricks. Samarra talks about her all the time. I'm surprised she hasn't talked your ear off about her."

"Really? What do you know about her?" I asked, my curiosity piqued.

"Miss Hendricks? Nothing really, but to hear my child talk about her, she's almost an angel."

"I saw her a few weeks ago at the office. She must be a patient." I faded for a minute as I thought about the times I'd seen Miss Hendricks, not to mention all the times she'd popped up in my thoughts since then. "She seems sad."

"Little brother has a crush, huh?" Moira's teasing snapped me from my thoughts.

Trying to downplay my interest, I waved Moira off. "I just noticed it about her."

Moira scoffed but she didn't say anything else.

Daniel joined us in the kitchen. He kissed Moira's temple as he reached for his mug of tea. I loved their relationship. I often hoped that I would find a love like theirs one day. It wasn't that they didn't have problems, everyone does, but I liked the way they loved each other so effortlessly. Leaning against the counter, Daniel stood as close to Moira as he could. "Did you tell him?"

I looked back and forth between them. "What?"

"I'm pregnant."

I jumped to my feet and rushed around the island, pulling my sister into a hug. I was so happy for her. I gave Daniel a brotherly hug. "Congratulations."

I left them a little while later after we talked about the pregnancy and I gave my promise to not mention it to our parents until she told them. Driving home, I thought about the happiness and contentment in my sister's eyes as we talked. I wanted her to always have that.

Pulling up in front of my house, I stared up at it through the rain. It was a two-story Tudor-style home I'd bought earlier this year. The house was dark because I kept forgetting to turn on a light. The walkway thankfully was illuminated by solar lights. I got out of the car and jogged up the walkway and let myself in.

I hated coming home to an empty house. My footsteps were loud on the hardwood floor. The house was cold and impersonal because I refused to decorate it. I wanted my wife to make our house a home. I wanted kids, light and laughter, homework, carpools, ballet, and baseball. I wanted someone to share my life with.

An image of Miss Hendricks invaded my mind. Was she married? Did she have a boyfriend? Was she sitting at home wishing for a good man in her life? Something about that woman lingered as I went about my evening, getting ready for the next day.

Chapter Eleven

Rachel

As I stepped into the warmth of the restaurant, a shiver ran down my spine. The weather had changed drastically since I left home this morning, and I was glad I had a sweater in the car because I was cold. A hostess smiled at me as I stepped up to her station.

"Rodriguez," I said, giving her Rosie's last name.

"This way." She led me down an aisle. Rosie sat at a table in front of one of the large windows that ran the length of the room.

"Miss Hendricks?"

My footsteps slowed as I looked at the man who sat at a table to my left. It took me only a moment to recognize Samarra's sexy uncle. He was sitting with a very attractive woman. I smiled at them. "Hello, Mr. Carmichael."

"Please, it's Saxon."

The way Saxon was smiling at me sent shivers of heat across my belly. His hazel eyes were warm and sexy in his pale, handsome face. "I'm Rachel."

I noticed the way the woman looked from Saxon to me, the way she was scrutinizing me before she cleared her throat. I smiled at her, nodding.

Saxon glanced at her. "Oh, this is my friend Natalie. Natalie, Ms. Hendricks is Samarra's teacher."

The woman gave me a brittle smile. The sneer on her lips was almost comical. I saw the disdain in her icy eyes, but I was unfazed. "Well, it was nice to see you." I waved the hostess away, indicating that I would seat myself. "I hope you have a good evening. Tell Samarra I said hello."

"How is Samarra doing in school?" His question stopped me from walking away.

Studying his pretty eyes, I told him, "She's doing well. She's one of my star pupils."

"Good. I'll be sure to tell her parents you said that. I know Samarra loves you."

I flushed. Saxon's hazel gaze fixed on me so intently that butterfly wings brushed against my belly. I didn't know why he was looking at me like that or why his gaze made me feel warm all over.

"Thank you. That's nice to hear. Five- and six-year-olds don't really make you feel appreciated." Glancing at Rosie sitting at the table, I gave her a little wave. "Well, there's my friend. It was good seeing you. You both have a good night."

I gave Saxon's companion a big smile. She didn't remove the bland expression from her face. I chuckled as I threw my hand up and walked away.

"Good night, Rachel." Saxon's voice was raspy.

I made my way to Rosie and removed my sweater as I sat across from her. Glancing out the window, I saw the moon riding low in the sky. Stars and constellations were bright and easy to identify.

The waiter appeared at the table. "May I take your order?"

I ordered lemonade. Rosie ordered tea. Once we were alone, she looked at me with a sly smile. "Who is that?" She looked across the room to where Saxon sat with his friend. She didn't bother trying to be discreet.

"Stop that." I laughed, playfully slapping her hand across the table. "He's the uncle of a student. I met him a couple weeks ago when he picked her up from school."

"Hmm . . ." Rosie ignored me completely while still studying Saxon. "I remember him. He was there the night I picked you up to go to Talon for dinner."

"Right. Now stop staring. I don't think his date is going to appreciate it. She didn't seem too friendly."

Rosie turned her gaze to me. "I would guess not with the way he was looking at you."

Waving her off, I shook my head. She was always trying to hook me up with someone. "Girl, please. That man was not looking at me any kind of way. Anyway, are you still coming with me to the doctor tomorrow?"

This would be my third appointment, and Rosie had been asking if she could come. She was excited about hearing the baby's heartbeat. I had to admit it felt good to share this with someone.

"Of course. Are you kidding? I can't wait to hear my niece's heartbeat."

I laughed at her. "How do you know it's a girl?"

"I just know. How have you been feeling?" Rosie's smile turned to concern.

"I'm good, just tired. Very tired." I knew Rosie was worried about me. So were Anna and Paul. I tried to assure them I was okay, but they weren't going to let me be. They were going to take care of me and make sure I took care of myself.

Rosie's eyes hardened. "Have you heard anything from Errick yet?"

"No. Anna and Paul have talked to him. He's adamant that he doesn't want the baby or to know anything about it. I don't expect to hear from him." I tried not to sound hurt, but I was. My throat burned with tears, but I wouldn't let them fall from my eyes. I wanted to be done crying over Errick's ass. He was right. I'd made up my mind. I was keeping my baby.

Anna and Paul sat me down and told me about the conversations they'd had with Errick. As much as it hurt, I appreciated the honesty. They were hurt by his reaction to the pregnancy, but they loved their son. I didn't expect any less. They would stand by him, but they also didn't make me feel bad about my decision.

"Bastard. I still can't believe he would do this to you," Rosie hissed through clenched teeth.

I couldn't believe it either. In the weeks Errick had been gone, Anna and Paul did all they could to make sure I wasn't in this alone. I purchased a few more pieces of furniture after Rosie and Anna bought the living room stuff. I didn't want to do a lot because I still wasn't sure what was going to happen to the house. Paul made sure the house was secure with new locks and an updated alarm system. They insisted on helping me with the mortgage, which I appreciated but tried to turn down. I was overruled. There were times I wondered if they felt guilty for what their son had done, but they never showed me pity. Instead, they made me feel like family. I loved them for that.

"Yeah, well, that's life." I tried to keep my voice light, but I wasn't fooling Rosie. I wasn't fooling myself.

Chapter Twelve

Saxon

Trying not to stare at Rachel Hendricks as she crossed the restaurant to her table, I didn't do a good job of it.

"Seriously, Saxon?" Natalie huffed. She was looking at me crazy.

"What?" I played dumb.

"What the hell was that? You were almost drooling over that . . . that woman," she hissed through clenched teeth.

Natalie and I had been on a few dates, but it wasn't serious between us. I shouldn't have been checking Rachel out, but Natalie was doing too much.

"I just spoke to her." I shrugged. I'd done more than speak to Miss Hendricks, but there was no way I was admitting it.

"I saw the way you were looking at her. You might as well have undressed her right here. I can't believe you would disrespect me like that." Natalie's voice cracked.

Shaking my head, I didn't say anything. I was wrong for checking out Miss Hendricks, but there was something about that woman that had me thinking of her at odd times.

The rest of the dinner was awkward and silent. Natalie sulked. I didn't really have an appetite, and the only thing that kept me from getting up and walking out were the glimpses of Rachel that I could get. What was it about this woman that had me so out of character?

Chapter Thirteen

Rachel

A knock at the door brought my attention from the papers I was grading. The kids were learning their alphabet and drawing pictures to represent the letters.

Moira Stewart was standing there. I stood, greeting her with a smile. "Mrs. Stewart, how are you today?"

"I'm good. I hope I'm not interrupting."

"No, not at all. What can I do for you? Samarra has already been picked up."

Mrs. Stewart smiled. "Yes, I know. I actually came by to invite you to dinner. Samarra loves you. She's been asking if you could come to dinner, and I promised her I would ask you."

I was flattered by the unexpected invitation. "Well, thank you, and please tell Samarra thank you as well, but I really wouldn't want to impose."

"No imposition at all. We would love to have you. It won't be anything fancy, but Samarra would be thrilled." Moira Stewart's smile was open and bright, her hazel eyes flashing. I liked Mrs. Stewart. She was always a fun room assistant when it was her turn. She also chaperoned every field trip. Samarra was one of my favorite students, so I agreed.

"Great, why don't you come on Thursday?"

"Sure, that sounds great."

I double-checked that her address and contact information I had from my class records were up to date. I was glad that I accepted. I began to put away my work, straightening my desk. Mrs. Stewart waited while I finished. She insisted that I call her Moira, and I told her to call me Rachel.

As I pulled my coat on, we left my classroom, making our way outside. The sun was setting. Already, long shadows were spread out across the parking lot.

Rosie pulled up in her dark green Altima. She rolled the window down and yelled, "Are you ready? I'm so excited to hear the baby's heartbeat."

Moira turned to look at me, surprise written across her face. "You're pregnant? Oh, my goodness. I'm pregnant too. When are you due?"

I laughed at her excitement. It felt good to share this news with someone. I was supposed to be ecstatic to become a first-time mom. Moira was the first person other than friends and family I'd shared my pregnancy news with. I felt lighter, like the secret wasn't weighing me down anymore. We chatted a few moments longer before I climbed into the passenger seat of Rosie's car with a promise to see Moira on Thursday.

We got to the doctor's office, I signed in, and we sat in the waiting room until my name was called. Rosie was bursting with excitement as the doctor prepped my belly by spreading gel across it. She was enthralled by the sound of the baby's heartbeat. Tears swam in her eyes, and she beamed as she stared at the monitor that showed the baby. She asked the doctor more questions than I did. I tried not to laugh at her, but she was too funny.

Once I was dressed, Rosie rushed to my side, throwing her arms around my neck. "I'm so glad you're having this baby."

I burst into tears, startling her. Her face scrunched up with concern as she rubbed my back, checking to see if I was okay. Getting myself under control, I wiped the tears from my face with the discarded gown I'd tossed over the exam table. "I'm just happy."

Laughter tinged our tear-filled moment. Neither of us would ever forget it.

Saxon Carmichael was coming toward us as I stood at the scheduling counter. I watched as "flirt mode" turned on automatically for Rosie. She couldn't help herself.

"Hello," Rosie almost purred.

Shaking my head, I spoke to him as well. "Hello, Dr. Carmichael."

"Saxon," he corrected me with a light chuckle.

His smile was beautiful. His lips were on the thin side, but they looked very kissable surrounded by his mustache and beard. "Saxon."

"Dr. Carmichael, what kind of doctor are you?" Rosie flirted, batting her eyes.

"I'm an ob-gyn."

"Aah. Maybe I should make an appointment?" This girl was outrageous.

I finished with the lady behind the counter. Turning, I saw Rosie eyeing Saxon with a devilish grin on her face. He deftly sidestepped her flirting.

"You can always call my scheduling office." Then he turned to me. "We seem to keep running into each other."

"Yes, we do. I hope you're having a good day."

"I am. What are you doing here? I mean, I've seen you in the office a few times. Who's your doctor?"

"Dr. Charles. He's wonderful."

"John is one of the best," Saxon agreed. "Well, you ladies have a good afternoon. It was nice to see you."

"You too," I told him. Rosie and I said our good-byes, and then we watched as he walked away. His tall, well-built frame moved with a sensual sway. This man screamed sex appeal.

We left the doctor's office. The cold wind took my breath away. Our hair whipped around our faces as we hurried across the parking lot to her car. We slid in, Rosie started it, and the warm air felt good as I shivered while we waited for the car to warm up.

"Girl, that man is fine."

"Yes, he is." I could do nothing but agree.

"I saw the way he was looking at you." She smirked.

"You are silly. You keep saying that, but that man is not looking at me in any kind of way. He is not thinking about me." I waved her off.

"Yeah, right, keep telling yourself that." Rosie laughed.

"Besides, I'm pregnant."

She looked at me intently, and her smile turned to a curious frown. "Do you really think that would stop a man from being interested in you?"

"I think it would. No man wants to be involved with some fat, pregnant woman whose 'baby daddy' left her because she was pregnant with his child."

I tried to hide the pain that sometimes bubbled to the surface. It burned my heart at times. I could hear it in my voice. Errick leaving me, his abrupt dismissal and disappearance from my life, left me distrustful and brokenhearted. Shaking off the sadness that threatened to overwhelm me, I was determined to look at my baby's birth as a blessing. This baby was wanted and loved.

Chapter Fourteen

Saxon

The afternoon sun beamed down from the washed-out pale blue sky, but there was no warmth to it. The wind beat fiercely as my cousin Josh and I hurried to my front door. I had to jiggle the key to get the lock to open it was so cold.

"Damn, man, it's freezing out here," Josh said, blowing on his hands as I opened the door.

Leading the way through the empty house, I led Josh to the only room in the house that was fully decorated: my den. This was where I spent most of my time. Three steps led down into the room. Two walls were covered in built-in bookcases stuffed mostly with medical journals with a few recent bestsellers mixed in. A seventy-inch flat-screen TV hung on the other wall, with a sofa and two chairs grouped in front of it. A pool table sat on the far side of the room in front of the French doors that led to the lanai overlooking the backyard. Two shelves with vinyl records sat next to a stereo system. I turned on the system, and Jay-Z and Justin Timberlake played through the surround-sound system I'd installed throughout the house.

I grabbed a couple beers from the small fridge in the corner and handed one to Josh, then settled in the chair closest to where he was sprawled on the sofa.

"So what's going on with you? You've been quiet today," he said.

Shaking my head, I knew I had been absent-minded, but I didn't think it was that noticeable. Josh was my cousin on my mother's side. Our mothers were sisters, so we grew up close. He was my confidant, the one person I shared my personal business with. "I met someone."

Straightening from his slouched position, Josh looked at me. "That explains it. Who is she, and where did you meet her?

I told him about Rachel Hendricks and how she had been on my mind a lot lately.

"She's a patient in your office and Samarra's teacher?"

"Yep."

"And you're diggin' her? What about Natalie?"

Most of my family knew Natalie since we'd been dating for a while. "What about her? We aren't serious. She knows that."

Nodding, Josh looked at me skeptically. "Are you sure about that?"

"Of course."

"What are you gonna do about this woman?"

"That's just it. I don't know. There's something about her, man, something that attracts me. She has sad eyes."

Josh laughed, long and loud. "Is that what you see when you look at her?"

"She's not someone I would usually be attracted to. She's a big girl, pretty, with long hair about the color of—"

"Wait, wait. Are you telling me this woman is a big girl like a fat girl? You're diggin' on a fat chick?"

I was sure my expression showed how much I didn't appreciate his comments. He stopped laughing when he realized I hadn't joined him.

"My bad, man. Ain't nothing wrong with diggin' a thick chick."

"Yeah, no problem. I'm sure she's probably used to people looking down on her for being big. Anyway, she's not the kind of woman I've dated before, but I think about her at the oddest times."

I'd always been the type to go after what I wanted, but something about Rachel Hendricks made me want to move slowly, to handle her gently. Her eyes said she'd been through something and she didn't need any more pain or sadness in her life. I knew for certain that if I had a chance to make her happy, she would never have a moment of pain or sadness again in her life, not if I had anything to do with it.

"It's obvious you're into this chick. Go for it. See where something might lead with her. If Natalie isn't who you want, then you should move on and find out who is."

I listened to Josh. Even though my cousin was a clown sometimes, he always gave me good advice.

"Maybe you're right, cuz. Maybe you're right."

Chapter Fifteen

Saxon

I was in the kitchen washing dirty dishes as I waited for Moira while she took Samarra upstairs to clean her up. She needed a bath after helping her mom chop vegetables and chicken for dinner. I watched rain streak down the panes of glass in the window over the sink. It overlooked the backyard, which was closed off by a privacy fence. The temperature had turned unseasonably cold over the past week.

The ringing doorbell brought me out of my thoughts. I finished what I was doing until another ring came a few moments later. Grabbing the dish towel from the counter, I dried my hands while going down the hall. I passed a wall full of family pictures. Our mother had some of the same pictures on her wall. I did too. There were pictures of me and Moira when we were kids, our parents, our grandparents on my mom's side, and my dad's sisters and brother. There were also pictures of Daniel, his mother and stepdad, and his brother, Ben. Family was important to all of us.

Another ring of the bell hurried me along. Opening the door, I couldn't hide my surprise. Rachel Hendricks was standing there, rain pouring off her bright red umbrella. She was bundled in a brightly printed coat that was belted at the waist. The first thing I noticed was how good she looked, fresh-faced and eyes dancing.

"Um, hello. How are you?"

When she smiled, my stomach did a little flip. Rachel's smile was sexy even when she didn't mean it to be.

"Hi. I'm looking for Moira and Samarra." She glanced at the house numbers to the side of the door, making sure she was at the right place.

"Oh, yes, come in. Is Moira expecting you?" I didn't know why I suddenly felt unsettled with her this close to me. I was just thinking of her, but she was the last person I expected to see.

"Yes, she and Samarra invited me for dinner."

"Oh, okay." My middle clenched with nervousness, which was totally unlike me. I was confident with women, but something about Rachel brought out the gentle side of me. I became fiercely protective. I wanted to handle her like blown glass.

Seeing her standing there with rain running down her umbrella, her hair windblown, her breath coming out as vapor in the cold wind, I wanted to pull her into the house and in my arms to warm her. Instead, I invited her inside, telling her that Moira was upstairs with Samarra and they would be down shortly.

The next few moments seemed to happen in slow motion. Rachel stepped through the door, and before either of us knew what was going on, she slipped on the tile floor. My heart felt like it stopped, my breath catching in my throat as I reached for her but missed her windmilling arms. Rachel crashed to the floor, hitting her head against the corner of the small foyer table. The table overturned with a loud boom.

I could hear Moira rushing down the steps as I knelt beside Rachel. I checked her pulse and her pupil dilation. I ran a hand through her hair. I could feel a lump forming already.

"Oh, Sax, what happened?" Moira stayed out of my way as I checked her.

Without missing a beat, I told Moira what happened as I tried to make sure Rachel wasn't going to pass out on me.

"Sax, she's pregnant."

My heart slammed against my ribs. *Pregnant? Did I hear Moira correctly?* Running a hand over her midsection, I felt the tightness in her belly. "How far along is she?"

Rachel groaned. She was going to have a terrible headache. I wanted to do something to ease the pain she was going to feel. Disappointment flooded me as Moira's words sank in. Glancing down at her hand, I didn't see a ring, but that didn't mean anything. Lots of married people didn't wear rings these days.

Rachel's eyes fluttered open, and she looked around and moaned.

"Don't try to move. Lie still for a minute," I spoke softly.

"What . . . what happened?" Panic lit her eyes. Gone was the dazed expression, replaced by one of fear, her hand automatically going to her belly.

That moment of protectiveness gripped me again. I wanted nothing more than to comfort her. I wanted to remove the fear from her eyes. Instead, I let the medical professional take over, explaining that she'd fallen and hit her head. "Don't worry. I think you'll be okay, but I want you to make an appointment to see John in the morning. How far along are you?"

She glanced over to where Moira stood by the living room entry. Moira gave her an apologetic shrug. "I'm sorry. I had to tell him."

"I'm four months, um, four and a half," she said, answering my question after giving Moira a nod.

"I would feel better if you get checked out."

Rachel insisted that she was okay to sit up. I helped her to her feet and into the living room, where she sat on the sofa. She assured me she was okay even though a part of me wanted to insist she go to the emergency room. She promised she would go see John in the morning, and I knew I had to back off. She didn't want me to make a big deal out of it, but it was a big deal to me.

I heard Samarra's small feet pitter-pattering down the stairs and across the floor as she came and climbed into my lap as I sat next to Rachel. She was excited to see her teacher, but I told her to be careful.

"Are you okay, Miss Hendricks?"

"I will be. I had an accident. I fell and hit my head."

My heart almost stopped when Samarra looked at me with all the innocence and confidence of a child and said, "Uncle Sax, kiss her boo-boo. You can make it all better."

My eyes met Rachel's over the top of Samarra's head. *I would like nothing more than to kiss Rachel and make her feel better.* The way Rachel looked back at me made me wonder if she was thinking the same thing. We shared a smile, and it warmed me.

Excusing myself, I went into the kitchen to see if Moira needed any help and to give myself some breathing room. I slid onto the barstool while I absently watched Moira move around the kitchen as she heated her wok and began to cook the stir-fry. My mind was battling itself. The protective urges I was having where Rachel was concerned were new to me. I didn't know this woman, so why was I feeling this way? Seeing her laid out on the floor scared me, and I wasn't sure why.

Moira looked over her shoulder at me. "Is she okay?"

"Yes, she seems fine. Why didn't you tell me she was coming to dinner?"

She turned with a smirk. "I didn't know it would matter."

I knew then that she was playing matchmaker, something she rarely did. If I said anything else about Rachel, she would become relentless. She was always telling me I needed to find a good woman and settle down. Not that I would mind the help, but I had a feeling that Rachel wouldn't want anyone prying into her private life. Besides, she was already with someone, which was obvious from her pregnancy. Even if she wasn't, I wanted her to be willing to meet me halfway.

Later that night, I pulled up behind Rachel in the drive of a pretty cottage-style home. She told me she would be okay, but after her fall I felt better knowing she made it home safely. Rain still fell in a steady downpour, the dark streets wet and slick. I got out of the car and made my way over to help her out of hers. She huddled with me under the large umbrella I held over our heads as I escorted her up the walk to her porch.

Stepping onto the large porch, I held the open umbrella to the side while Rachel unlocked the door. "Promise me you'll call John in the morning," I repeated. "I want him to check you out."

"I promise." She smiled, giving me the Girl Scout sign.

We shared a laugh at her silliness. I loved the husky sound of her laughter. I was also glad to see her amusement made it to her eyes this time. I didn't want to leave, but I knew I needed to go. Rachel shouldn't have been standing out here in the cold.

"You lock up tight. I'm glad you're feeling okay."

"Thanks for making sure I got home safely tonight. You be careful driving in this bad weather."

I fought the urge to bend down and capture her lips. "I will. Good night."

We stood there just looking at each other for several heartbeats before I turned, forcing myself from the porch before I did something I wouldn't regret but Rachel may not have appreciated. I had to remind myself that she belonged to someone else. She was carrying his child.

She waited until I was at my car before she went inside. I slid behind the steering wheel and sat there a few minutes, my gaze on the place Rachel had stood just moments ago. Shaking my head, I needed to put her out of my mind.

Chapter Sixteen

Errick

Leaving the office, I crossed the parking lot to my car. I had a spring in my step and a smile on my face. I loved my new position. There was a lot to learn, but there was a great team in place, and the outgoing director had shown me the ropes. The VP came to me this afternoon, complimenting me on a job well done, and he told me he was happy with my work so far. Things were already turning around in our division, and I was glad I was making a good impression. He also told me that if I kept it up, another promotion may not be too far in my future.

Starting the car, I rolled the windows down and pulled out of the lot into rush-hour traffic. I wasn't even bothered by it today. It was seventy-eight degrees. The sky was clear and blue. I was loving life. John Legend poured from my speakers as I drove. I loosened my tie and sat back to relax as much as I could in bumper-to-bumper traffic.

My mind slipped to thoughts of the ski trip I was going on this weekend to Colorado with two of my single coworkers. The ringing of my phone brought me back. Without bothering to see who it was, I pressed the button to answer on my Bluetooth. "'Lo?"

My mother's voice filled the interior of the car. "Hello, Errick."

"Hey, Ma, how are you?" I hadn't spoken to my folks in a little while. Our relationship was strained because of the situation with Rachel. That was something else I could thank her for. Shaking my head, I put those thoughts out of my mind.

"I'm good. Just calling to see if you need anything and how my firstborn is doing."

I chuckled, shaking my head. In my mother's eyes, none of her children would ever be grown enough to stop needing her. "I'm good. Do you or Pop need anything?"

There was a long pause on the phone. "Only to see my son. When are you coming home?"

"Things are really busy here. I'm trying to get used to my new position and get acclimated with my surroundings, so I'm not sure when I'll be able to get home." Changing the subject, I asked about Dad and the rest of the family.

My brother, Jamie, was coming to visit me for Thanksgiving next week. I was ready. I missed my family, and it would be good to have him around. I hadn't made an effort to go home because I didn't want to see or deal with Rachel and her situation, but I knew my parents would do everything they could to make that happen. I refused to keep talking about it. Rachel had made her choice, and she would have to live with it.

My mom gave me the rundown on my dad and their plans for the holiday. My sister, Aimee, would be helping her cook along with my aunts and cousins. As I knew it would, the conversation turned to Rachel. She would be coming to dinner, of course. I stopped my mother before she got started.

"Ma, I really don't want to hear or talk about Rachel. Damn, that's one reason I don't call more often. You won't stop with all the bullshit." I didn't mean to snap at her over Rachel's fuckup, but I was tired of hearing it.

"Errick, she needs you. That baby needs you. This has been hard for her."

I heard the disappointment in my mother's voice. I also heard tightly controlled anger because of the way I'd snapped at her. I was sorry she was upset, I hated hurting my parents, but this time I wasn't giving in.

"You don't think it's hard for me? Never once did you or Dad or Aimee ever stop to ask me how I was feeling. Rachel broke my heart. I loved her, I trusted her, and she went behind my back and got pregnant."

My mother gasped. "Went behind your back? Do you think this baby is not yours?"

"Ma, that's not what I meant."

"So how did she go behind your back? Did she get pregnant by herself? No, you helped with that. You reaped all the benefits of practicing for a baby, but when you actually got one, you decided you weren't ready to step up to the responsibility of it. You know, I thought I raised my sons to be better men, but you're just like two-thirds of the male population. You want the woman to take care of it instead of being a man and helping to raise your baby."

I rolled my eyes as my mother went on and on, but then I was startled when I didn't hear anything for a moment. I looked at my phone. It was my screensaver. My mother had hung up on me. Tossing the phone on the passenger seat, I groaned in frustration.

When would anyone understand my side in this? When would someone see my point of view? How long would they continue to punish me for a mistake?

Chapter Seventeen

Rachel

Swiping my screen, I hit the speed dial for Rosie's office. I left the doctor's office. Dr. Charles told me to take it easy for a few days, so I was calling Rosie to see if she would like to have lunch. The phone rang as I thought about the visit. I was glad that everything was okay. No matter how strong I tried to be last night, I was worried about the fall.

"Hey, I was just calling to see if you wanted to have lunch with me," I invited Rosie when she answered the phone.

"Lunch? What time?"

"I was thinking now. I'm in your area. I can be there in a few minutes."

"You're off today?"

I knew Rosie would panic, so I just kept my voice calm. "I fell yesterday, so I went to the doctor to make sure everything was okay."

"What?" Rosie almost yelled into the phone.

"Everything is okay. I'll see you in five minutes. Bye." I disconnected the call before she could respond.

Laughing, I pulled into the parking lot of Optical Illusions, the interior design service Rosie owned. After parking, I went up the walk and opened the door. I stepped into a spacious showroom. I smiled at Desiree, Rosie's assistant. "Hey, how are things?"

"Hey, Rachel, things are great. How are you?" The younger woman smiled at me. I liked Desiree. She was in her early twenties and had just graduated from the Watkins College of Art in Fountain Square, and after she did her internship with Rosie, she hired her upon graduation. Rosie often said she didn't know what she would do without Desiree.

"Good, good. I'm going back." I indicated the back hall that led to Rosie's office.

Nodding, Desiree waved me off as she moved to greet a woman who was coming in. I went down the small hall to the left of the consultation area and knocked on Rosie's door. I waited until she called for me to come in before opening it.

"Was this fast enough?"

Rosie was on her feet and around the desk in just a few steps before I could get into the office good. "Are you okay? What happened? How did you fall? What did the doctor say?" Question after question tumbled out, all while Rosie was running her hands over my belly like she thought my bump was going to be gone.

"Calm down. Everything's okay." I tried to hide my amusement as Rosie finished her inspection. She finally backed off enough that I could sit down on one of the chairs in front of her desk. I told her what happened when I went to dinner at Moira Stewart's house the night before.

Rosie visibly relaxed as she listened. By the time I finished filling her in, she was smiling. "So the handsome doctor followed you home. How did that go?"

"Stop it, girl, you are dreaming." I laughed at her, always the matchmaker. I knew what she was hinting at. Her overactive imagination was running away with her. "He was concerned, nothing more."

"Well, come on so we can go feed my baby." Rosie grabbed her bag from the bottom drawer of her desk.

At the restaurant, we were seated at a table next to a window overlooking the parking lot and street beyond. I watched the ebb and flow of traffic while Rosie excused herself for a minute. I was lost in thought about the baby. I was so glad that everything was okay.

I heard someone call my name, and turning, I saw David. I smiled at Errick's best friend. I stood and hugged him. When I stepped back, I saw the way he was looking at me. I guessed that Errick hadn't told him.

"Hey, how are you? I haven't seen you in a while."

"I'm good. Ummm, you're pregnant?" He looked confused.

"Yes, I am. I'm four and a half months." I told him my precise time, and I could see that he realized Errick was the father.

"Oh, wow, congratulations. I didn't know."

Shrugging, I nodded. I ran my hand over my baby bump with a smile on my face. "Thank you. I'm excited."

He looked at me with compassion in his eyes. "Are you really okay?"

"I am, thanks, David. I'm due in May, and I'm already excited to meet this little person."

"That's great."

"Yes. Things between Errick and me didn't work out, but this baby was one of the best things to come out of our relationship."

David nodded. He gave me another hug and kissed me on the cheek. "It's good to see you, Rachel. You take care of yourself."

"I will, and you do the same."

Rosie returned to the table a minute later. "Was that David Chow?" She must have seen him walking away.

I nodded. "He came over to say hello."

"I bet he did. I'm sure he's already on the phone with Errick, telling him he saw you."

"Probably. Errick didn't tell him I'm pregnant. He was shocked when he realized it."

Rosie laughed, "They are as bad as women gossiping on the phone."

Laughing with her, I tried to push away the moment of sadness that hit my heart. Errick didn't want this baby, and every time I thought about it, it broke my heart. I was never going to let my child feel unwanted for even a moment. I was going to love this baby and be the best mother I could be.

Chapter Eighteen

Saxon

Ringing the bell, I tugged at the hem of my coat, adjusting it. I hefted the heavy brown paper bag I held. I was nervous. I hoped Rachel wouldn't freak out with me just popping up at her house. I assumed she was home because her car was in the drive and some lights were on in the house. I didn't have her phone number to call before I came over, and I hadn't seen her in the office this morning. My schedule was hectic. An unexpected delivery kept me at the hospital most of the day.

The sun had set long ago, and the temperature dropped with it. It was now in the high thirties, and my breath whipped from my mouth in the strong wind. Pulling my collar closer, I rang the bell again. I almost jumped when the door swung open immediately after. The surprise in Rachel's eyes when she saw me standing there made me smile while I ran my gaze over her. She looked great dressed in a pair of shorts, a long, loose T-shirt that still showed off her baby belly, and a pair of ankle socks. Her hair was loose, hanging in curls over her shoulders.

"Hi." I smiled at her, hoping she wouldn't turn me away.

She smiled back, even though it was a little confused, and warmth surrounded me. I didn't even think about how cold it was once she looked at me like that. Her smile alone could make me forget. When she crossed her arms over her breasts and shivered from a cold gust, I told her I wanted to check on her.

She invited me in. Stepping in the foyer, I glanced around. There was a staircase to my right. The living room was off to the left. A hall led toward what I assumed was the kitchen and other rooms straight toward the back. Following her into the living room, I looked around her personal space. The room was spacious with a sofa, a sofa table, two floor lamps, two chairs, and a flat-screen TV on a stand. The walls were painted a soft green, and a few green plants accented the room. The large window overlooked the front yard. No pictures hung on the wall. There were no mementos or knickknacks, no decorations or family mementos. The room didn't feel like Rachel.

"I'm sorry to pop up on you unannounced, but I wanted to check on you. Did you get to see John today?"

Her round cheeks flushed rosy. She was a little flustered from the attention. "You didn't have to check on me, but thank you. I did see Dr. Charles today, and he said everything is fine."

"Good. I was worried about you."

The pretty pink flush in her cheeks deepened. She opened her mouth to say something but closed it with a snap. "I'm okay, thanks."

Holding up the bag in my hand, I said, "I wasn't sure if you've eaten or what you might like, but I stopped for Chinese food. I got a little of almost everything. I thought we could have dinner together."

When she smiled at me this time, I felt that familiar tug in my middle. Her eyes sparkled, and her lips curved into a smile, full and sexy. "I love Chinese. I hope you don't mind if we eat here in the living room."

"Not at all." I didn't care where we ate as long as she ate with me.

Rachel left me to go into the kitchen. I took my jacket off, tossing it across a chair. She returned with plates and silverware, then left again. I fixed her a plate with a little bite of beef lo mein and chicken fried rice, an egg roll, Hunan beef with spring peas, and a couple other items. This time when Rachel came back, she carried a glass of tea for each of us. Settled on the sofa, we dug into the hot food, talking, relaxing, and getting to know one another.

"So you're an ob-gyn. That's an interesting choice. What made you follow that route?" Rachel really seemed to want to hear my answer.

"I knew I was going to be a doctor. I like babies, so I thought why not?"

I struggled not to lose my train of thought. I was distracted when she wrapped her lips around the egg roll and took a bite. Looking away, I got my thoughts together and away from where they were headed. This woman turned me on without even trying. I didn't think she was even aware of my interest in her.

"You enjoy the work, huh?"

"Yes, it's fascinating. I don't care how many babies I deliver. It always amazes me. I get to witness the miracle of birth and the development of the fetus until it is a full-term baby. I get to help in the process of caring for a life, keeping the mother healthy, monitoring the baby. It's a very gratifying feeling." I could talk about medicine and babies for hours, but I wanted to know about Rachel. "What made you choose teaching?"

"I am fascinated with children's minds. They soak up everything like a sponge. I am satisfied to know that I helped them learn, especially the little ones. Teaching them their ABC's and to read, helping to shape their minds—there's nothing like that."

Rachel spoke with passion. It was obvious she loved what she did. From the way Samarra acted and from what Moira told me, all the kids loved her.

We talked about other things. I loved that she liked sports, pop culture, music, and books. She had strong views on the world and politics. Her sense of humor was quick and wicked. She was articulate and didn't have a problem expressing herself. I liked a woman who could challenge me. That made her even more attractive.

After we'd eaten and I helped pack up the leftovers in the bag, Rachel carried them away to the kitchen while I made myself comfortable on the floor with my back propped against a chair. I was full. The food and the company were both just what I needed. Rachel joined me after she'd straightened up, sitting on the sofa close to me.

"When is your baby due?" I had taken a chance showing up at her place, but I didn't regret it. I was curious about the father and her status. I wanted to know if there was a man in her life.

"May second." She smiled, and that pregnancy glow that lit her from within gave her a soft, beautiful aura.

Looking at her, I wondered about her life. "Where is the father, if I may ask?"

As soon as the words left my mouth, I regretted them. The pain-stricken look that crossed her face made my heart ache. I wanted to take the words back immediately, take her in my arms and wrap her in my protection, and tell her everything would be okay. She would be surprised to know how much I wanted to make it okay. She glanced away from me, but not before I saw the tears glistening in her eyes. It took her a moment to collect herself, but in that moment, I wanted to wring the neck of the shadow man who had hurt her. I wanted to wring my own for dredging up what was obviously painful to her.

"He's not here." That was it. She didn't say anything else about him.

Not that I needed an explanation. It wasn't a good situation for her. It was obvious from the pain on her face as she stood, excusing herself. I kicked myself. I didn't mean to be inconsiderate. I was just trying to make sure there weren't any surprises in store for me if I acted on what this woman had me feeling. Every time I saw the sadness in her eyes, my protective urge reared. I wanted to keep her safe from any harm or sadness. I wanted to put a smile on her face and keep it there. What was it about a woman I barely knew that made me feel the need to wrap her in my arms and keep her safe and happy?

I was just starting to worry about Rachel when she returned to the living room. I could tell from her puffy eyes and red nose that she'd been crying. My stomach flipped. I was the reason she was upset. I wanted to do something to make her feel better, but I didn't know what. Rachel picked up the conversation like nothing was wrong, so I left it alone.

It was after nine when Rachel walked me to the door, where we said good night. It had been a good evening after that one little blip, and I hated to leave.

"I had a good time tonight. I'm really glad you let me have dinner with you. Maybe next time you will let me take you out?" I smiled, trying to keep it light.

A flicker of uncertainty crossed her face. "That would be nice, but . . . are you sure?"

"Of course I'm sure. I'll call you."

"Won't you need my number?" We shared a laugh.

I pulled my cell from my pocket and programmed in her number before saying a final good night. I stood on her stoop after she'd gone inside and closed the door. I wanted to knock on her door and kiss her when she opened it, but I would wait. I wanted to make a move, but I was willing to take my time. I wanted Rachel to want me as much as I wanted her.

Chapter Nineteen

Errick

I was excited as I pulled up in the fifteen-minute parking area at the airport to pick Jamie up. I climbed from the car and stood beside it to wait for my brother to come through the doors. I hadn't seen him since I moved to Phoenix, and I was happy he came. I missed my mom and dad, my brother and sister, and the rest of them, but with everything going on with Rachel, I knew it was best to keep my distance.

"What's up, man?"

Looking over, I saw Jamie with a duffel bag over his shoulder and pulling his rolling bag behind him. Jamie was an inch or so shorter than me, with shoulder-length dreads. His skin was the color of fresh coffee, and he wore a mustache and goatee.

"What's up?" I dapped my brother up, then pulled him into a man hug—that half hug, half slap on the back thing. I was glad to see my little brother.

We jumped into my Challenger and headed into traffic. It was seventy-three degrees on Thanksgiving Day, the sky clear with only a few clouds floating lazily. I loved this weather. I drove from Phoenix to Tempe, the suburb where I lived. Instead of going to my apartment, I drove to a beautiful Neo-Mediterranean house.

"Damn, who lives here?" Jamie looked around the perfectly landscaped yard when we climbed from the car.

"A friend of mine. Grab your bag. You can take a shower, and then we'll have dinner," I said over my shoulder. I smiled at the beautiful woman heading toward us.

"Hey." Amber—a beautiful half-Spanish/half-Black woman with waist-length auburn hair, smooth olive skin, and the sultry beauty associated with Spanish women—stopped in front of me, pulling me into a hug.

"Hey, Amber, this is my brother, Jamie," I introduced them.

I saw Jamie checking her out. Hell, I didn't blame him. Amber was sexy as hell with her thick thighs and tiny waist. Any man would give her a second glance. Jamie nodded hello, reaching out a hand for her to shake. I saw the flush creep up his neck when Amber hugged him instead. I had the same reaction when I met her.

"Come on in, fellas."

We followed Amber inside. She led the way through the large foyer and down the hall past the staircase. The game room was to the left, and the formal dining room and living room were to the right as we passed the stairs. There was an eat-in kitchen and a den with double doors that led to a covered lanai.

White wicker furniture was grouped on one side of the lanai. A black wrought-iron table with a large white umbrella and chairs were placed on the other side by the barbecue grill. There were five steps leading down from the deck to the Olympic-size pool. A pool house was connected to the lanai on the far end. There was another beautiful Spanish woman draped over a lounge chair in front of it. She wore a lilac tank top and a pair of white jeans that looked painted on, with her long hair pulled up in a ponytail.

"Errick, Jamie, this is my cousin Isabel," she said, making introductions.

I led Jamie into the pool house. We passed a living area with glass walls that opened toward the pool, a small bedroom, and the connecting bathroom with two shower stalls. "Man, what's going on?" Jamie asked, stopping outside the bathroom door.

"What's up?" I was curious.

Jamie looked at me like he was exasperated. "What's up with you and these chicks? I mean, you living like a rock star out here, ain't you? I'm not trying to get in your business, but it hasn't been that long since you and Rachel broke up, and you're in with someone else like that already?"

"Amber and I are just friends. We date. Nothing serious. And as you stated, Rachel and I broke up, so I'm doing exactly what she needs to be doing, and that's moving on with life. Look, bro, I know you're concerned, but I'm just enjoying myself. Take your shower, and we'll swim before dinner." I slapped his shoulder.

Jamie looked at me like he didn't know me and shook his head. Without a word, he left me standing there. Frustration rushed through me. Once again, my family was forcing me to think about Rachel. Jamie bringing her up dredged up memories and feelings I had pushed away. It was hard enough, but to hear it all the time was tiring.

Leaning against the wall, I thought about when I proposed to her a year ago today. We were supposed to be married a couple of months from now, but everything was different. That part of my life was over.

Running a hand over my waves, I pushed those thoughts out of my mind. Things with Rachel and I were over, and I was moving on with my life. My family was just going to have to get used to that.

Chapter Twenty

Saxon

My mother opened the door as I juggled sodas and ice that Moira asked me to pick up on my way. The house was filled with good aromas as I followed her down the hall toward the kitchen. My mother, Ellen, and my father, Connor, still lived in the house that I grew up in. It was a cozy little three-bedroom, with two and a half baths, an eat-in kitchen, and my mother's favorite spot: the porch that wrapped around the front and one side of the house.

Moira was in the kitchen with my aunts Lynn and Bert, my mother's sisters. The house smelled like Thanksgiving and Sunday dinner with my dad's family. I set everything down on the table, then kissed my aunts and my sister. I grabbed my mother in a hug, spinning her around as she laughed.

"Boy, put me down."

I stood her back on her feet, then started meddling in the pots. Moira chased me out of the kitchen with a dish towel. Laughing, I went down the short hall to my dad's den. He and my uncle Lonny were watching the pregame show.

"What's going on, *Athair?*" I greeted my dad, calling him the Irish name for "Father." "Uncle Lonny." I shook his hand.

Soon the house was filled with other aunts, uncles, cousins, and friends. Daniel's folks and sister came with her husband. The smells of good food and sweets filled the air along with chatter and laughter. It was good to spend the holiday with my family.

I was in the den with my dad and several other guys. We were talking shit about the football game and anything else we wanted to mess with each other about. I was sitting at the end of the sectional closest to the sliding glass door leading to the patio. Glancing outside, I noticed my parents' neighbor, Ms. Claudie, hanging her Christmas wreath on her front door. Rachel popped to mind, and I wondered what she was doing for the holiday.

Thinking of Rachel made me think of her pregnancy. Where was her baby's father? Why wouldn't he be there for his baby? For Rachel?

Ms. Claudie caught my attention again when she went inside. She plugged in her lights, and her house became a winter wonderland. There were reindeer and inflatable characters like Santa Claus, Rudolph, and Mickey. I smiled. Ms. Claudie had been doing it big for Christmas for as long as I remembered. I looked forward to having holiday traditions with my own family: decorating the tree, drinking hot chocolate with marshmallows while watching cheesy movies and shows, wearing matching pajamas, making special food or crafts with the kids. I wanted to be a husband and father.

Once all the food was done, my uncle blessed it, and then we served ourselves and sat around the house in groups and clusters. Moira, Daniel, and I sat with my cousins Isla and Veronica. As usual, the conversation turned to me and my dating life.

"When are you going to introduce us to whoever you're dating?"

"I date casually. No one is meeting my family anytime soon."

Moira looked at me with a sly smile. "I think I've already met her."

The cousins pounced just like she knew they would. Who was she? Was it serious? Why didn't they know about her?

I laughed at all of them. "Moira is tripping. Y'all don't believe that. I haven't met anyone. Yet."

Rachel crossed my mind again. I didn't know anything about her, but I wished she were here with me. She was the one I wanted to introduce to my family.

Conversation turned to other things, and I was relieved to be out of the spotlight. I spent the rest of the evening just hanging out with my people.

Chapter Twenty-one

Rachel

After pulling into the drive, I sat a long time in the car, long enough to hear the ticks and clicks as it cooled. The wind blew fiercely, the cold seeping into the car quickly without the heat running. Laying my head against the headrest, I exhaled. It had been a long, tiring day.

Thanksgiving.

I had so much to be thankful for, but it was hard not to be sad. I spent part of the day with Anna and Paul. That was the hardest. This time last year Errick proposed to me, and we were excited to be making wedding plans. This year I was an unwed mother-to-be. Anna and Paul had done all they could to lift my spirits, and I had to admit, I did enjoy spending time with them and their family. Aimee and her boyfriend were there. She was so excited to be an auntie that she kept rubbing my belly anytime she got close to me. Jamie called from Phoenix while I was there, and he and Errick spoke to everyone. I had to excuse myself to go cry in the bathroom. I was mad at myself for shedding tears over Errick again, but the pain was sharp. To know he was on the phone and didn't want to talk to me was like a stab in the heart.

I left shortly after they finished their call. Anna tried to convince me to stay, but I didn't want to bring anyone down. I promised I would take care of myself and reassured her I would be good alone tonight. Before I left, I gave her a card to thank her for doing all that they had to help me, and inside I tucked a sonogram picture of the baby. I knew she and Paul would love it. I thought I would be fine alone, but now, sitting here in front of this empty house, loneliness burned my chest. Tears stung my eyes. I tried to stop them, but soon they were rolling down my face. Breaking for a moment, I sobbed. I cried for me and my broken relationship. I wept for my baby. How could Errick not want this baby? I didn't understand how he could be so cold toward his child.

A pair of headlights flashed in my rearview mirror as a car pulled into the drive behind me. I reached into the glove box and grabbed some napkins and tried to wipe my tears. I wasn't expecting anyone. I knew it wasn't Rosie. She was visiting family in New Jersey. I waited to see who would get out of the car. I was stunned when I saw Saxon Carmichael climb from the gray BMW. I stepped out of my own truck. I could tell he was surprised that I was sitting in the car.

"Hi." I walked to the back of my truck, where he met me. I was beginning to feel the weight of my pregnancy. My lower back was tender, so I reached behind myself, trying to stretch a little.

Saxon looked at my middle even though he couldn't see my belly through the sweater I was wearing. When he smiled, my evening unexpectedly felt like it was going to be okay.

"Hi yourself. I wasn't sure of your plans, so I stopped by to see if you'd like to have a late dinner with me?" He walked around the car and took two large paper bags from the passenger seat. "I'm sorry I didn't call first."

Normally I would be mad if someone just popped up at my house, but I was glad that he did. I was just thinking how I didn't want to be alone, and he'd appeared. "It's okay, come on in. You need any help?"

Saxon shooed me away from the bags, then followed me up the walk to the porch and waited patiently for me to open the door. I took him to the living room, where he began to unpack the bags on the sofa table. I stood watching him from the doorway. He moved with a masculine grace. I could imagine the muscles beneath his shirt moving under my fingertips. I'd only known him a few weeks, but watching him here, in my private space, he felt very familiar to me. That scared me a little. Hell, it scared me a lot. After everything with Errick, I was in no shape to be looking at or thinking about another man. Besides, Saxon was just becoming a friend.

Leaving him to finish his unpacking, I went to get plates, utensils, and something to drink. By the time I joined him, he had everything unwrapped. There was traditional Thanksgiving fare—turkey and dressing, sweet potatoes, and green bean casserole—but there were also dishes he told me his father grew up on in Ireland. I knew he was mixed, but I had no idea that Saxon's father was Irish. He explained what they were. There was cider pork with apples, which was a browned pork dish cooked with onions and sliced apples, and sausage plait, which was made from browned sausage and cooked with ketchup and herbs with a braided crust across the top. Both were delicious. I found myself eating until I was stuffed. I was glad Saxon brought food because I really hadn't eaten when I was with Anna and Paul, and I was hungrier than I realized.

After dinner, Saxon uncorked a bottle of red wine, pouring me half a glass. We sat on the sofa. *A Christmas Carol* with Alastair Sim was playing quietly on the TV, but we weren't paying attention. I was tuned into the conversation.

"Why aren't you with your family tonight? Not that I don't appreciate the company, but I'm sure that you have other things to do." I wanted to ask about the woman I saw him with at the restaurant that night, but it wasn't my business. More and more lately, Saxon had been on my mind. I knew it was because he was nice to me, and after everything with Errick, his kindness was welcome.

"I spent most of the day with my family. My parents always have a big thing for Thanksgiving at their place. I thought about you, and I wanted to come by to check on you. I didn't know if you had plans for the holiday."

I tried to tell myself that the pleased feeling that came over me meant nothing. It just felt good to have someone show that they cared about me. "Well, I'm glad you did. I really wasn't looking forward to being alone tonight."

Our eyes met, and we held each other's gaze. I knew before it happened that Saxon was going to kiss me. He pulled me close, sucking on my bottom lip, nibbling on it before slipping his tongue in my mouth and exploring with restrained passion. I kissed him back, and the desire I felt exploded through my body from everywhere his body touched mine. Deepening the kiss, I became the seductress, licking, sucking, pulling, tugging, taking, giving, until I felt breathless and out of control. Inhibitions aside, I wanted him. My body was molten, liquid, hot, raging with desire. Saxon made me feel things I hadn't felt in a long time. I wanted him, and I was going to have him.

Breaking the kiss, I stood. Our eyes never left the other's as I unbuttoned my blouse, revealing my pale peach lacy bra. Next, I kicked off my shoes and the black skirt I wore. I was standing there in matching panties. My pregnant belly was on display, but I didn't flinch under his scorching gaze as he took me in. His heated expression sent shivers down my spine. I was exposed to him with all my insecurities on display, but I felt sexy and powerful to see him in a lust-filled daze.

I thought I was going to faint when Saxon bent to his knees in front of me. He slid his large, strong hands over the swell of my belly before placing a kiss on it. The heat that had pooled in my stomach now seeped between my legs. They trembled. Sinking to my knees in front of him, I took over, leading the way to ecstasy as we came together right there on the living room floor with the Spirit of Christmas Yet to Come on the screen showing Scrooge how things could be in his future.

Chapter Twenty-two

Errick

Waking early the morning after Thanksgiving, I lay in bed staring at the ceiling, thinking about the day Jamie and I spent with Amber and her cousin. Amber was a cool chick. She was mad sexy, and she held her own. When I met her, she made it clear that she was looking for a good time, nothing serious, and since I wasn't trying to be in a relationship, I was good with that. We had a good day as far as I was concerned, but there were times I found Jamie watching me. He never said anything, but I could tell he was wondering what was going on with me and Amber. He never asked questions and seemed to relax after a while.

I got out of bed and went over to grab my laptop from the dresser. I propped myself against the headboard so I could check emails and my social media. I went to Instagram first and scrolled down my timeline. There were the usual pictures of all the food people had cooked, family pictures, and messages. I scrolled through some pics that Aimee posted when I came across one that stopped my hand from moving forward.

There was a group picture with Aimee, my cousins Mylyn and Kinzy, and Aimee's best friend Stephanie. What stopped me was Rachel standing in the middle of the group with the women's hands on her baby bump. I studied her face, and my heart skipped painfully. Rachel looked the same with the exception of the weight she'd gained with her pregnancy. Her face was a little fuller, her breasts a little heavier, and her hips a little wider. My eyes kept going to the small, round belly she sported under the multicolored blouse, then to her eyes. She was smiling, but there was something about it that didn't reach her eyes. Shaking myself, I closed the picture out.

I opened my emails. The first was from my dad. A note informed me that the attachments were pictures from Thanksgiving. The first one made me smile. My mom was feeding my dad a piece of pie. The next was of Aimee, her boyfriend, and both sets of parents. Then there were family members—aunts, uncles, cousins—family friends, and coworkers of Aimee's and my parents'. My parents' house was the spot where everyone congregated when we had any kind of occasion. They loved having family functions. Our cousins and friends were fixtures at our house during the summers and school breaks. I missed those days. I missed my mom's greens and sweet potatoes. I missed my aunt Patty's peach cobbler. Chuckling, I felt a little melancholy.

The next picture stunned me even more than the picture of Rachel. It was a sonogram. In the upper right corner, it read **Baby Hendricks**, the date, and the time.

That's your baby.

No.

I clenched my teeth in anger. This was not my baby. I couldn't think of it as my baby. It was a mistake that should never have happened. I shut my computer off, and my mood changed that fast. I was pissed because Rachel was right back to the forefront of my mind. She hurt me, and she broke my heart. I couldn't regret my decision to leave.

Anger pumped through me. I knew why my parents wouldn't let it go, but they were pushing me away. I loved them, but this was a decision they couldn't change my mind on. I needed to work some of this stress off, so I went to tell Jamie I was going to the gym on the top floor of my building.

Two hours later I had showered and dressed, and my muscles were killing me because of the grueling workout I put myself through. I tried to take all my anger and aggression out while I was working out. All I could think about while I did was that I was not ready for a baby. I'd made that very clear when Rachel and I discussed our five-year plan. I'd also made it clear to my parents and everyone else that Rachel made this decision on her own.

Jamie and I went to grab some breakfast after he showered and dressed. We were at a little mom-and-pop diner I'd found not far from my condo. The food reminded me of home, so I frequented it.

"Have you heard from the folks?" Jamie asked, setting his coffee down.

"Yeah. Dad sent an email of pictures from Thanksgiving."

He heard the anger in my voice, and his facial expression said it all. "What's that about?"

"He included pictures of Rachel and a copy of her ultrasound."

"I take it you're not happy about that?"

"No, I'm not. Rachel broke my heart. No one seems to think about how hard this is for me. I love Rachel. I wanted to marry her. She decided that she wanted something else."

Jamie was quiet while I vented. When I was done, he didn't say anything for a while. When he finally responded, he gave me some advice. "The only thing I can say is don't be too hard on the folks. This is their first grandbaby, and they're excited. Don't close them out because you don't agree on things in your life. They love you."

"Sometimes it's really hard to tell," I muttered, but I knew my parents loved me. I just wished they would respect my decisions in this situation.

Chapter Twenty-three

Rachel

Closing the door to my classroom, I was so glad it was Friday and the children had all gone home. It had been a long day and an even longer week. The kids were getting excited about the upcoming Christmas break, and they were getting a little unruly. I stayed longer than I intended so I could finish grading papers and get the room ready for Monday. I was going to surprise the kids with a little pre-holiday party, so I wanted everything in place. All I could think about while I worked was going home to a long, hot shower and propping up my swollen feet.

Once the decorations were up and the desks arranged as I wanted them, I took a final look around the room before I left and made my way toward the exit. I was surprised to see the principal's office door still open when I was passing the office. He stood up from his desk, calling my name.

"Please shut the door," he instructed when I stepped into his office.

I did so and took a seat across the desk from him. Alfonso Rivers was an attractive man. He was my height with brown skin, was clean-shaven, and wore wire-rimmed glasses that made him look bookish. We went on a couple of dates before I met Errick, but we decided we would be better friends. Now, a few years later, he was principal of the school.

"Miss Hendricks, you know that we want our school to be a comfortable learning environment for our children, a place parents can be confident in sending their child to learn, a place where teachers can enjoy their work."

I wondered where he was going with this. Starting out by calling me Miss Hendricks sounded very official. "Yes?"

"Is there something you would like to tell me?" His expression said it all.

Sitting back in my seat, I knew I should have said something earlier, but I didn't want to deal with the questions or explanations on top of everything else I was dealing with. I smiled wryly. "It's getting obvious, huh? I apologize that I didn't say anything before."

The stern expression on his face deepened when he said, "Miss Hendricks, perhaps you should consider taking some time to deal with your situation. We don't want your students to be . . . exposed to anything that could be construed as a . . . bad influence."

When his words sank in, my blood began to boil. I was hot all over at his implication. "Bad influence?"

"We wouldn't want the students, or their parents, to think that your situation is the example we want to set." He continued to look down his nose at me.

"My situation? The example we want to set? Are you trying to say you think I'm in my classroom teaching my five- and six-year-old students inappropriate things?" I knew what he was getting at, but he was going to have to say it. I was angry and embarrassed that he would even come at me like this. I'd done nothing but love and nurture my students over the years.

"No, but your situation still remains."

"Explain to me what you mean then, Principal Rivers."
I sat up in my chair, leaning in closer toward his desk as I
waited for him to finish his accusations.

"I think you should consider the welfare of your impres-
sionable, young students."

Sitting there with my body trembling, I had to take a
few deep breaths to keep calm. Rage threatened to con-
sume me. I'd worked at Blakemore Academy for several
years, and never once had I had a complaint or a problem
with any parents or coworkers. Now he was implying that
I would do something to harm my students? Fury shook
me, but I had to stay calm.

"Is there anything else?" My voice was as hard and cold
as his stare.

"Think about what I've said. I know you'll do the right
thing. That's all."

Just like that, I was dismissed. I made my way out of
the school with rubbery legs. I could still see the smug
look on Principal Rivers' face, and that look told me I'd
become just another statistic: an unwed black woman
about to have a fatherless child. As I climbed behind the
wheel of my car, the tears I'd fought to control began to
roll down my face. I sat there a long time crying, long
enough to see Principal Rivers come out of the building
and climb into his own car to leave the premises. I was
seething. *How dare he question me? Like I would really
do something to harm these kids.* I slammed my hand
against the steering wheel until it hurt. I yelled out in
frustration. I was pregnant and alone, and now my job
was in jeopardy.

"Damn you, Errick," I hissed through clenched teeth.

My tears continued to fall. I had to brush them away
over and over as I made my way through traffic. Dark
had come long ago. The temperature was in the high
thirties, and it was as cold inside as it was outside. When

I reached the house, I headed straight for the shower. After, I was wrapped up in my favorite old terry-cloth robe, settled in the middle of my bed. Tears continued to run down my face from time to time. I pulled my knees to my chin, wrapping my arm around them.

I didn't know what to do. I loved teaching. I loved watching the children's faces when they discovered something new, and knowing I was helping them in such a small way made my heart full. This hurt was a physical pain in my heart. Not bothering to turn on any lights, I lay down, my hands rubbing my belly as I prayed for guidance. It felt like from the moment I found out I was pregnant, my life kept taking left turns. Errick left me, took all my furniture, didn't want the baby, and turned me into a statistic, and now I could lose my job. When I thought about my baby, none of the rest of it mattered in the long run. It was hard right now, but I wanted this baby. I loved the baby already, and I promised to do everything I could to make sure he or she made it here safely. I would give them the best life I could. My stomach growled, but the thought of eating made me a little nauseated. The ringing of my phone brought me out of my dark thoughts.

"Hey, beautiful."

Just the sound of Saxon's voice brought more tears to my eyes and longing to my heart. I broke. Sobs burst from me before I could stop them.

"Hey, hey, what's wrong? Baby, talk to me. Are you okay?"

The concern in his tone made me cry that much harder. It took me a moment or two before I could answer. I finally managed to get the sobs to subside. I took a deep breath. "I'm okay. I just . . . I need you right now."

It took a lot for me to admit that, but I did. It had only been a few weeks since we'd taken things to the next level, and it was too soon to depend on him for support, but in this short time, that was what he'd become: my person to lean on.

"I'm on my way," he replied without hesitation.

True to his word, I was in his arms twenty minutes later, clinging to him, my tears soaking his shirt. When I finally calmed down enough to tell him what had happened, his indignation made me feel better about the whole situation. Saxon encouraged me to do what I felt was best, promising me he would be there for me no matter what.

I lay with my head in his lap, and he stroked my hair, massaging my forehead, soothing the worry lines there. The living room was dim. The only illumination was from the light of the TV. Thinking back over the weeks to when I met Saxon, I didn't know when or how he'd become the person I turned to first when I had something happen. It didn't matter if it was good or bad. Saxon was there. From the moment we'd had dinner at his sister's, he'd been there for me in any way I needed without asking for anything in return.

"Saxon?" I said, my voice low.

"Hm?"

"My baby's father's name is Errick. We dated for three years, and he asked me to marry him." I held nothing back as I told Saxon about Errick and the way our relationship ended. I actually felt relieved once I got it off my chest. When Errick walked out on me, he left me with all the fear of being a new mother and single parent. He'd hurt me when he disappeared from my life. How hard it had been, dealing with everything on my own. My emotions were a jumbled mess, preparing for the baby, all of that. "Errick hurt me bad. I swore to myself I didn't want to meet anyone for a long time. I didn't know if I would ever get over the pain and anger of what he did. You make me want to."

Saxon pulled me up into his arms. Settling against his chest, I laid my head on his shoulder. He kissed my forehead and then my lips. The way he looked at me made me feel safe, secure.

"I'm here for you, Rachel. It's his loss. You're a beautiful woman, and if you'll let me, I'll be here for you and the baby, too."

Throwing my arms around his neck, I kissed him, hanging on tightly. I was afraid that if I let go, I would float away and never get back to him.

Chapter Twenty-four

Saxon

Rachel and I spent time together every day. Since the night she told me about her ex, we had grown closer. Holding her head high, she still went to school every day. She hadn't decided what she was going to do, but I encouraged her to speak with an attorney. Whatever she decided, I was going to support her. Since we were spending time together, I made sure to leave my office no later than six or six thirty every night. I would grab dinner if she didn't feel like cooking and go to her place, where we would hang out watching movies or reading. After our intimacy on Thanksgiving, Rachel pulled back from me, but I wasn't having it. I understood she needed to take her time to get through the pain her ex had caused her, but I wasn't giving up on her. I tried to make sure she was as stress free as possible. I tried to be patient, and things were comfortable between us.

The Wednesday before Christmas, Josh and I were doing our shopping, picking up a few last-minute items. Decorations were everywhere, and it made me think about Rachel. She hadn't done anything to make her place festive.

We took a break, going to Ruby Tuesday in the mall. We were at the bar, talking, having a beer.

"You're really into this woman, huh?" Josh asked me.

"I am. She's a good woman. She's got her head on straight, and she doesn't let the fact that her baby's dad isn't in the picture stop her from doing what she needs to do."

"Damn, I see she got you gone." Josh started laughing but stopped suddenly. "Wait. This chick has a kid?"

"Well, she's pregnant. Why?" I looked at him, wondering what he was thinking.

"I don't know, man. You may wanna check this chick out for real. Does she know you're a doctor?"

"Yes, she knows."

"What if she's just looking for a father for her baby? How do you know if dude shows up, she won't run right back to him?"

I wanted to deny what Josh was saying, but I knew it happened. I just had to believe that she wouldn't do that. Her ex broke her heart, left her while she was pregnant with his child. On the other hand, she was attached to the man in a way I didn't understand. I pushed the doubt aside. I was going into this situation with open eyes. I believed in the possibility of what we could have, and I wasn't going to worry about the what-ifs.

"Rachel is through with that clown. He dumped her while she was pregnant. I don't see her getting past that."

Josh didn't push. He just looked at me with a smirk. "All right, man. Just watch yourself."

"Man, this ain't some hood chick. She's fully capable of taking care of herself. She doesn't need my money."

"Shit, a lot of them are capable, but that doesn't mean they want to." He held his hands up in a surrender gesture when he saw the frown on my face. "I'm just saying I don't want to see you taken advantage of. Just be careful."

I was glad to leave the restaurant after that conversation. I shook off my irritation. Josh and I got back in the mood of things as we made our way around the mall. I picked up several things for the baby. I saw Josh's mouth twitch a few times, but he kept any comments to himself. We left the mall a little while later, loaded down with gifts. I stopped at a Christmas tree lot we passed on the way. Josh got out with me while I looked around. When I found the perfect tree, Josh and the man from the lot helped me tie it down to the roof of my car. We made another stop at Target to get ornaments and lights. I filled the cart with things before paying and loading the car.

"I take it you're spending Christmas with this woman?" Josh asked once we were settled back in the warmth of the car.

"If she'll let me."

"Saxon, for real, are you sure you want to be a ready-made family?"

"Aren't you jumping the gun?" I chuckled, but he was shaking his head before I even got it all the way out.

"No, once that baby is here, you're part of a ready-made family."

I didn't say anything as I made my way through traffic so I could drop Josh off at his place. What Josh said was true. Rachel was a ready-made family. If I wanted her, I had to accept all of her, and that included her baby.

After helping Josh carry his stuff inside, I dapped him, told him I would call him later, then went back to my car. Traffic was heavy as I headed straight to Rachel's. I knocked and waited nervously for her to open the door. She answered wearing joggers and a large T-shirt that was clinging to her round belly. Her feet were clad in fuzzy slippers. Fresh-faced and casual, she was beautiful. In that moment, I knew I was ready. Rachel and her baby were a package deal, and I was okay with that.

"Hey, boo." She accepted the kiss I dropped on her lips.

Rubbing her belly, I told her I would be right back. I went to the car, cut the cord that held the tree, and pulled it from the roof. It took me a few minutes of struggling to bring the tree inside. Rachel watched me from the porch, giggling as I finally managed to get it in and propped against the wall.

"What are you doing?" she asked through laughter.

I shook loose needles from my coat while Rachel shut the door against the cold. Pulling her into my arms, I kissed her thoroughly this time. She pressed her warm body against me, wrapping her arms around my neck and kissing me back.

When the kiss ended, I looked down into her warm brown eyes. "We're decorating a Christmas tree. This is our first Christmas together, and we're going to celebrate."

Rachel's eyes got watery, but she wore a smile. "Thank you."

"Have you eaten?" I asked, rubbing her firm belly.

Her voice was low and husky. "Not yet."

I loved that she was bashful with me sometimes. It made teasing her so much easier. "Okay, I'm gonna get the rest of the stuff from the car. Order something, and we can decorate the tree while we wait." I gave her a light push in the direction of the living room.

Opening the door to get the rest of the stuff, I was startled by an older couple who were about to ring the bell. They had gaily wrapped bags and packages in their arms.

"Hello, is Rachel here?" the man asked. His voice was deep, his eyes wary as he looked me over. I knew he was inspecting me. I wondered if he was Rachel's father.

Calling for Rachel, I stepped back to allow them to enter.

"What is it? You need some help?" Rachel was carrying a pizza menu with her.

I saw the way she reacted when she saw the couple standing there. She looked nervous, even a little scared. Taking a step closer to her, I held out my hand to her, but the woman stepped between us, wrapping Rachel in a hug with a smile on her face. When she released her, the woman ran a hand lovingly over her belly. That seemed to make her relax, and she smiled.

"Sorry we just popped up, but we wanted to surprise you and to deliver these gifts before we leave tomorrow." The woman turned her attention to me, extending the hand that wasn't on Rachel's belly. "I'm Anna, and this is my husband, Paul."

"Um, Anna, Paul, this is a friend of mine, Saxon Carmichael. Saxon, this is Anna and Paul Martin."

Shaking hands with both of them, I saw the open appraisal in their eyes. They looked at one another. They were having a conversation with no words. It was obvious they were so familiar with each other that it didn't even take long.

Anna noticed the tree against the wall for the first time. She gave a very girly squeak of excitement. "You got one. I'm glad you changed your mind."

Rachel laughed at her before she glanced at me. "Saxon bought it for me. He was just bringing it and all the decorations."

"You should stay to help us decorate it," Anna said to me. She took Rachel's arm and led her into the living room.

"I'll be right back. I'm going to get the rest of the stuff from the car," I told Rachel.

"Let me help you," Paul offered, following me out into the cold.

Pulling boxes and bags from the car, I laughed at how overboard I'd gone. I wanted to make this a Christmas that Rachel would remember. I wanted our first Christmas to be special. Paul grabbed a few bags. It didn't take long before he started to question me. I didn't hesitate to answer when he asked how Rachel and I met. I had nothing to hide, and although I usually wasn't into answering strangers' questions, I could tell he was only concerned for Rachel.

"I'm glad to know that someone is looking out for her. Anna and I worry about her. We want our grandbaby to be healthy and happy," Paul told me, taking some of the bags, and we made our way back up the walk.

The connection hit. It had been in the back of my mind since I heard their last name, but for some reason it didn't come to me until now. Anna and Paul Martin were Errick's parents.

"I worry about her too. Trust me, I'll take care of her if she'll let me."

Paul studied me for a long moment before nodding when we stepped up onto the porch. "I believe you will."

The four of us spent the evening decorating. We left the tree to the ladies until it got too high on the seven-foot spruce. Paul and I hung garland and lights around the windows. I learned a lot more about Rachel listening to the teasing banter between the three of them. They didn't exclude me, but I kept quiet because I wanted to know the carefree Rachel they talked about. She was so reserved since I met her, but it was because she'd been hurt. This Rachel, the one with the quick laugh and dancing eyes, was the one I wanted for her.

"What are you two doing for the holiday?" I asked them as I climbed the ladder to put the ornaments where the ladies couldn't reach.

"We're leaving tomorrow to visit our son," Anna replied.

I saw Rachel freeze just for a brief moment. Our eyes met and I smiled. She relaxed and smiled at me, and things moved right along.

The older couple left us shortly after, declining the pizza that was delivered as we finished up. Wishing us a merry Christmas, they promised Rachel they would check in on her and see her when they returned.

Once we were alone, we relaxed on the sofa with the lights off so we could enjoy the clear, twinkling lights on the tree.

"I like them. I can see they love you," I told her, speaking of Anna and Paul. I took a deep drink from the bottle of beer I held.

Rachel smiled, laying her head on my shoulder. "I love them too. They've been good to me."

I didn't know how to broach the subject without upsetting her. The last time I asked anything, I'd made her cry. I took a deep breath and asked anyway. "Do you hear anything from him?"

"No." She sighed. "When Anna told me he moved to Phoenix, I knew it was totally and completely over. He's made it clear from day one that he doesn't want to hear about me or the baby. He feels I got pregnant on purpose. He blames me for everything."

I could hear the hurt in her voice, but it didn't seem to be as strong as it was when I first met her. I hoped I had something to do with that. "I'm sorry."

"Thank you, but you don't have anything to be sorry for. I'm getting used to it. I don't want to dwell on it. Besides, if it weren't for Errick leaving me, I would have never gotten to know you." She looked up at me, her dark eyes shining. "Thank you for everything. I know you're trying to cheer me up, and I really appreciate you."

Tapping my shoulder, she sat up, and I stood. Taking her hands, I pulled her gently to her feet, wrapping her in my arms. I needed to leave. The way she was looking at me had me wanting to take her upstairs. Kissing her lightly, I told her I would call her later. I wanted her to ask me to stay, but I respected that she wanted to move in her own time. Patience was a virtue, and Rachel was worth waiting for.

Chapter Twenty-five

Rachel

The incessant ringing of the doorbell brought me slowly from the depths of sleep and my comforter. Turning over, I sighed, aggravated, certain I was dreaming, but the dream was so real. When the bell rang again in quick succession, I pushed the covers from me. I knew I was awake. I groaned as I pushed myself up from the bed. The sun was barely up, the house still dim and shadowy. Tossing a robe on over my nightie, I went down the stairs as fast as my growing belly would allow. Rubbing the sleep from my eyes, I tried to smooth down my mussed hair, pulling it away from my face.

Another quick round of rings had me groaning and clenching my teeth. "I'm coming. I'm coming."

Yanking the door open, I let out a yelp when a blast of cold air followed Saxon in the house. Grabbing me, Saxon hugged me.

"You're warm." He buried his cold face in my neck, dropping kisses against my skin and making me shiver. He whispered softly against my ear, "Merry Christmas to you."

Squealing, I wiggled to get out of his arms. "Saxon, you're cold."

Laughing, he let me go. Slapping my ass, he pushed me lightly. "Go in the living room. Go."

"Give me a minute." I went back upstairs to wash my face and brush my teeth before going back downstairs and into the living room.

I didn't know what Saxon was up to, but I was excited. *Christmas morning*. I opened the curtains, turned on the Christmas tree lights, then took a seat on the floor next to the tree. Rubbing my belly, I wished the baby a merry Christmas. I couldn't wait until next year when we would celebrate together.

"Ho, ho, ho. Merry Christmas." Saxon came in wearing a Santa beard and hat. He was pushing a stroller filled with gaily wrapped gifts.

"Oh, my." Tears immediately sprang to my eyes. My hand flew to cover my mouth. "What have you done?"

Saxon came to sit beside me on the floor where I had my face buried in my hands. He gently pulled my hand away, bringing it to his lips and kissing gently across my knuckles. "I hope these are happy tears. Come on, open them."

His smile melted me. I wanted to put my arms around him, hold him tight, and stay that way forever. Instead, my face flushed. I looked away bashfully. This man and the attention he paid me had my heart all aflutter. Saxon did all this just to make me smile.

I was glad I was sitting down. I was sure my weak knees wouldn't support me as I looked at all the packages inside the convertible stroller. Saxon's excitement became contagious as I tore into the presents. There were bottles and bibs, a diaper bag, diapers, onesies, footies, a baby tub full of shampoos, lotions, and wash, powder, and ointments. When the last gift was opened, I sat amid the piles of torn paper and empty boxes. I burst into tears again. Saxon's kindness was overwhelming.

"Hey, hey, what's wrong?" Saxon moved closer, pulling me against his chest. Holding me, he rubbed his hand along my back in soothing circles.

Shaking my head, I couldn't answer over the lump in my throat. I didn't understand how Saxon could be so good to me when my child's father, the man who claimed to love me, couldn't. I would never forget how special Saxon made this day for me.

Sitting up, I brushed my tears from my face, took a deep breath, and gave Saxon a small smile. "I'm okay. It's just . . . I didn't expect all this. You . . . I just appreciate you."

Kissing my temple, he held out his hand. "Here. You missed something."

I could only look from him to the box.

"Take it. Go ahead."

My fingers trembled when I took it. I opened it, and my heart skipped. The tears that just tapered off started again. Inside the box, nestled on the white interior, was a thin silver chain with a silver locket. A filigree design was etched on the front, with lots of swirls and curlicues entwined around an R. On the back, it was inscribed "From S, 12-25" and the year. Taking the chain from my hands, he put it around my neck, securing the clasp. Leaning over, I kissed him, a light brush against his lips, but I felt that brief contact all the way to my toes.

"Thank you so much. You've made this day very special." My cold fingers brushed the locket.

We made breakfast together, and then after breakfast, I showered and dressed, coming downstairs in a long denim skirt and a maternity top. I'd taken time to put on makeup, and I made sure to put my locket back on. I heard Rosie's voice as I made my way down. I found her and Saxon in the living room talking.

Rosie looked over, winking at me. "Merry Christmas, boo."

Hugging my friend, I accepted and opened the gifts she brought. There were more things for the baby and a day at the spa for me. I gave her a fire engine red dress that would look fabulous on her.

Taking me aside when Rosie went to get a cup of coffee, Saxon wrapped his arms around me. He kissed the tip of my nose. "Hey, I'm gonna go. I've gotta stop by my parents' house and Moira's. You know, you can always come with me."

"No, you go see your family." My face flushed at the thought that he wanted to introduce me to his family. "I'm sure your family wants to spend time with you and not some stranger you bring along."

"You're not just some stranger," he said sternly.

My heart melted. He made me feel so cherished.

"Go, enjoy your day." I pushed him toward the door playfully.

Catching my wrist, he pulled me close again, kissing me. The kiss was hot, lingering, taking my breath away and making my body hum.

"Ahem." Rosie came through, clearing her throat.

I jumped, trying to push my way out of his arms. He wouldn't let me go. Instead, he kissed me again, and I stopped struggling immediately. When he broke the kiss, his eyes met mine, staring at me intently. "I'll see you later."

I could only nod. My heart skipped in my chest, and the way he looked at me made the butterfly wings brush my belly.

"Bye, Rosie," he called, and then he was out the door.

Chapter Twenty-six

Saxon

My parents and my aunt and uncle were in the living room when I arrived. I knew my mother and Aunt Thelma made breakfast. It was their Christmas tradition. Aunt Thelma and her husband, Uncle Ben, lived about two streets over, and the sisters took turns having holidays at their places.

"There he is," my mother said when I came in. I gave her and Aunt Thelma a kiss, then shook my father's and Uncle Ben's hands.

"Are you hungry? Your sister and Daniel should be here shortly with my baby," my dad said.

"No, I had breakfast with a friend this morning." I sat on the sofa next to my mother. I knew we would open gifts when Samarra arrived. My parents wouldn't even start the Christmas celebration without their only grandchild.

"A friend?" Aunt Thelma questioned.

"Yes, a friend." I chuckled. If I gave my auntie any indication of how I felt about Rachel, she would run with it and be planning a wedding for next week. She had dubbed herself the family matchmaker.

Before she could reply, there was a knock at the door. Moira, Daniel, and Samarra came in in a whirlwind of voices and laughter.

"Merry Christmas, Grandma and Grandpa," Samarra yelled, running to give them both hugs and kisses.

She then ran over and jumped into my arms. I scooped her up and kissed her all over her face before putting her down. I hugged Moira, whose stomach was getting bigger by the day, then gave Daniel a man hug. We settled down in the family room to open presents, allowing Samarra to pass them out as we oohed and aahed over our gifts. Samarra kept us laughing as she ran around overloaded with excitement and the treats my parents kept giving her.

Spending the morning with them, I enjoyed myself, but I kept thinking of Rachel, wondering what she was doing, how she was feeling. I had to force myself not to call her. I wanted her to enjoy her day with her friend.

Dad and Uncle Ben put steaks on the grill, and Mom and Aunt Thelma made the sides while Daniel, Moira, and I played with Samarra and talked. It wasn't long before family and friends began to stop by. My parents had several friends in the neighborhood, and they began to fill the house. My mom was in her element, entertaining and making sure everyone was okay.

Daniel caught me alone on the deck when Dad asked me to get the food from the grill.

"What's going on with you, brother-in-law?" He took a drink from the beer he carried.

"Just working and trying to maintain. How's things with you?"

We talked a few minutes while I finished on the grill. Daniel was cool. He was good to my sister, and he was crazy about Samarra. I liked him, and we hung out a few times a month.

"How are things going with Ms. Hendricks?"

He caught me off guard. I hadn't mentioned anything about Rachel to him since the night I followed her home. He'd never brought her up before.

"Um, she's good."

He laughed, shaking his head. "How are y'all doing? I know you've been seeing her."

"What?"

"You've been different since the night at our house. I see you smiling in your phone, and I heard you call her Rachel a couple of times. I put two and two together."

I wasn't trying to hide my situation with Rachel. I just didn't know what it was at that point, and I didn't want to put any pressure on her by pushing for a relationship. "We've been hanging out."

"I hear you. I think she's a good look for you," he told me before Moira stuck her head out the door and called him.

I finished with the grill, grabbed the pan, and went inside. Lunch was full of laughter. We sat around the large dining room table and reminisced about Christmases past. These were times I really enjoyed being with my family. After lunch, we went into the family room and watched football, just like we always did.

Chapter Twenty-seven

Rachel

Saxon wasn't gone but a short while when Rosie started hitting me with questions. "You and Saxon are getting close, huh?"

I smiled. "He's been good to me."

"Are you good to him?"

Confused, I frowned at her. "What?"

"That is a good man. You need to get past Errick and recognize that where he failed you, Saxon has taken up the slack. I never thought I would say this, but I'm glad you have Saxon in your life. He's good for you. Look what he did for you today. That man is crazy about you. I just want to see you give him a chance," Rosie said, lecturing me.

She was right, and I knew it. Saxon did all the little things for me that a boyfriend or husband would, fixing small things around the house, cleaning up my car, making sure my oil and things were okay. He gave me kindness and encouragement. Saxon was all the things I needed in my life. We'd only known each other a short while, but if felt like he'd been a part of my life forever.

Rosie and I spent the day together. I threw together lasagna for dinner. Saxon returned in the early evening. I realized I missed him. I stood against the doorframe leading into the living room, watching while he took his coat off and hung it in the closet. Turning, he caught me staring. I blew him a kiss. When he smiled at me, my heart sang.

Anna and Paul surprised me just as we were about to sit down for dinner. They came back from Phoenix early so that I wouldn't be alone for the holidays. Anna came into the kitchen as I removed the lasagna from the oven. She gave Rosie and me hugs and kisses. Washing her hands, she took the sweet potato pie from the counter, sliding it in the oven.

Almost absently, she said, "I think that young man is in love with you."

My heart slammed in my chest. *Love? No.* I just looked at the older woman. "Saxon and I are friends."

Anna and Rosie looked at each other, then laughed.

"I've been trying to tell her," Rosie said to Anna.

"I know I'm older and all, but in my day, when a man did all that Saxon seems to do for you, he was more than just a friend." Anna stopped my protest before I could even begin. "Errick is my son. I love him with my whole heart, and you know I'm sorry for the way things have turned out between you, but Saxon isn't Errick. He's in love with you. Even though you are pregnant by another man, he loves you, and you're on your way to being in love with him. I see it in your eyes, so don't try to deny it. Don't fight it either. You deserve to be happy, to be loved. Don't stand in your own way. Don't be scared because you've been hurt before. We've all been hurt, but if Saxon wants to love you, let him."

I hugged Anna. I was glad I had her in my life since I didn't have my mother anymore. I knew I could talk to her about anything and she would give me the truth. She was right. I had to let go of the pain and anger that Errick left me with.

It was nice to have my small adoptive family around me. Dinner was filled with chatter, laughter, and warmth. I was tired when we finished, and I was glad the men offered to clean up the kitchen. Anna, Rosie, and I were in the living room. I sipped the half a glass of wine that my doctor told me I could have. Once the men were finished, Anna and Paul left with another round of hugs and kisses. Rosie left shortly after.

I walked her to the door, where she hugged me, whispering in my ear, "Don't let him get away."

I swallowed over the lump in my throat as I squeezed my friend. "Thank you. I love you. You be careful and let me know you made it home."

Closing the door behind Rosie, I turned to find Saxon standing right behind me. He'd seemed a little distracted this evening, but I didn't say anything about it. I wondered if something happened at his parents' house while he was there. He wrapped his arms around me, holding me for a long time without saying anything. I felt good in his arms.

Finally, he said, "I better go too."

"I want you to stay with me." I looked into his hazel eyes. I needed him tonight. I didn't want this feeling to end. If he stayed with me, I would feel loved and protected—everything he always made me feel.

"Are you sure?" He studied me.

Saxon didn't want to pressure me. I knew that. Right now, I was pressuring him. Taking his hand, I kissed him softly.

"I want you to stay with me."

I led the way upstairs to my bedroom, where I made love to him late into Christmas night.

Chapter Twenty-eight

Saxon

Spending time with Rachel was something I looked forward to every day. The dynamic of our relationship changed after Christmas. I stepped right into the role of her man even though we hadn't put a title on things. I met her in John's office for appointments. When she hit her five-month mark, we found out she was having a girl. I dropped a few tears when John told us. Rachel laughed at me. I didn't care. I felt like the baby she was carrying was a part of me. I was fascinated by her pregnancy and the changes I was experiencing with her. We spent evenings going over ideas for the nursery, and I helped her get the room decorated, painting it and setting up the crib and changing table. I made sure she had everything she needed, often making late-night runs for ice cream, which she craved by the bucket.

Josh still questioned Rachel's motives, but he didn't say much anymore because he could see I was happy. I was falling in love with Rachel. She was everything I wanted. The time we spent together since Christmas showed me that.

It was the beginning of February when I picked her up on a cold early evening that threatened a rain/snow mix. I rang her bell. She answered dressed in a pair of black pants and a brightly printed maternity top. She was almost seven months pregnant now, and I thought she was absolutely beautiful with her big belly and glowing skin.

I kissed her full lips, running a cold hand over her belly. "Hello, ladies."

"Hello, handsome." Rachel laughed at me. Grabbing her bag and coat, she stepped out into the cold night with me. Helping her down the stairs, I was careful that she didn't fall. I laughed a little on the inside. I was hovering, but I couldn't help it. I didn't know what I would do if something happened to her. Helping her into the passenger seat, I went around the car, sliding behind the wheel. When I looked over at her, I wanted to forget about going out. I wanted to take her inside, strip her naked, and spend the evening in bed.

I didn't tell Rachel where we were going. We made small talk while we drove, and she was distracted looking up stuff for her registry on her phone, so she wasn't paying attention to where we were. When I stopped, she looked up. She frowned a little when she saw we were at Moira's place.

"Saxon, you know I don't want Samarra to know we're seeing each other."

Rachel left her position with Blakemore Academy after the Christmas break. She was stressed, and the principal was making it uncomfortable for her to work there. Since she'd been Samarra's teacher, she didn't want her to think that I was the father of her baby.

Taking her hand, I kissed her fingertips. "She's at a sitter's. Don't worry. C'mon, let's get inside."

Ringing the bell, we stood waiting for someone to answer, so I pulled her closer. Rachel giggled as I buried my face in her neck, kissing her lightly.

"You are so bad."

"Only with you." I planted small kisses against her ear. "I love you."

A flicker of panic shaded Rachel's eyes. Her mouth fell open, but nothing came out. I kissed her, this time a little more deeply, until she kissed me back and I felt her relax a little. Rachel had to know how I felt about her. How could she not?

For weeks I'd been telling myself that I wasn't sure if what I was feeling was real. I thought about her when we were not together. I wanted to protect her and make her happy. I wanted to make sure the baby in her belly was loved and protected as well. Wasn't that love? I thought so, and being with her right here on my sister's doorstep, I knew for sure that I didn't want to ever be without her.

The door opened, and I was scooped into a fierce hug. Passed from one set of arms to the next, I never released Rachel's hand I was holding. When I was released from the hugs I received, I tugged her a little closer.

"Rachel, meet Ellen and Connor Carmichael, my parents."

Chapter Twenty-nine

Errick

The weather in Phoenix was overcast and rainy. The sky was gray with low-hanging clouds that blocked the normally beautifully shining sun. My game of golf was canceled due to the rain, so I came to the club I was now a member of to play racquetball with one of my colleagues. After an invigorating game, we showered, then went to the restaurant in the clubhouse to have an early dinner.

Over orders of grilled shrimp and salmon, Calvin Collins, my colleague, and I enjoyed drinks. Cal was the only other black VP in my area of the company. He was cool, a smart guy, worked hard, ambitious. I liked hanging out with him.

"You don't have any family living here?" Cal asked.

"Nope, everyone's in Nashville."

"I'm sure there's some lucky lady waiting for you to come back."

I laughed, but Rachel's face popped into my head—her bright smile and sparkling eyes. Pushing her image away, I shook my head. "No, I'm free and single."

"Don't let my wife hear that. She'll have you fixed up and married off before you know what hit you."

"Not me. I was almost married, but it didn't work out. That's enough for me right now," I insisted. Relationships and marriage were the last things on my mind.

"Almost married doesn't count." Cal chuckled. His laughter died off when we saw three women dressed in tennis outfits that accentuated their tight bodies stroll by our table.

I didn't miss the look Cal gave them. "Man, you're married."

"Married, not dead."

Shaking my head, I couldn't help but start liking this guy. He was funny.

Leaving the club later, I ran through the parking lot to my car, but I still ended up soaked. Traffic was slow and heavy, giving me time to think about the conversation with Cal about his wife marrying me off. It made me think of Rachel, something I managed not to do for a while. I couldn't help thinking about the last time I saw her. My heart was broken, and I was furious with her for putting me in this situation. Now that time had passed and my anger wasn't so white hot, I could think about her and remember some of the good things. I couldn't help wondering how she was doing, what she looked like now, how far along she was, if she knew what she was having. I missed her. It was getting easier, but I tried not to think about her often.

My cell rang. Answering on my Bluetooth, I smiled when Amber's warm voice filled my car.

"Hey, *papi*."

"Hey, what are you doing?"

"I was thinking about you. You wanna come over and play?" The invitation in her voice was unmistakable.

Laughing aloud, I told her I would be there soon. Amber was just what I needed right now. Thoughts of Rachel were something I didn't want to deal with, so a nice diversion was welcome.

Chapter Thirty

Rachel

His parents? He brought me to meet his parents, my mind screamed. I could tell from the looks on their faces that Ellen and Connor Carmichael were just as surprised as I was.

"Hey, you two." Moira broke the tableau, pushing past her stunned parents to pull me into a hug. Then she led us all inside out of the cold.

Following Moira into the living room on wooden legs, I tried to compose myself. I could feel the eyes boring into my back as Saxon's parents looked me over. I was going to kill Saxon later. *How could he do this with no warning? His parents?*

Moira took our coats, giving me the opportunity to study Ellen and Connor out of the corner of my eye. Ellen was attractive with salt-and-pepper hair cut into a fashion-forward bob that framed her pretty face. She had a smooth chocolate complexion and dark eyes, which at that moment rested on my large belly. Connor was his wife's exact opposite. Tall like Saxon, he had sparkling green eyes and reddish-brown hair that was streaked with gray and still tumbled over his forehead, giving him a boyish look. I could see where Saxon and Moira got their looks from. They were almost the spitting image of their father.

"You guys have a seat. I'm going to check on Daniel. I left him alone in the kitchen. Can I get you something to drink?" Moira offered.

Taking the chair, I tried to control the nervous knots in my belly. I asked for a ginger ale. Saxon and I spent a lot of time with Moira and Daniel lately, and since she was pregnant as well, she kept a stock on hand.

I glanced at Saxon when he sat on the end of the love seat closest to my chair. I couldn't believe he would spring his parents on me like this. When he reached over, taking my hand, I wanted to strangle him. When he brought my hand to his lips, kissing the back of it, I couldn't stop the small smile even though I didn't want to react that way. I was mad at him. He shouldn't be able to make me smile so easily. But that was the effect Saxon had on me.

Ellen and Connor settled beside one another on the sofa. Ellen didn't bother to hide the fact that she was scrutinizing me. It was obvious from the moment the door was opened and she saw me standing there with her son.

"How was your trip?" Saxon inquired.

His parents just returned from a month's visit to his sister at the homestead in Ireland. Saxon told me it was something his parents did a couple of times a year.

Connor started to answer but was interrupted by his wife. I felt her eyes on me, so I made certain to look directly at her.

"Excuse me." Ellen patted her husband's leg, gave him a sweet smile, then looked back at me. "Young lady, is that my grandchild?"

Saxon and I exchanged a look. I knew this question would come up if we dated. I wasn't sure what Saxon told his parents, so I wasn't sure how to respond. From the looks on both of their faces, he didn't tell them much about me. Saxon gave me an encouraging smile. I wanted to kick his ass.

"No." I sat up a little straighter. "No, it's not."

A look was exchanged between husband and wife. Then she looked to Saxon. "Son?"

"Rachel and I met after she knew she was pregnant," Saxon answered his mother's silent inquiry.

"Are you trying to find a father for this child?" Ellen turned her attention back to me.

Anger ran through me at her implication. "My child has a father. He just happens to not be in the picture."

"Mother," Saxon said in a scolding tone.

"It's okay, Saxon. I think this is something we need to get on the table right now. I don't want your family thinking I am after you for anything other than being who you are." I smiled at him. I couldn't avoid this if I was going to be a part of Saxon's life. I just wished he had given me some kind of warning that today would be the day. Turning my attention back to Ellen and Connor— Ellen really because she would be the one to convince—I repeated, "Saxon and I met after I knew I was pregnant. What else would you like to know?"

"I want to know how you feel about our son and where he fits into your situation," Ellen came back immediately.

I was a little taken aback by her abruptness but understood her concern for her son. If it were my child, I would want to protect them as well. Saxon bringing me home big and pregnant had his mother's nerves worked, I was sure.

"Saxon and I have grown very close over the last few months. He's a wonderful man." I glanced at Saxon with a smile. He was a good man. I wanted him to always know how much I appreciated him.

"And?" Ellen indicated I should continue.

And? How did Saxon fit into my situation? He fit perfectly. He was everything I needed him to be whenever I needed it from him. There were many times he knew what I needed before I did. .

"I love you."

Those words, his words, played in my mind, making my heart race. Fear rushed through me. *How could Saxon love me? We've only known each other for a few months.* I was pregnant by a man who left me because I was pregnant with his baby. How could Saxon want to step in as the man in my life when Errick, the man who claimed to love me for years, so easily walked away? I couldn't deal with that right then, so I pushed those thoughts away.

"And he's very special to me."

Ellen watched me closely. I could feel her dark eyes. It was like she was trying to look through me. After what felt like a long time but was only a minute or two, she nodded her head once.

"Good." Ellen looked at her husband. "I like this young lady. She doesn't back down, and I can't make her say something she doesn't feel."

Tension left my shoulders. I relaxed in my seat a little. Saxon smiled at me, winking and bringing my hand to his lips to kiss the tips of my fingers. I smiled back at him, feeling like I passed a test. I glanced over to the entrance of the dining area. Moira was peeking around the corner. She gave me a thumbs-up. I winked at her.

The doorbell rang. Moira moved from her hiding space to answer it. Another surprise was in store when Rosie and her friend Charles followed Moira back into the room.

Standing, I hugged Charles first, then turned to Rosie. She didn't bother to hug me. Her hands went straight for my belly. As she talked baby talk to my bump, I asked what she and Charles were doing there. I was surprised when she said Moira invited her to dinner. I didn't know they knew each other except for the time I introduced them at school.

Introducing Rosie and Charles to his parents, Saxon wrapped an arm around my waist, smiling down at me. He thought he was slick, but he wasn't getting off that easily.

Chapter Thirty-one

Saxon

Taking Rachel's hand, I stopped her when Moira told us dinner was ready. When we were alone in the living room, I kissed her on her soft lips.

"You were great," I murmured as I nibbled at her bottom lip.

Pulling away, Rachel scowled at me, her face scrunched up in a mean mug. She punched me in the arm, hard. "Uh-uh. Why didn't you tell me you were bringing me here to meet your parents?"

"Come on, you two." Moira stuck her head around the corner.

We all laughed.

"Behave," I playfully scolded as I ducked from the next punch to my arm. I tried to kiss her again, but Rachel held up a hand in my face, and my lips connected to her palm.

"Oh, no, you will not get off that easy." She was acting upset, but I could tell by the twinkle in her eyes that she was pretending.

"Come on, let's get in here before Moira sends my mom after you."

Taking her hand, I led the way to the dining room, where Daniel and Moira were bringing out the last dishes from the kitchen.

Over dinner, I watched the way Rachel interacted with my family. I was happy with the way she handled my mother and her questions. I should've warned her she was going to meet my parents, but I was scared she wouldn't have come tonight if I did. Rachel was still holding back from me, and I didn't know what to do to break down that wall. I understood her hesitation about getting involved with me. Her life was complicated when we met, but she swore she didn't want to go back to the man who broke her heart. I just wanted to be the one to help hers heal.

Rachel fit in with my family like she'd known them for years. Even Rosie and Charles felt like family. As the evening progressed, it was obvious that Rachel had my father's approval. She laughed and teased him. She even made him blush a couple of times. My mother was more reserved, but when she found out Rachel was a teacher, she seemed to soften a little. Rachel talked books and the educational system with Daniel. It was a discussion they'd had several times before. She talked babies with Moira, she asked about my parents' trip to Ireland, and she and Rosie shared stories with us about them growing up together.

I thought about my parents' marriage. Thirty-two years and my dad still thought my mom was the most beautiful woman in the world, and he treated her like that. Their relationship was solid and filled with love. Moira and I witnessed it growing up. It was still obvious. They were affectionate, and they touched each other unconsciously whenever they were close to each other. They finished each other's sentences. I wanted that in my life. Glancing at Rachel as she joked around with my dad, I felt warm inside.

After dinner, the men cleared the table and brought in dessert: thick slices of chocolate cake with whipped cream and cherries drizzled over it. I made it a point to be the last one to leave the kitchen. Peeping through the door to make sure everyone was at their place, I rejoined the table, setting Rachel's plate in front of her.

My pulse was racing. With small beads of sweat dotting my forehead and upper lip, I was struggling to keep my breathing normal. When Rachel smiled her thanks at me, her brown eyes sparkled, and I knew I was making the right decision.

I watched, waiting as Rachel picked up her fork and started to cut the cake. Her fork stopped midway to the plate before slipping from her fingers, making a loud clank against the china as it fell. When she looked at me, her eyes were full of questions. Uncertainty, disbelief, stunned—all those expressions crossed her pretty features in quick succession.

Looking back down at her plate, tears swam in her eyes. Nestled in the rich chocolate of the cake was a two-carat, marquise-cut diamond ring. Her ring. All she had to do was say yes.

One by one, those at the table realized what was going on and fell silent. I took her hand.

"Rachel, I know this is sudden, and you don't have to answer right now, but I love you. I feel like all my life I've been waiting for you. I want to be the man you need, the one you depend on. You and the baby both. I know you're a package deal, and that's a package I'm ready to open and cherish. I love both of you, and I want you to be my wife." Holding up my hand to stop her before she could respond, I continued, "Please, just think about it."

Taking the ring from the cake and cleaning off the band, I slid it on her finger. Tears caught in the back of my throat. I looked around the table. My mom looked stunned, and my dad gave me a knowing look, one that said we would be talking later. Moira and Rosie had excited smiles. Daniel nodded. Rachel's tears finally overflowed her lids, rolling silently down her cheeks as she looked at the ring.

Rosie jumped to her feet and rushed around the table, followed by Moira. She grabbed Rachel's hand, and they both exclaimed over the ring. My mother told me it was a beautiful choice. The men laughed at the women's excitement.

That night, when I took Rachel home, I walked her to the door, kissed her good night, then waited while she unlocked the door. Once she was inside, I turned to leave.

"You're not staying?" Rachel's smoky voice stopped me.

Shaking my head, I pulled my coat closer around me. The temperature had dropped from the time I picked her up earlier, there were light flurries blowing around, and our breath was like vapor in the cold. It was hard for me to leave, but I knew if I stayed, I would push her for an answer, and I wanted her to come to her decision without me harassing her.

"No, but I'll call you when I get in. I love you." With a last, lingering kiss, I left her, leaving my heart right there with her.

Chapter Thirty-two

Errick

With the day at a perfect sixty-nine degrees, with very little breeze and a clear blue sky overhead, I was getting spoiled. The weather in Phoenix made me realize how much I was loving it here. Not having to deal with the frigid cold that Nashville had during the winter was a definite bonus to moving here. Traffic moved easily as I made my way home after a round of golf with some colleagues. We spent the morning on the golf course talking business and making plans to attend the Suns game the next day. My networking base was growing, and I was meeting a lot of people who could be great contacts to have. My boss was pleased with my work and showing confidence by letting me hire a couple more designers to my team. This was exactly where my life was supposed to be. This was what I envisioned for my career.

What about love?

What about it?

You know you miss Rachel.

My inner dialogue was messing with me. Shaking it off, I put it and any thoughts of Rachel from my mind.

Twenty minutes later, I was at the house. After a quick shower, I tossed on some basketball shorts and a T-shirt before flopping down on the couch to channel surf. Nothing caught my attention, so I left it on some

National Geographic programming, then tossed the
remote aside on the sofa. Grabbing my cell from the sofa
table, I scrolled through until I got to David's number.
Hitting him up, I thought it would be a good time to catch
up. We'd been missing each other lately with our busy
schedules. I was actually surprised when he answered.
We talked for a while, filling each other in on what we
were missing in our daily lives. Then David's voice grew
serious. "I saw Aimee yesterday."

"Oh, yeah?" I hadn't talked to Aimee in a while. We
weren't as close as Jamie and me, but I loved my little
sister. "What's she up to?"

"She's chillin', said she's been working and all that."

Getting up, I went to the kitchen to grab a beer from
the fridge. "That's cool."

"Yeah. I, uh, I also saw Rachel. She was with Aimee."

Almost choking on my beer, I didn't say anything. I
didn't have to because David continued.

"Rachel's not working at Blakemore anymore. She said
there was an issue about her being unwed and pregnant.
They asked her to take a leave."

Slamming my beer on the table, I fought not to yell at
the top of my lungs. Every time I talked to someone back
home, no matter who it was, it never failed that Rachel
came up in the conversation somehow. *I'm sick of it. I'm
sick of everyone throwing her in my face.*

"I'm sure she'll be all right," I said once I got the anger
in my voice under control.

The silence on David's end of the line stretched for several long moments. Disapproval hung in the air between
us. David changed the subject, but I could hear the
disdain in his voice, so we shortly ended the conversation.

Feeling more restless after the conversation with David,
I paced the confines of my apartment, thoughts of Rachel
clouding my mind. My family, and obviously my friends,

thought the way I handled things was wrong. None of them could, or took the time to, understand how hurt I was by this situation. I loved Rachel. Everyone seemed to think the decision to leave was easy, but it wasn't. It tore my heart to shreds to walk away from Rachel, but it was obvious by the decisions she made that she didn't want to be with me. A year ago, I would have never imagined my life without her. Funny how time changed everything.

Sitting down on the sofa, I closed my eyes. My parents stopped sending stuff about her. Aimee brought her up from time to time, but Rachel was part of my past, and I didn't want to keep being reminded of her. Shaking all thoughts of her off, I jumped to my feet. Grabbing my wallet, cell phone, and keys, I jetted out the front door. Dialing Amber, I waited for her to answer. She would make me forget all about Rachel. At least for a little while.

Chapter Thirty-three

Rachel

"Rachel?"

Turning, I stopped in my tracks when I heard my name called. A smile curved my lips when I saw David standing behind me, looking at my huge stomach. I walked over, giving him a hug, my big belly all in the way. The baby kicked at the unwanted pressure, and we both laughed.

"Wow. You're really out there," David said, looking me over.

I laughed again. "A word of advice—that's not something you tell a woman who's nine months pregnant."

"Right, you're right, but I meant it as a compliment. You're glowing. Pregnancy suits you."

"Yeah, it suits me if I like looking like a whale."

I was due any day now, and I was feeling enormous. My ankles were swollen, the baby refused to move from my bladder, and I waddled when I walked. That was not what I thought of as attractive. Today I decided to get out of the house, so I was at the mall on my way to meet Rosie for lunch.

"Anyway, what about you? How've you been doing?"

"I'm good, good. Oh, this is my cousin Josh. Josh, this is Rachel," David said, introducing me to the man who was with him. He hadn't said anything since I walked up on them, not even cracking a smile.

I reached to shake his hand, but David stopped me, grabbing my wrist. He pulled it closer. I knew he was checking out my ring.

"Is this . . . Are you . . ." The look on his face was comical. His eyes were wide with disbelief, and his mouth was hanging open with shock.

Looking at my swollen finger, I couldn't stop smiling. I'd been wearing this ring since Saxon gave it to me. I still hadn't given him a definite answer. *Saxon.* Just thinking of him made my smile brighter. Saxon was still sticking around, still putting up with my emotional outbursts and three a.m. cravings. He was still being good to me when I was an evil bitch.

"It is . . . and I think I am. I haven't said yes yet."

David's eyes filled with disbelief. "Wow."

Bursting into laughter, I nodded. "Yeah, that's what I said."

David's cousin didn't say anything, but I saw that he kept studying me. I gave him the same look as I openly studied him. He stood my height and was clean-shaven. He was very good-looking, and he looked familiar, but I couldn't place him. Brushing him aside, I hugged David again, then said my goodbyes. David made me promise to let him know when the baby was born. I agreed, then walked, or waddled, off to meet Rosie.

Arriving before Rosie, I ordered for both of us. Settling back in my chair, I was thankful to be off my feet. Everything ached, and this baby lived on my bladder. Breaking open a warm roll, I covered it in butter, eating it absently. Seeing David made me think about Errick. At least thoughts of him now weren't so painful. Saxon helped ease a lot of the hurt associated with thoughts of Errick. When I first met Saxon, I never imagined he would be interested in me, let alone proposing to me and giving me time to make up my mind on my answer.

Studying the ring Saxon placed on my finger, I wondered what it was that kept me from telling him that I would marry him. He said he loved me, and he showed me that he did in so many ways. No matter what was going on in his life, he always made sure that I was okay. *That's love, right? So what is it? What's holding me back?*

I'm scared.

The thought hit me fast and hard. That was all there was to it. I was scared. I was terrified of being hurt again. Although Saxon managed to get past a lot of my barriers and insecurities, I couldn't help but wonder what would happen if I gave in completely like I did with Errick.

Rosie rushed in, flushed and breathless but still looking like she stepped from the pages of one of her design magazines. Kissing my cheek, she slid onto the chair across from me. "Sorry I'm late."

"As usual." I laughed at my friend. "I just ran into David."

"David, Errick's friend?"

Nodding, I told her about seeing David the day Aimee and I were shopping then running into him today.

"Did he mention Errick?"

"No. There was no reason to bring him up. There's really nothing left to say, and I don't want to hear shit about him all these months later." I felt Rosie staring at me. Propping my elbow on the table, I put my chin in my hand, looking at her. "What?"

"When are you going to accept Saxon's proposal?" She gave it to me straight.

"I was just thinking about that actually." Straightening up, I took a sip of my lemonade, then looked back to Rosie. "I'm scared."

"What?" Rosie exclaimed loudly. Looking around, she smiled sheepishly at the people at the table next to us.

Lowering her voice, she continued, "What? Why are you scared?"

Tears pricked my eyes. Taking a deep breath, I exhaled, trying to keep them under control. "I don't want to be hurt again."

Rosie's face softened. She reached across the table, taking my hand. "Rach, don't be scared to love Saxon. You already love him, don't you?"

Nodding, I couldn't speak over the lump in my throat. I loved Saxon with everything in me, but was that enough? Would my love be enough that he wouldn't walk away when we got to a situation he didn't like or wasn't ready for?

"Don't let what happened with Errick keep you from being with a good man. Saxon has proven that he's not selfish like Errick. He loves you, and he loves this baby. Don't run from something good because of a bad experience in your past. Shit, Saxon treats you like you're made of glass. I wish I had a man like that."

This made me look up, confused. "You have Charles."

"Yeah." Rosie smiled. "But he still doesn't treat me the way Saxon treats you. Rach, marry that man. Put him out of his misery."

That was why I loved Rosie. She always knew what to say whether I was right or wrong.

Chapter Thirty-four

Errick

"You know, I've been thinking." Amber stretched her body over mine so that she was lying across my chest. She ran her finger up and down my breastbone.

"Yeah, about?" I had my eyes closed, but I wanted her to know I was listening.

"About us."

"What about us?" I didn't want to ask, but I needed to. I knew where this was going, but I knew Amber needed this.

"About taking things a little more seriously between us. I know you're not ready for a relationship, but what about exclusivity? What about dating? We never go out or do anything really."

"Dating? Exclusivity?" Now I opened my eyes, looking into Amber's pretty face. "Amber, I know things aren't going the way you want them to, but I'm not into that. I just want to relax and have fun when we're together. I don't want the expectations or the responsibilities of dating or exclusivity."

I saw in her eyes that her feelings were hurt, but I wasn't going to sugarcoat anything. The woman I loved betrayed me and broke my heart. I wasn't ready or willing to go down that road again.

Sitting up, Amber climbed from the bed, moving across the room. I watched the sway of her ample hips as she walked over to the chair, removing her robe from it and slipping it on.

"Errick, I like you, but since this isn't going to move forward, I think it best we stop altogether." She spoke calmly as her dark eyes met mine.

Propping myself up on my elbows, I looked at her. I could see in her eyes that she was serious. That was my cue. Getting out of bed, I went to the side she'd just vacated and picked up my jeans from the floor. Less than three minutes later I was dressed.

I moved in the direction of the door. Neither of us had spoken a word since Amber told me to leave. I didn't want things to end on a bad note. Amber was a cool woman.

"Take care of yourself. I know you'll find the man you want a relationship with," I said over my shoulder, but I didn't stop walking. I wasn't going to force something I wasn't feeling, and I wasn't going to feel bad about that. I gave Rachel my all, it wasn't enough, and I didn't have time to go through that heartbreak again.

Anger pumped through me as I realized that Rachel was right back in the center of my life. She was still affecting it even when we weren't together. In the car, I slammed my fist on the steering wheel, pissed that so much had changed all because of a simple mistake.

Chapter Thirty-five

Saxon

Leaving the delivery room, I felt the weight of the world on my shoulders. Heading to the doctors' lounge to shower, I couldn't get the faces of the mother and father from my mind. Their baby was born with the cord wrapped around her neck, and despite everything I and my team did, we'd lost the baby. That brought thoughts of Rachel to mind. Moving mechanically, I showered and dressed, all the while thinking about Rachel and what we would do if something like that happened to us. I already thought of us as a family even though Rachel hadn't given me a definite answer yet. I already loved the baby as much as I loved her. I never really thought about the baby not being biologically mine.

It was late when I left the hospital. It was dark, and the night sky was filled with stars twinkling brightly. I wished they could cheer me up. I wanted to go see Rachel, but I needed to get my thoughts together first. It was never easy losing a baby.

Driving around for a long time, lost in thought, I had no destination in mind. My thoughts were dark and jumbled. I hated this part of my profession. I always felt responsible when a baby died, no matter what I tried to do to help the success rate of births. I always felt like I should have done more, even though I knew some things were out of my hands.

It felt like summer already. It was still hot at eight thirty. I thought about the birth of Rachel's baby. I was glad that Rachel included me in every aspect of the pregnancy. When she started talking with me about baby names, I couldn't have been happier. Now all we needed was to get married so we could become a real family. I hadn't told Rachel yet, but I wanted to legally adopt the baby. Once the adoption process was finished, I would be able to put my name on the birth certificate.

My cell rang. I smiled when I saw Rachel's number. Answering on my Bluetooth, I felt a little more relaxed when I heard her smoky voice fill the car.

"Hey, how was your day?" Rachel always asked after me, and it made me warm inside.

"Long. How was yours?"

"Interesting. I was hoping you were coming by tonight?"

"Yeah, I was going to." I wondered what she meant by "interesting." She never usually asked if I was coming over, so I wondered what was going on with her.

"Good. I ordered Chinese. Should I keep it warm in the oven or will you be here soon?"

Rachel took care of me in a hundred little ways. She made sure that I had a warm plate no matter how late I got to her house. There were a few times that she was sleeping, but most nights she was up if I came late. She made sure I slept. She did my laundry since I was at her house most of the time. She cooked for me. That was how I knew she loved me.

"I'll be there in about ten minutes." I was unconsciously already heading in her direction, so it wouldn't take me long to get there.

"Okay, I'll see you then."

Fifteen minutes later, I pulled into the drive at Rachel's place. Shutting off the car, I sat in the darkness for a few minutes just looking up at her house. If I had my way, she wouldn't be living there much longer. I'd been trying not to push Rachel, but I thought we needed to have a talk about my proposal. *I need her with me.* It was getting harder and harder being away from her when I did go home.

I wasn't ready for the intimate scene Rachel set up in the living room. She'd spread a white cloth over the sofa table, a few candles glowed in the dim living room, and her favorite blue earthenware dishes and silver were placed on decorative servers. Chinese food containers waited in the middle of the table to be served.

Rachel kissed me until we were both breathless. Breaking the kiss, I looked at her, and she was glowing.

"What is all this?" My eyes roamed the setup again.

"Do you remember the first night you came over here?" She led me to the pile of pillows on the opposite side of the table from where she would sit.

I was curious where she was going with this. "Yeah?"

"You brought me Chinese food and came to check on me."

I was quiet while she spooned helpings from several different dishes on my plate. Setting it down in front of me, she then settled on the sofa across from me.

"You're not eating?" She knew how I felt about that. She needed to feed the baby, and I knew she was being careful of what she'd been eating lately because she was scared I would think she was too fat. She never said it to me, but I'd seen her in the mirror enough times to know she was concerned.

"Not until I tell you something," she said with a smile.

"Okay?" I was concerned. Rachel was acting a little strangely. Was the baby's dad back? Was that what this was? Was she trying to butter me up to tell me that this fool was back and she was leaving me? My heart pounded in my chest as my adrenalin kicked in.

"I love you, Saxon, and I want to marry you."

Shock. Elation. Uncertainty. Jubilation. Excitement. Fear. All these emotions warred within me in a matter of milliseconds. I jumped to my feet and was around the table in two steps, pulling Rachel to her feet. Gazing into her eyes, I was searching for certainty. I needed her to be sure this was what she wanted because once she really said yes, there was no leaving.

"Are you serious?" I sounded like a teenager, but I needed her to say it again. "Are you really going to marry me?"

"I'm going to marry you."

Wrapping her in my arms, I held her tightly. Rachel loved me. She was going to be my wife. The only thing that would be better than this moment would be when our baby was here with us. Dinner forgotten, I kissed Rachel again and again. I wanted to make love to her, but John warned against it in her last couple of weeks. My heart was filled with joy, and I knew a way to celebrate without the strain of sex. Settling her back on the sofa, I knelt in front of her and brought her to the same heights of happiness I was in.

We're getting married.

Chapter Thirty-six

Rachel

"Well, it looks like Mr. Rivers did not have the school board's approval to approach you regarding your pregnancy. They are doing an investigation of their own, but it looks like you have a good chance of winning your case," Luanne Bridges, my attorney, told me.

After talking things over with Saxon, I decided to bring a discrimination suit against Principal Rivers and the school. My pregnancy hadn't hindered my ability to teach my students, and I wasn't the first teacher on the payroll to have a baby. The way the principal handled the situation was unfair, and I wanted to make sure no one else was treated the same.

"What's the next step?"

After meeting with the attorney, I felt better about the situation. Things had been looking up for me lately. Since I accepted Saxon's proposal, we decided to sell the house I lived in. I had to deal with Errick to do that since both of our names were on the deed. When I talked to Anna and Paul to ask him to call me, he refused. He worked with his dad on his end. It was a process, but we managed to get his name removed from the deed so I could proceed with listing the house.

I had also spent a lot of time with Moira and Ellen. She had warmed up to me over the last several weeks. I was glad because I wanted to have a good relationship with Saxon's family. I wasn't sure how things would go since Saxon sprung me and my pregnancy on his parents. Once we got to know each other a little better, Ellen was right there to give me advice and encouragement.

The early afternoon sky was clear, and the temperature was seventy-one degrees. Spring had settled in, and the weather was perfect. I left the lawyer's office and decided to stop by Rosie's shop to see her. I wanted to talk to my bestie about decorating Saxon's place. I'd been to his house several times since we'd started seeing each other. After our engagement, he told me to start getting the house together. He wanted everything done as soon as possible, and I was excited about getting started. Almost nine months pregnant, I wasn't sure what I would be able to get done before the baby came, but Rosie would help me with anything I needed.

Inside Optical Illusions, I was surprised to find Rosie instead of Desiree in the showroom.

"Hey, best friend." I gave her a hug.

Rosie immediately rubbed my bump. "How's my baby?"

I gave her a teasing frown. "Dang, I can't even get a hello?"

She waved me off. "I see you are doing fine. It looks like you've dropped."

Taking a seat in one of the chairs in the showroom, I rubbed my bump. The baby was moving like crazy. "That's what Anna said. Three more weeks and my baby will be here."

"What brings you by?"

Filling her in on the appointment with the attorney, I also let her know it was time to get started on getting the house together. She pulled out her iPad and several books that held samples and ideas. I spent a couple of hours going over things. I took pictures of things I wanted to show Saxon and get his input on and told her some of the things he wanted for his man cave. Rosie and I left together. She had a date, and I went home to make dinner for my fiancé.

Chapter Thirty-seven

Saxon

The gentle shaking brought my eyes open slowly. I smiled at Rachel. My vision was bleary with sleep, but her face was glowing as usual. Her soft smile gradually turned into a twisted grimace. I bolted up in bed. My eyes ran over Rachel. She leaned over my side of the bed, one hand bracing herself and the other on her belly as she breathed slowly. She was dressed in a loose purple dress. Her long hair was brushed up into a ponytail. The window over her shoulder showed that it was still dark outside. The clock said it was 4:47 a.m.

"What is it?" I rubbed the remnants of sleep from my eyes. "What's wrong?"

"It's time," she was finally able to get out.

Springing up, I rushed to pull my jeans on. I grabbed a shirt from my drawer, then stepped into a pair of Vans I kept by the side of the bed. All my medical training flew out the window. I was just an excited expectant father. Taking Rachel's hand, I helped her down the stairs. She stopped midway, a contraction gripping her and making her face scrunch up against the pain as she breathed through it. I held her, my arm around her shoulder, wishing I could take her pain. Once the contraction passed, I helped her the rest of the way down and out to my car. Her bag was already in the trunk. We'd packed two because we didn't know whose car we would be taking, so we had one in each.

The twenty-minute ride to the hospital felt like an hour as Rachel's contractions quickly grew closer and harder. I called my parents then Anna and Paul to let them know she was in labor. I did my best to keep Rachel calm as the contractions took her breath and had her grinding her teeth with their intensity.

Anxiety settled in my chest. It didn't matter how many babies I'd delivered. This one was mine. This was a different experience, and I felt like any first-time father. We reached the hospital and were taken to a birthing room, where I watched the nurses prepare her for delivery, and I stayed out of their way. Twenty-five minutes later, Rachel was prepped and ready, breathing through her contractions. I never left her side, coaching her, encouraging her, feeding her ice chips, and wiping her brow. She was more beautiful in this moment than I'd ever seen her.

Anna and Rosie were taking pictures and videos to Rachel's disgust and my amusement, which I made sure to hide.

John came in to check on her. He told her it was time and that the baby was ready to make her appearance. My heartbeat began to race as I held Rachel's hand and dropped a kiss on her lips.

"I love you. You got this," I whispered as she took a few breaths, then began to push.

It felt like she pushed for hours but was probably only thirty minutes when John looked up.

"Saxon, the baby's head is crowning. Do you want to see the baby be born?"

Rosie stepped in to take my place at Rachel's side. I kissed her forehead, brushing random strands of hair from her face. I smiled, winked, then went to join John.

Coaching Rachel to push again, I watched as the baby's head slid from the birth canal. She had thick, dark hair and pale peanut skin, and she whimpered while John cleared the nose and mouth with the blue syringe a nurse handed him. Instructing Rachel to give one more push, he turned the shoulders, then eased the goop-covered baby free from her body. John slapped the bottom, and a loud wail flooded the room.

Tears filled my eyes as they met Rachel's. She burst into tears at the baby's cry. She was looking at me, her face flushed, tears running freely down her face. She was absolutely beautiful.

"She's perfect," I choked out over the lump in my throat. Tears burned my eyes, and my heart swelled with a love I'd never experienced before. I was head over heels from the first glance of her chubby face.

"You want to cut the cord?" John held out the scissors to me.

Our eyes met, tears swimming in both pairs. Rachel nodded. Taking the scissors, I cut the lifeline between her and our daughter. *Our daughter.* I laughed aloud at the thought. Our little girl was here, and she was gorgeous. I felt like I would burst with happiness. I wanted to laugh, cry, shout with joy, tremble with fear—all those emotions engulfed me. This little girl changed my life.

Chapter Thirty-eight

Rachel

The nurse laid the goop-covered baby on my chest, and the past six hours melted away. Tears filled my eyes as I looked at the little miracle, counting fingers and toes, running a gentle hand over her thick hair. I looked at Saxon as he stood beside me. He was watching the baby like she was the most spectacular thing imaginable. She was. Our eyes met. I couldn't stop smiling at the man beside me. Saxon was this child's father in every way except biologically.

"What is my niece's name going to be?" Rosie asked, snapping more pictures. Her eyes were red and wet from the tears she was shedding. She and Anna were trying to see the baby while staying out of everyone's way at the same time.

"Meet Kiernon Renay Hendricks," I said, introducing the crying little girl to her grandmother and *tia* Rosie.

While the nurses had me cleaned up, Rosie and Anna went to deliver the news to the family in the waiting room, and Saxon followed the baby to the nursery to get her settled. A short time later, Paul, Anna, Connor, and Ellen came to my room. Saxon pushed the bassinet in right after, and all of them cooed over Kiernon. They stayed for a little while, each of them holding her. Anna cried when she held her. I saw Paul wipe his eyes a time or two when he had his turn. Rosie, Aimee, Jamie, and others stopped by throughout the day while I dozed.

That evening, Saxon walked Moira and Samarra to their car after their visit. Samarra was so excited about the baby she wanted to hold her the whole time she was there. I lay back in bed, waiting for him to return. I closed my eyes briefly while waiting, thinking about all that happened today. My eyes popped open. It was dark in the room, the only light from the TV and through the crack of the bathroom door. I turned my head to see Saxon stretched out in the pullout recliner. The sight melted my heart.

"Hey, beautiful," he said softly. Standing, he moved to stand beside the bed. He brushed my hair from my face. "How are you feeling?"

Laughing, I winced. "Like I birthed a Thanksgiving turkey."

His whole face lit up. "The nurse will bring you something for that. Rach," he said, his voice breaking, "she's beautiful."

Aches and pains were forgotten when I thought of my baby, my little girl. I immediately fell in love with her. "She is, isn't she?"

"Like her mother," Saxon insisted.

"I want to see her."

"Okay, we'll be back shortly." Saxon kissed me long and slowly. There was something in this kiss. Was it gratitude? Appreciation? He stayed beside me for several long moments just looking at me. His eyes seemed to be searching, like he wanted to see into my soul. I blushed, my face warm with heat when he kissed me again. "I love you."

He left me alone to go get our daughter. My face hurt I smiled so hard at the thought. *Our daughter*. I managed to get out of bed by myself. By the time I emerged from the bathroom, Saxon had returned with the baby.

"How are you feeling, mommy?" the nurse who followed Saxon into the room asked as she checked my vitals.

"Sore."

"I'd be worried if you weren't, but you'll be fine."

Gratefully I swallowed the pain medicine the nurse gave me, then took the baby from Saxon. Slowly, carefully, I unwrapped the little bundle from the blanket she was snuggled in. Tears filled my eyes as I studied the perfect miracle before me. The baby emitted a little squeal of protest when the cool air hit her. Her skin was the color of fresh peanuts, her hair thick and straight. She was balled up, and another squeak came when I tried to open her little fingers. My heart raced when her eyes peeped open. They were the same soft brown as mine.

Wrapping her up, I placed her against my heart, and it immediately calmed both of us. I was overwhelmed by the flood of emotions that raced through me, but I felt serene at the same time. I'd never felt a love like this. There was no way I could even describe what I felt the first time I saw this little person. Wiping away a tear that managed to escape, I looked up into Saxon's hazel eyes. I felt so much love for this man that I couldn't help the tears that flowed harder. He loved me and the baby. He showed me in a million little ways every day. Having him in my life made it complete.

Saxon watched me with Kiernon, the expression on his face awestruck. "Thank you."

I could only nod. My throat was too tight with tears to speak.

Glancing around the room at all the balloons, a huge stuffed teddy bear, and flowers from family and friends, I felt nothing but love. Kiernon was here. Her big, blended family was excited for her arrival, and the tokens of happiness said it all. I was full of happiness and satisfaction as I kissed my baby's soft brow. Kiernon couldn't have had a better birthday.

Chapter Thirty-nine

Saxon

"Hey."

Glancing over, I was surprised to see Rachel moving up beside me. I didn't know how long I'd been standing here in front of the observation window just watching Kiernon sleep. I didn't want to take my eyes off her. She didn't seem real. She was wrapped in a light gray blanket with yellow and pink designs, and her little lips were pursed as she suckled in her sleep. All this felt like a dream I didn't want to wake from.

"Hey." I wrapped my arm around Rachel's shoulders. I felt her weight settle into my side. She felt right against me, like she belonged at my side. "What are you doing up?"

It was late, and everyone had finally left a while ago. Rachel was exhausted, so I told her I would be back and headed to the nursery. I was glad she and Kiernon were being released the next day. I was ready to get my family home.

"I couldn't sleep. You're just standing here watching her?" Rachel wrapped her arm around my waist, resting her head against my shoulder.

"She's perfect. I . . . almost . . . feel like she's mine." She was only twenty-four hours old, but she had my heart.

Rachel's head snapped up, her eyes crashing into mine. A frown twisted her mouth, and she squeezed my waist. "Hey."

I didn't want to look at her because I was emotional. I didn't want Rachel to see me cry. She didn't say anything until I met her gaze.

"She is yours. Never doubt that. Kiernon is our daughter."

The tears fell, and I didn't care now. Hearing Rachel say that put me at ease. There were a few times during the day that she seemed sad, far away, and I knew she was thinking of Errick. It hurt me, but I knew it would be natural for him to be on her mind. What hurt most was that Errick didn't deserve her thoughts, her sadness. I wished I could wipe all the pain, sadness, even the memory of him from her life, but if I did that, I would have never met Rachel and I wouldn't have this beautiful baby.

A thought hit me. It actually wasn't a new one, but every time I had it, it sent chills down my spine. What would happen if Errick came back? What if he wanted to claim my place? What if he realized that he wanted Rachel and Kiernon? *Fuck that. I am Kiernon's daddy. I've always been Kiernon's daddy.* Nothing Rachel's coward-ass ex could say or do would change that.

"Come on, let's get you back in bed. She'll be up for a feeding before you know it." I kissed her temple.

Walking Rachel back to her room, I was caught off guard when she thanked me.

"For what?"

"For doing this with me. For being here with me. For being the man Kiernon and I need. Thank you for loving us."

One Year Later

Chapter Forty

Errick

As I drove around, memories invaded my mind. I'd driven past David's place, past Pitts Park where I used to play basketball, past TSU and Fisk. Being back in Nashville, I felt like I never left. There were changes of course. There was always construction going on around town. The weather was perfect as I drove. The sky was a clear, vibrant blue with no clouds in sight. Late spring was in the air. Birds chirped, chasing each other from tree to tree, and kids were playing in some of the neighborhoods I drove through.

I found myself parking on the opposite side of the street in front of my old house. Rachel's house. I kept telling myself I didn't want to be here. When I got to town last night, I found that this was the first place I wanted to see.

I didn't tell anyone I was coming. I wanted to surprise my family. They definitely weren't going to expect the news I had for them.

Rachel had been in my thoughts since I left Phoenix. As I drove around today, my memories of her were overwhelming. It seemed like no matter where I went or what area of town I drove through, something about it brought her to mind. Now I was parked across the street from her house, watching it. Tulips, all yellow, lined the walkway.

There were no ferns on the eaves, but two large planters filled with bright flowers sat in pots at the base of the stairs. I saw Mrs. Stanley out in her flower garden. I couldn't help but smile at my old neighbor. I was sure she was still looking out for everyone in the neighborhood.

The door to Rachel's house opened, and my heart thudded in my chest as my breath caught in my throat. A tall white man stepped out onto the porch, and a young boy who looked to be around 6 or 7 ran out right past his legs. I slumped lower in my seat, wondering who the man and boy were. Maybe they were just friends of Rachel's. The man was followed out the door and down the steps by a very pregnant brunette woman. She turned, locking the door with a key before following. For some strange reason my heart fell. Rachel obviously didn't live here anymore. What was I doing here anyway? Why had I come here? To skulk and wait to see a glimpse of her? Rachel was a part of my past.

Yeah, my conscience taunted me, *a part you haven't been able to get out of your head more than a few days at a time over the last eighteen months.*

Shaking those thoughts off, I started my car, took a long last look at the house, then pulled away. It was best that Rachel didn't live there. There was nothing either of us needed to say at this point. That relationship was long over.

I had to park a little way down the street from my parents' house. There were cars lined up and down both sides of the street. I could smell a grill going and hear music as I got out of my car. Even though this was a quiet neighborhood, most of my parents' neighbors were retired like they were, and it was obvious someone was having a get-together. Once I made it to the sidewalk, I saw that it was my parents' house where the party was underway. Bundles of pink, green, and yellow balloons hung in clusters from the mailbox and from weights on either side of the door. Ringing the bell, as I waited, the smell in the air made my stomach rumble. I wondered what the celebration was. Maybe they were hosting something for one of their friends.

My brother stepped into view through the glass storm door. I could see surprise etched all over his face. He hurried to open the door for me, pulling me into a brotherly hug.

"What's up, man? What are you doing here?" Jamie's voice was loud with excitement. "C'mon in. Ma. Ma. Guess who's here."

Stepping down the short hall to the living room, I was surprised to see all the people there. I tuned them all out when I heard my mother's voice.

"Is that my baby?" she called, coming from the direction of the kitchen. She was wiping her hands on a dish towel, her steps faltering when she saw me. "Errick?"

"Hi, Ma." A rush of love poured through me when she tossed the towel over her shoulder and moved swiftly across the floor into my arms. I lifted her from her feet in a fierce hug. I missed my mother. I missed my whole family, but my mother and I were always close. This time away from my family was harder than I realized until this moment. All the anger and disagreements weren't worth being away from this lady.

Once I set my mother on her feet, I saw my dad coming in from the back patio. He wore an apron, so I knew he was the one on the grill. Jamie must have gone to tell him I was here. Crossing the room, I stopped in front of him. My old man was stern at times, but he loved his family. I wrapped my arms around him and couldn't stop smiling when he did the same.

Aimee came from the back patio, following my dad, I was sure, and she let out a loud squeal when she saw me. She rushed over, and I had to brace myself when she threw herself into my arms. After I greeted my immediate family, I was met with hugs, kisses, and fist pounds from aunts, uncles, and cousins. I met the Stewarts and the Carmichaels, friends of the family. Some of their extended families were there as well.

I saw the birthday banners hanging throughout the house, but it was really just dawning on me now that the introductions and greetings were out of the way. I was standing with my arm resting over my mother's shoulders. She had a glow on her face, and I knew she was happy to have her family all together again.

"Whose birthday?" I asked her. I didn't think I'd spoken that loudly, but several of the people closest to us stopped to look at me strangely.

"Kiernon's," my dad said from where he stood talking to my uncle Rod.

"Kiernon?" I was trying to think if I knew a Kiernon, but the name wasn't familiar to me.

"Rachel's daughter," my mom informed me. Her eyes flashed with hurt, anger, regret, and pain. Turning away from me, she headed toward the kitchen.

I nodded at her words, but I was completely stunned by the announcement. Watching my mother walk away from me with her shoulders slumped made me feel terrible. When my father said it was Kiernon's birthday, I couldn't believe a year had passed since Rachel's baby was born. Establishing my career and social life in Phoenix kept me busy, and the times I thought about Rachel, I usually remembered her the way I saw her last.

Following my mother in the dining room, I wanted to apologize for hurting her, but she had put on a smile, finishing things for the party. She and Aimee were bringing snacks from the kitchen to set buffet style on the sideboard. She was busy, so I stayed out of her way. I would talk to her later.

The doorbell rang. A few moments later, I saw Jamie coming in, carrying a large cake box. He was followed by Rosie Rodriguez. When she saw me, the look on her face was priceless. She did a double take. I knew she was stunned to see me here.

"Hello, Rosie, how you been?" I spoke while Jamie took the box in the kitchen.

"I'm good."

Her answer was short. I knew she wasn't fucking with me. I hurt her friend. It was only natural. "You're looking well."

She cut her eyes at me. If looks could kill, I would have been laid out right where I stood.

"Look, I know you don't like me—"

"That's just it," she interrupted me, shaking her head. "I did like you. I thought you were a great guy—"

Sounds of laughter and excited chatter stopped her short and brought me face-to-face with my past.

Rachel stepped into my eyesight, and it was like there was no one else in the room. Everyone else faded into the background, and I drank in the sight of her. She was dressed in a long butter yellow sundress with a bright orange design stitched around the bottom. She had lost weight in some places and gained some in others, but she was still full and lush. Her hips were wider, her breasts were larger, but it was all good. Rachel was laughing and teasing when she came in. Her cheeks were flushed, her eyes sparkling. I couldn't seem to take my eyes off her. It was like time stood still as I watched her tuck a lock of her long hair behind her ear.

Damn, Rachel looks good as hell. My body instantly reacted. My heart raced, and my dick was getting hard as I stared at her. I knew I needed to get myself together.

Rachel was laughing. Her smile was a thousand watts as she looked at the person beside her. It was then I noticed the man. She laid a hand on his arm, and I knew from just that touch he was someone special in her life. Jealousy twisted my gut as she smiled up at him. He was tall with sandy brown hair and gray eyes. He was a nice-looking guy. I could see the resemblance between him and the woman I met, Moira. It was obvious they were related. They looked almost identical. The resemblance to the older Carmichael guy let me know they were family. Seeing the way this dude looked at Rachel, like she belonged to him, had me feeling like choking the shit out of his ass.

Guess it's true what they say—there's nothing sexier than your ex with her new man. And dammit, Rachel is sexy as hell right now.

Seeing her here like this when I'd been thinking about her since my flight out of Phoenix seemed surreal. I wasn't thinking about her as my ex at this moment. Rachel was the woman I loved. Seeing her with another man made me realize just how much I wasn't over her. For the past eighteen months I'd lied to myself, and I was just now realizing it.

A child's peal of laughter made me tear my gaze from Rachel. It landed on the little girl in the man's arms. I couldn't breathe. I struggled over and over to take air into my lungs. There was no doubt she was Rachel's daughter. My daughter.

From where I stood, I could see the little girl was a mixture of me and Rachel. She had skin the color of roasted peanuts and Rachel's soft brown laughing eyes, but she had my nose and my smile. Four teeth peeked out of her smile. Her eyes turned up in the corner when she laughed. She was wearing the same soft yellow as her mother, hers in a yellow blouse with orange shorts and yellow sandals. She had orange and yellow barrettes in her hair. She was beautiful.

The high trill of her laugh brought an epiphany to me. Rachel was right. She'd been right all along. How could I have ever wanted her to kill this child? How stupid was I to walk out on them?

The little girl patted the man's face, her smile loving, trusting. He kissed her little, round cheek, and she laughed again. My insides were clenching. Her laughter mingled with his was like nails on a chalkboard against my nerves. *What have I done?* Until this moment I never stopped to think about what I was giving up when I walked away from Rachel. Anger and jealousy gripped me as I watched the tableau: Rachel gazing up at the man with love in her eyes, and the man holding the baby, my baby, looking at both of them like they were his.

I felt sick to my stomach. It churned painfully, and my breathing became shallow. I wanted to show my ass, but I kept my cool. I actually felt like I was punched in the stomach. Rachel had done exactly what I told her to do—move on with her life. Now that I was seeing that up close and personal, I selfishly wanted everything to be like it was before I walked away.

Chapter Forty-one

Rachel

Running behind as usual, I hurried from the car, grabbing the diaper bag and the bag of presents while Saxon got Kiernon from her car seat. I watched the two of them as they teased each other and laughed playfully. Kiernon said several words, but she still hadn't mastered the art of sentences. That didn't stop her from jabbering with Saxon like she was making the most sense in the world. She had him wrapped around her finger. Anytime she said, "Daddy," he melted into a puddle. She had that effect on all the men in her life. Her Pawpaw Paul, *Daideo* Connor, and Uncle Jamie were no better than Saxon, falling all over themselves to make her smile.

Eighteen months ago, I would have never imagined my life like this. The past year had flown by: our engagement, my resignation from Blakemore, the subsequent law suit I'd filed against them, Kiernon's birth, and finally, my marriage to Saxon six weeks ago. God was definitely smiling on me. When Errick walked out of my life, I thought I lost the man of my dreams only for God to send him to me a few weeks later.

It hadn't all been easy. Dealing with the lawsuit was taxing. We went back and forth with the school board, mediation, meetings with attorneys, depositions, and delays. Principal Rivers denied any harassment. I was glad I started making notes when he began making comments. I was also thankful that a couple of the teachers I worked with saw this behavior more than once and were willing to testify on my behalf. I spent several months crying out my frustration, but Saxon was beside me every step of the way. He encouraged me to not give up and assured me that, no matter what, he had me.

There were also growing pains in our marriage and settling into being first-time parents. Kiernon was a good baby, but it was hard to get her on a schedule. I was exhausted. Saxon was working more than ever, and we didn't spend a lot of time together. He came home from the office late, ate, played with Kiernon, then crashed before doing it all over again the next day. Things finally smoothed out, and I was happier than ever.

Going up the walk, I took Saxon's hand, lacing our fingers together. He carried Kiernon in his free arm. Letting her ring the bell when we got to the door, I laughed as she began to swat the balloons beside the bell. She bounced in her daddy's arms, talking in her baby language. Aunt Jacks, Errick's auntie, answered the door with hugs and kisses, tickling Kiernon until she shrieked with delight.

Samarra, who was now seven, raced to throw her arms around her uncle Sax's legs in a hug. He bent to kiss her, but she was more interested in getting to Kiernon, although she kissed the side of his lips absently. The girls adored each other. Kiernon followed her around, wanting to be a big girl, while Samarra was patient with her. She had her very own live dolly to play with. Samarra gave me a quick hug before following us down the hall, begging Saxon to put Kiernon down.

The house was filled, and I was glad to see so many people come out to celebrate my baby. Anna and Paul had gone all out to make this a family celebration. Streamers and clusters of balloons and banners in pink, green, and yellow filled the corners and walls of the room. There was a huge stuffed giraffe in one corner with a ribbon in the same colors as the balloons tied around its neck. As I was swept up in greeting everyone, it took me a few moments to see the man standing in the dining room. My smile slipped when I looked into Errick's deep brown eyes. I was caught off guard, stunned really, to see him standing there. I stiffened, my suddenly cold fingers gripping Saxon's tightly, making him look down at me curiously. The tension in the room was thick immediately. Even Kiernon seemed to pick up on it as she began squirming to get out of Saxon's arms. Paul moved over to take her from Saxon. He winked at me. I nodded slightly.

What the hell is he doing here?

Still at Saxon's side, I met Errick's dark gaze again. He looked good. Still fit and trim, still sexy. I couldn't stand him. Why was he here today of all days? He was looking at me, staring at me really. I felt the way his eyes roamed over me like a physical touch, and it wasn't something I wanted.

"Hello, Errick." I kept my voice light. I didn't want to give him the impression that his popping up affected me in the slightest.

I felt the muscles in Saxon's arm stiffen. He pulled me closer, wrapping an arm over my shoulder. I leaned into him, looking up at him with a soft smile. He was always my rock.

"Hello, Rachel."

Errick's gaze moved from me to Kiernon, where Paul was bouncing her on his lap. A few of the other kids were around his legs, including Samarra, who was waiting for her to be put down. Panic fluttered in my chest when I saw the way he studied my baby.

"Saxon, this is Errick Martin. Errick, Saxon Carmichael," I introduced them.

The men moved closer to each other to shake hands. That meant I had to move too because Saxon hadn't let me go. Once they exchanged greetings, Anna stepped in.

"Let's eat, Rachel, and then the children can go out to play, and we can have cake and presents a little later."

"Sounds good to me." I smiled up at Saxon. His expressive hazel eyes were filled with love and concern. I was so glad he was here with me. I didn't know what I would do without him by my side. Errick's unexpected appearance threw me. I was angry, sad, disgusted, and confused. What made him show up today, and why did I have to run into him at all?

Saxon bent to kiss me, a gentle brush of his lips against mine. No words were spoken, and none were needed. The one thing about Saxon I knew without a doubt was that he would be right there if I needed him.

Leaving him with a final kiss, I followed Moira and Rosie into the kitchen. I spoke absently to the women who were already there. Helping Aimee, we took the giraffe-shaped cake from the box. My baby was obsessed with giraffes. I was lost in my thoughts, still trying to process Errick's appearance. Anna and Ellen were at the sink with their heads close together. They must've felt my eyes on them, because they both sent me encouraging smiles. I didn't think Anna would keep something like this from me, so I was sure she was caught off guard by him showing up.

"You okay?" Rosie asked me quietly.

Nodding, I said I was, but I really wasn't. Seeing Errick brought back all the pain, the humiliation, the anger, the desperation I felt when he walked out on me.

Moira put the 1-shaped candle on the cake. She smiled at me, her eyes full of compassion. Moira, Rosie, and I grew close over the last year. Our friendship was tight. She knew my history with Errick. We'd had several long talks about it.

"Shocked?"

"That's an understatement," I said quietly. "What is he doing here?"

"I think everyone was surprised to see him from their reaction," Moira assured me.

"You can say that again. Mom and Daddy have been trying to talk Errick into coming home since he left. Believe me, we were not expecting him today. What are you going to do?" Aimee put an arm on my shoulder.

"What is there to do? I'm not going to let it ruin Kiernon's big day." I shrugged.

We joined everyone else outside so we could eat and start this celebration.

Chapter Forty-two

Saxon

Rachel's introduction of Errick caught me by surprise, but I took my cue from her. We concentrated on making Kiernon's birthday special. The cake Rosie ordered was a big hit with Kiernon. She was fascinated by giraffes. Her excitement when we sang "Happy Birthday" made her little face shine, and my heart melted like it did when I saw her smile. She jabbered along with everyone else as she bounced and clapped in Paul's arms. Kiernon made a mess of herself with the miniature cake Rachel made sure she had. Rachel caught a picture of us as Kiernon tried to feed me a piece of her cake and wiped icing on my face in the process.

I saw the way Errick watched Kiernon as the afternoon progressed, looking at her as she played with Samarra and some of the other children. Moira's son, Dathan, and another baby were in a pack and play on the patio while Rachel, my mother, Anna, and the others were watching the kids play on the bouncy house Paul and my dad rented. Kiernon had taken her first steps recently. She was still unsteady on her feet as she toddled after Samarra. She was jabbering and clapping at all the excitement around her. Errick's eyes followed her, his expression blank but his eyes studying, watching.

I hated to admit it even to myself, but I was feeling a little insecure. This was something I would never tell Rachel. I would never tell anyone that I worried about Errick showing up again. It scared me. The thought of this man coming back up, this invisible specter showing up, the one who claimed a biological connection to my daughter trying to claim her scared me. I pushed the thoughts from my mind. *I'm Kiernon's daddy.* Nothing Errick could do would change that.

"Damn, cuz, you straight?" Josh came to where I was standing, watching as grandparents took pictures and video.

"Yeah, man, I'm straight. I can't believe this fool shows up today of all days."

"Yeah, odd how he shows up on li'l bit's birthday."

I looked at Josh. "What you trying to say, man?"

"I'm just saying it's odd. You don't think his family may have told him it was her birthday?"

"Nah, man. Anna and Paul aren't going to do that to Rachel. They love her like a daughter, and Kiernon is everything to them."

Josh was still skeptical about Kiernon's biological father. I couldn't blame him. What kind of man walks away from a woman like Rachel when she was pregnant with his child? I was glad Josh got over his reservations about Rachel. They'd spent time together since we made things official, and they actually had a decent friendship now.

Out of the corner of my eye, I saw Kiernon lose her balance. Jumping up, I rushed over as Rachel hurried to scoop her up in her arms to soothe her after she bumped her head. Anna and my mom both moved in to help, but Kiernon was squirming in Rachel's arms, holding her arms out toward me.

"Dada. Dada," Kiernon cried.

My heart lurched when I saw her red face and her crocodile tears running over her chubby cheeks. I took my baby from Rachel, my hands running gently over her head and making sure there were no boo-boos. Kiernon buried her face in my neck, whimpering and holding on to me tightly while I bounced her gently and rubbed her back.

I looked up, and my eyes met Errick's. He was sitting on the lawn with some other men, watching us. The look in his eyes made me wonder if for the first time he was realizing all that he lost when he walked away.

"I think it's time to get this one home," Rachel said, kissing Kiernon's cheek.

We thanked Anna and Paul. I was glad that Rachel helped straighten up earlier with some of the aunts and cousins because my pretty girl was tired.

Another round of hugs and kisses, then my girls and I were on our way. Kiernon was asleep as soon as the car was in motion. Glancing in the rearview mirror, I smiled at my baby. Her little mouth was open, and she was blowing spit bubbles.

The sun was riding low in the western sky. The day was wonderful. Kiernon and the other children had a ball in the bouncy house. Glancing over at Rachel, I could see she was wrapped up in her thoughts. I took her hand with my free one, raising it to my lips to kiss her fingertips.

"I love you."

She smiled and my heart thumped. This woman had all of me. Every moment that I had to wait for her to come to me had been worth it. She and Kiernon brought so much to my life. I didn't know what I would do without them.

"You okay?" Seeing Errick after all this time had to be affecting her some kind of way.

When she sighed, I knew she was tense. "Yes, I'm okay. I just can't believe that he showed up today of all days."

I thought about Josh's words. "Do you think Anna or Paul would have told him about the party today?"

"No. From what Aimee said, they couldn't have been more surprised to see him."

"Well, you handled it great."

"You did too. I love you, you know."

Just those words from her set my mind at ease. At home, Rachel went to put Kiernon down, and I went to our bedroom to run a hot bath. We both needed to relax. I dropped in some of Rachel's favorite milk bath beads, lit several candles, then went downstairs to pour us each a glass of wine. Returning, I found Rachel undressing in our room.

"C'mon, babe."

She followed me into the bathroom, smiling when she saw the bathwater and candles. I helped her into the tub, handed her our glasses, then climbed in with her. She nestled between my legs. My body reacted, so I had to get control of myself. That would come later.

"Kiernon had a good time today. She's out," Rachel said.

I stroked her hair. "I think the grandparents had more fun than the kids. Paul and Dad are punks when it comes to them."

We shared a laugh because it was true. My dad and Paul never said no to any of the children. All Kiernon and Samarra had to do was bat their eyes and it was over.

"You say that like you're not the same way," Rachel teased with a laugh. "Ellen asked me today when we were going to have another one."

"Another one? Another baby?" I was surprised. I knew my parents wanted as many grandchildren as they could get, but I didn't know she was asking my wife about more.

I wanted a large family, but I wanted Rachel to be sure she was ready. I told her before we married that we could wait, but I couldn't wait to have Rachel pregnant again. She was sexy as hell to me when she was carrying Kiernon.

Turning to face me, Rachel playfully splashed water at me. "Are you ready for another baby?"

Setting our glasses on the floor, I tugged her up until she straddled me. Her full lushness had me reacting, and this time I wasn't going to fight it. Her full breasts were buoyed by the water, brushing across my chest as she settled against me. Rachel rocked her hips. I could feel her center when she pressed against my hardness. She kissed me, her tongue sliding in my mouth to tangle with mine. She moaned low in her throat.

"Well?" she asked when she broke the kiss.

"I want to have lots of babies with you." My voice was deep, my body hard with desire.

"Really?" Rachel seemed surprised. She reached between us, grasping me, stroking until I groaned. Moving, she slid down my hard length, her eyes fluttering closed before she opened them again. "How about we get started on the next one right now?"

I gazed into her root beer eyes as she moved over me slowly. Slowly, the tension began to build. With a groan, I lost myself in my wife.

Chapter Forty-three

Errick

Lost in thought, I was drawn inward after my encounter with Rachel. She took my breath away. Seeing her was a jolt to my system. After the time I spent in Phoenix, I knew I was over Rachel. I was certain of it. Seeing her today, I realized I wasn't over her at all. Not even close. All the bullshit and insistence that she needed to go on with her life, and now that I'd seen that she had, I didn't want to know anything about it. That was nothing but smoke. I was mesmerized when she came into the room. I couldn't get over how good she looked. Her skin was glowing, and her long, thick hair hung loose over her shoulders the way I loved it. Her smile was devastating, and I felt like I was sucker punched when I saw her.

Then there was Kiernon. She was amazing. Her soft, laughing eyes were so much like her mother's. She seemed to be a happy baby. There was no question that Rachel was a good mother or that motherhood suited her. In the few short hours that I was around them, I could tell that she loved her daughter.

My daughter.

It was crazy. I never expected it, but when I saw the chubby little girl for the first time, I was floored. Fascinated. I couldn't keep my eyes off her as she was passed from one family member to another. It was obvious that Kiernon was part of my family. I was the only one who didn't know her.

She toddled around my parents' house like she owned it. Kiernon was her own little person. She was adventurous, and she followed the older children around as best she could. The older little girl was loving toward her, and Kiernon seemed to adore her. I also saw she had a stubborn streak when she wanted to do something on her own.

I stayed in the background during the party, feeling awkward in my parents' home. When they sang "Happy Birthday" to Kiernon and she opened her presents, her excited laughter made my heart sing. When she toddled around aimlessly, rubbing her sleepy-looking eyes, I wanted to hold her until she slept. I thought about the tumble she took. It scared the shit out of me. I actually started from my place where I was sitting with some cousins, but seeing Rachel and the man with her comforting her stopped me. It was like a knife piercing me on the inside. Jealousy, strong and fierce, hit me as I watched this man comforting my daughter.

"Errick. Yo, man, what's up?" Jamie nudged my shoulder. "You all frowned up. You okay?"

My eyes moved around the crowded room. We'd come to the sports bar after we left our parents' house. This was the same place me and Rachel came to the day we met. Shaking my head, I couldn't escape memories of Rachel anywhere I went.

Realizing I hadn't heard anything Jamie said, I shook my head. "Sorry, yeah, I'm cool." I took a long pull of my beer, draining the bottle. I felt my brother's gaze on me. "It was just seeing Rachel today. That was crazy."

"You know she and the fam are close. I'm sure you expected to run into her sometime."

Chuckling, I nodded in agreement. "Yeah, just not as soon as I walked in the house. I still can't believe it." Pausing a moment, I met Jamie's eyes again before asking, "Is that her boyfriend?"

Jamie drained his bottle, motioning for another round. I was beginning to feel anxious. Why was it taking so long for him to answer? Finally, Jamie met my eyes. "Saxon is her husband."

Husband? Husband, my mind screamed. Rachel was married. *Married?* I actually felt dizzy. It took a minute before I could really get my mind around what Jamie just said. Was he serious? I knew Rachel would go on with her life, but I'd only been in Phoenix eighteen months. In a year and a half, she fell in love with someone and married him?

"Rachel's married?" I choked the words out. I didn't bother trying to hide the panic I felt from Jamie. There was no use. He knew me too well and would see it anyway.

How the fuck was Rachel married? This shit hurt. As much as I said I was done, I still loved that woman, and for her to be married to someone else was a blow.

"Yep, they were married a few weeks ago."

Regaining my composure, all I could say was, "Wow."

Jamie only nodded.

"No one said anything." I turned my head because before he could even respond I knew what he was going to say.

Shrugging, Jamie said, "You made it clear that you weren't trying to hear anything about Rachel or her baby, so we stopped telling you. I understood you weren't ready to be a father, but I never told you I wasn't going to be in the baby's life."

Taking a deep drink of the fresh beer the bartender set before us, I ordered two double shots of Cîroc. I didn't say anything about Jamie's comment. He was right. My family made it clear they weren't going to turn their backs on Rachel. I was the one who insisted they stop trying to tell me anything about Rachel or her pregnancy. I just wanted to forget about it. I did a pretty good job at times.

Slapping me on the shoulder, Jamie said, "Kiernon's a doll, right?"

"Yeah, yeah, she is. Like her mom." The raspy whisper didn't sound like me.

"Errick, let it go. This is what you wanted."

Nodding, I changed the subject, but Rachel and Kiernon stayed on my mind.

Late that night, lying in bed in Jamie's spare room, I couldn't sleep. Thoughts of Rachel played over and over in my head. I thought about the last time we ran into each other before I moved out. We were in the hallway that morning as we were getting ready for work. Rachel looked tired, her face was pale, dark blotches had settled under her eyes, her shoulders were stooped, and she looked devastated. I looked just as bad. I wasn't sleeping. I was angry, and the tension between us was thick. I let her leave for work that morning with no words for her. A last look in her tired eyes, and that was it. I hadn't seen or spoken to her since.

Then there was Kiernon. It was more than obvious that my family loved her. My parents were whipped. Aimee and Jamie loved her. Aunts, uncles, and cousins made it clear she was family. Something I didn't expect was the way I felt when I saw how Rachel's husband's family fit in with mine like they'd known each other for years. Why was I feeling betrayed and cheated? I was the one who made the decisions that led here. I didn't want a baby. At least that was what I thought. Seeing Kiernon today, I knew I couldn't have been more wrong. I walked away from the woman I loved. I walked away from my child.

Kiernon was my daughter, and she knew another man as her daddy.

How could I have left her? How could I let another man step in to raise my child? To be the man who loved her? How could I not be her daddy?

Chapter Forty-four

Rachel

Sitting on the balcony with my feet up on the railing, I inhaled the scents of late spring. This was my favorite time of year. The leaves on the trees were new, budding to deep, rich greens. Flowers were blooming, and the air held the sweet scent of honeysuckle and freshly mown grass. The sun was riding low in the west. The sky was darkening from light blue to navy with several shades in between on the horizon. A few stars peeked out even though it was still early.

Rosie came out, handing me a glass of lemonade spiked with our favorite lemon rum. Settling in the chair beside me, she mimicked my pose, sinking into the chair and propping her feet up on the rail.

"So what's going on? Have you heard from Errick?"

After taking a long swallow of my drink, I set my glass on the table between us. I looked at her curiously. "No, why would I hear from him?"

"Because no matter what he said or did, I saw the way he was watching you at Kiernon's party. He's still in love with you."

I laughed a full, deep belly laugh. "Girl, you are too much. That man is not thinking about me."

I did see the way he watched Kiernon though. I didn't like that. Not one bit. As relaxed as I may have seemed on the outside, I'd been tied in knots on the inside when I saw Errick. I definitely wasn't expecting him to be here for Kiernon's birthday party, but what could I say?

"Hmmm, okay. How are you?" Rosie changed the subject. I was glad.

"Good."

"Good? Just good? Girl, you just got married and you're just good?"

Face flaming, I couldn't stop the blush that ran up my neck into my cheeks. "I'm great, actually. Saxon and I are talking about having another baby. I want to make sure Kiernon isn't too much older. I'm not working right now, so it's perfect."

"That's great." Rosie was excited for me. She always told me she was glad I gave Saxon a chance and that he was just what I needed. She was right.

Thinking about my husband, I was thankful for him more than anything. Saxon came in and changed so many things in my life, but most importantly, I never doubted his love for me or Kiernon.

My face clouded, my smile slipping away as different thoughts popped to mind. "I don't know what me and Kiernon are going to do while Saxon's gone on this trip. It's the first time he's been away from us for more than an overnight delivery at the hospital since Kiernon was born."

Reaching over, Rosie pushed me playfully. "You're sickening."

Snorting laughter, I reassured her. Her day was coming.

Later that night, when I got home, I found Saxon sitting in bed reading. Standing in the doorway, I watched him for a few minutes. He was in pajama bottoms and a white T-shirt, the wire-rimmed glasses perched on his nose making him appear bookish. His short brownish red hair was mussed where he'd absently run his fingers through it while he was reading. Kicking off my shoes, I crossed the thickly carpeted floor and crawled into bed next to him, snuggling close but careful of the laptop on his lap.

"Hey, you." I placed a kiss on his shoulder. "I went to check on Kiernon. Your parents or Anna and Paul?"

Removing his glasses, Saxon rubbed his eyes before smiling at me and kissing my temple. "She's with Anna and Paul. They stopped by to see her. You know they weren't leaving her when she threw a fit to go with them."

Chuckling, I could imagine Kiernon putting on a show. "She's got them both whipped."

"Yeah, me too." He joined my laughter.

Looking up into his hazel eyes, I smirked. "So that means I have all night to ravage my husband?"

Saxon's eyes fluttered closed the moment I ran my nails gently down the side of his leg. Making my way back up, I crept under the edge of the laptop, stroking a moment before he caught my wrist, groaning. He protested that he had to finish reading over his information for the conference, but I had him. Twisting my wrist from his grasp, I increased the friction, rubbing, stroking, concentrating on the inside of his thigh.

"Go ahead, read," I teased, taking little nips against his shoulder.

Saxon fought it a few minutes longer before putting his laptop aside and rolling me over on my back. I loved the feel of his weight against me, his arms around me. I felt safe and protected. When Saxon kissed me, I thought I would explode with desire.

Later, much later, Saxon lay across the foot of the bed with my feet propped on his chest. He massaged them, every now and then placing a kiss on one or the other.

"What did you and Rosie get into today that got you coming home taking advantage of me?"

"Nothing. I just wanted to come home and do it with my husband."

"'Do it,' huh?" He laughed at the expression.

Nudging his side with a toe, I laughed too. "Stop making fun. I'm gonna miss you." My face scrunched up in a pout when I thought about Saxon being gone the next four days.

Turning on his side to face me, he ran a hand slowly up and down my leg. "I'll miss my girls too. Why don't you have Rosie come stay a couple of days?"

"I already beat you to the punch," I said with a giggle. "She's gonna stay at least one night."

I wasn't sure if he heard my answer since his hands were replaced by his lips placing kisses up my leg. This time it was Saxon who wouldn't leave me alone.

Chapter Forty-five

Errick

Tipping up the bottle of beer I was drinking, I watched the TV absently, not really paying attention to what was on. My mind was a jumble of thoughts, but the ones that kept in the forefront were of Kiernon and Rachel. From the moment I saw them, I couldn't stop thinking about them.

"What's up, Errick?" Jamie came into the family room and took a seat in the recliner next to the couch.

"Chilling. What you up to?"

"Nothing. Just stopped by to see what Mom cooked."

Jamie knew how to cook, but he didn't like to do it, so he would hit Mom up or order something most days. Mom would always feed his spoiled ass. We settled into a familiar pattern, talking and watching TV while we waited for Mom to finish dinner. Dad came in with Aimee a short time later. Mom called us all to the dining room. We washed our hands, set the table, then took our seats while Aimee helped Mom bring out the food.

It had been a long time since we sat down together as a family. It was familiar, listening to everyone talk about their days, teasing and laughing, discussing world events, sports, anything we could think of. I missed all of this living in Phoenix.

"I have an announcement to make."

Everyone quieted down and gave me their attention.

"I put in for a transfer back to the Nashville office. It was approved the other day."

Shock covered my mom's face. My dad's expression didn't really change.

"You're moving home?" Mom's voice trembled a little.

That was another reason for my trip. I wanted to deliver this news in person.

"Yep. I'll be back in Nashville in about a month."

Aimee jumped up from her seat, ran around the table, and threw her arms around my neck as she giggled. "I'm glad you're coming home."

Mom got up to hug me as well. Tears rolled down her face. I wiped them away. Dad wanted to know what happened, so I told him about the move. I accepted a transfer, and the VP I worked for previously was excited to have me back on board. I would actually be getting a pay increase without a promotion because I would be working on a project that would bring the company millions of dollars.

"I also want to apologize to all of you. I was an asshole when I left and took it out on you guys. Y'all didn't deserve that." I treated my family badly when they just wanted me to do the right thing. They deserved an apology.

"Thank you, son." Dad clapped me on the shoulder.

After apologizing, I felt much better. The time in Phoenix showed me how much I loved and needed them in my life. I would make sure to do better with how I handled them moving forward.

Chapter Forty-six

Errick

"Good morning," I called, closing the door of my parents' house. I was moving into my apartment later today, but I wanted to stop by to see my parents before I got busy. Our relationship was still a little strained, but I was trying my best to fix things. The apology was a start, but I still had work to do.

The smell of bacon and sausage made my stomach growl as I made my way down the hall.

"In here," my mother called.

I found them in the kitchen. My mom was at the stove making breakfast, and my dad sat at the table, trying to coax a sticky-faced Kiernon to eat her eggs. They were strewn over the tray of the high chair where she sat. My steps faltered when my eyes landed on her.

"Morning, son," my dad greeted me over his shoulder, then turned back to the little girl as she struggled to eat with her fist balled over the spoon.

The table my dad sat at beside Kiernon was in front of a large window where sunshine streamed in. My mother's flowers were bright, in full bloom.

Kiernon slapped her spoon against the tray and said, "Pfffftthhhtt."

My dad's smile was as bright as the sun shining outside.

Crossing the kitchen, I kissed my mother's cheek.

"Morning. You want some breakfast?" she asked.

"Yeah, it smells great." I joined my father at the table, sliding into the chair across from him. Looking at Kiernon, I studied the little girl. She was pretty, chubby cheeked with dancing eyes and an infectious smile. She chattered away in her baby language with a word I recognized thrown in every so often. I was amazed at the transformation in my dad. He was captivated, laughing and making faces at the baby while she tried to feed him eggs. Every now and then he would take a little bite, and Kiernon would clap gleefully. The longer I watched her, the stronger the feeling of disappointment grew in me. She didn't know me. I was a stranger to this pretty little girl, and it was all my fault.

When my mom set my plate in front of me, I saw Kiernon watching closely. I took a bite of my eggs. Kiernon smiled, her top four teeth showing, and she clapped excitedly.

"Yeeeeaaaahhhh," she exclaimed.

I flushed, and pleasure ran through me, catching my breath in my chest. The feeling was overwhelming. It struck fast and hard, and it made me want to make Kiernon smile over and over again.

"Come on, ladybug, let's get you cleaned up." My mom took the baby from her seat, propping her on her hip. She left us alone in the kitchen so my dad could eat. Before he dug in, he washed the baby's tray and swept the floor. I watched, struck by how changed my dad seemed since Kiernon was born. I felt a sharp stab of resentment. I wanted to know Kiernon. I wanted to hold her, to know what it felt like for her to love me. I wanted to have unconditional love for her. From the moment I saw her, I felt drawn to her. It was crazy because I was convinced I didn't want to be a part of her life.

I had tossed and turned several nights with Rachel and Kiernon on my mind. I still couldn't believe Rachel was married. I asked myself over and over why I cared, and the only thing I came up with was because I still loved her. When I saw her that day, it was like I had never left. The love I felt for her, the love I kept saying wasn't there, hit me in my gut.

"Dad?"

"Yeah?" Dad answered absently.

"Jamie told me that Rachel is married."

Dad rinsed the rag he wiped the counter with, hung it over the rod below the window, then came to sit down across from me. He started eating, but he looked at me a long time before he said anything. "How do you feel about that?"

For a minute, I wanted to deny I felt anything about it, but my dad knew me too well. He had always been able to read me. Shrugging, I knew I probably looked as miserable as I felt.

"Stunned. Numb. I still can't believe it. How can she be married?" My eyes met my dad's, and I knew before he even said a word what was coming. "I know, I know. I brought this on myself. Trust me, I realize that. I saw Rachel walk in the house that day, and the first thing that came to mind was I love her."

My voice cracked on those words. I knew I fucked up. Big time. I'd been home for a week and a half, and I already realized that nothing in my life was the same.

"What did you expect, son?" Dad asked, setting his fork down on his plate.

What had I expected? That I would come back to find Rachel alone, sad, and lonely? Why did it bother me so much that she wasn't any of those things?

"I didn't expect her to be sitting around waiting for me, but I sure didn't think she would be married. It makes me wonder if she really loved me."

"Wait a minute, Errick," Dad said, his tone stern. "That girl was sick when you walked out on her. She waited and waited for you to call, to come back, to say you were sorry, anything. She fought her feelings for that man not only because she felt like she was betraying you, but because she felt like moving on while she was pregnant was betraying me and your mom as well. You never did anything to make her think things would change. You made choices and decisions, and you can't blame her for doing what was right with the situation she was in."

I knew my dad was right, but fuck that. I wasn't trying to hear that. I knew it was my fault and no amount of regret was going to make it right between Rachel and me, but I didn't want to hear about her being happy with the next man either.

"I know, you're right. But when I saw Rachel . . . and Kiernon . . ." Shaking my head, I didn't think I could make my dad understand what I was feeling. My eyes were damp thinking about her. "Kiernon is beautiful."

Another smile split my dad's face. "She is. Anna and I are so thankful to Rachel for her. She's been a blessing, not just to us but to her extended family, Saxon's family, as well. I know you didn't want a baby. It was your decision, and once I saw how much it bothered you, I tried to stay out of it, but I love that little girl in there. Saxon stepped up, accepting the responsibility of a child who is not his, and his family loves her, so I'm giving you a word of advice. Rachel is happy. Remember that. She deserves to be happy, and so does Kiernon."

I knew Rachel deserved to be happy. I knew that. The question now was, how would I deal with it?

Chapter Forty-seven

Rachel

Dinner with Rosie out of the house was just what I needed. Saxon had been gone several days, and I was missing the hell out of him, so getting out was great. Kiernon was with Ellen and Connor. They were keeping her and Samarra this weekend. I took advantage of the downtime.

"What's going on with you?" I hoped she was seeing someone. I wanted my girl to be as happy as I was. Since her breakup with Charles, she was on a "no man" kick.

"Just working. You know me, about my paper." Rosie took her business seriously.

"What about dating?"

"What about it?" She balled her face up in a frown.

Laughing, I shook my head. "Girl, you need to get back out there. I'm waiting for my niece or nephew."

Looking like she wanted to slap me, she shook her head. "Girl, please. We both know that ain't happening anytime soon."

"But why not?" I pretended to pout.

The waitress came, saving me from a cursing out. Once we ordered, Rosie changed the subject. "When is Saxon back?"

"Tomorrow." My cheeks flushed as I thought about my husband. I couldn't wait to see him.

I still couldn't believe Saxon was my husband. I'd never felt this way for any other man in my life, including Errick. The way he loved me and Kiernon was something I couldn't have asked for.

"Look at you over there blushing with your nasty ass," Rosie teased me.

It was good to be out with my girl. We laughed, talking about nothing and everything. After dinner, we parted ways with a hug. I went home to get some laundry done and clean the house before Saxon returned. I wanted everything to be straight so I could concentrate on him when he got back.

Chapter Forty-eight

Errick

Taking a deep breath to calm my racing heart, I opened the door. I knew I should say something, but the sight of Rachel and Kiernon took my breath away. The resemblance between mother and child was obvious in their dark eyes, both sets of which looked at me curiously right now. Rachel shifted the baby higher on her hip. Kiernon hid her face in Rachel's neck, peeping at me.

"Hello, Errick. Is Anna home?"

An electric tingle ran through me when she said my name. Her honey voice recalled memories of when she'd called out to me under different circumstances. "No. She ran to the store but said she'd be right back."

Glancing at her watch, Rachel muttered an expletive under her breath, then glanced quickly at the baby to make sure she hadn't heard.

"Come in. She won't be gone long," I said. I found myself hoping that she would agree. I wanted to talk to her. I could tell that she was hesitant as she glanced at her watch again. "Come on," I coaxed.

Rachel stepped into the foyer, and the scent of vanilla hung in the air behind her as she moved toward the living room. She was wearing white capris, a white-and-black-patterned halter top, and black-and-white low-top Converse sneakers. Her long hair was pulled away from

her face by a large white band. Kiernon was dressed simi-
larly in black shorts, a white-and-black top, and the same
Converse sneakers her mother had on. Her hair was done
in ponytails with black-and-white barrettes. They were a
cute mother-daughter pair.

Kiernon watched me as Rachel moved into the living
room, crossing the floor to settle on the sofa. She was
peeking over her mother's shoulder at me, and then she
studied me straight on when Rachel settled her on her
feet. Kiernon clung to her leg. She was shy around me.
Unexpected pain squeezed my heart when she looked
at me with uncertainty. *My daughter doesn't know me.*
This beautiful little girl was mine, and she was scared of
me. *My own fault.*

"Can I get you something to drink?" I asked Rachel,
tearing my attention from Kiernon.

"No, thanks."

My eyes moved back to the little girl. She released her
grip on her mother and was toddling slowly around the
room. I smiled when she stopped to look at a picture of
my mother, then turned to Rachel with a big smile and
said, "Ammah."

Rachel's whole demeanor softened. The love she
had for Kiernon was etched in her features. "Yes, that's
Ammah."

I watched the interplay between them, and the tightening in my chest left me breathless. "What is that she's
saying? 'Ammah'?" I asked Rachel.

Rachel glanced at me, and her face darkened. "That's
what she calls your mom. 'Ammah' is her version of
'Grandma.'"

Rachel answered me, but I could tell she was impatient
as she glanced at her watch. There was tension in the air
between us. It was my fault. Her reaction to me was my
doing.

"You don't have to worry about us," Rachel assured me. "I'm sure you have better things to do."

The dismissal in her voice was unmistakable, and it stung like a bitch. I waited a long moment just inside the door. "Rachel . . ." I waited until she looked at me. Her eyes were cold, filled with disdain. "She's beautiful."

Shock registered on her face, but her eyes remained cold.

"I know I was a bastard about this from the beginning. I can't blame you if you hate me for the way I treated you, but when I saw you that day . . ." I shook my head, trying to get my thoughts in order. "I still love you. As much as it will surprise you, it surprised me even more. I want Kiernon, and you, in my life. I keep asking myself how I could have treated you that way, but more importantly, how could I have turned my back on her?"

Rachel stood. She struggled to keep her anger in check. "Obviously it wasn't too hard for you. Errick, this conversation is totally unnecessary. Things happened, and that's the way it is."

"Rachel, let me say this—"

"No." Her vehemence made the baby jump and stare up at her mother with round, wide eyes. "You had months and months to do this. After all this time, it's really not something I want to discuss with you."

"What about her?" I asked, pointing to where Kiernon stood looking up at both of us. Her little face was balled up in confusion, like she didn't know if she should cry.

Rachel froze. Something wild and frightened flickered in her root beer eyes. "What about her? Kiernon is fine. She has a mother and father who love her. Grandparents, aunts, uncles, and cousins make her life complete."

"I'm her father." Saying it aloud made me feel proud and sad at the same time.

Snorting, sarcastic laughter made me flinch as Rachel's eyes flashed at me. "Saxon is her father. He has been since before she was born."

I watched Rachel. She was furious and flustered as she gathered Kiernon's bag and her own. She picked up Kiernon, propping her on her hip. I wished I could do something to ease the anger in Rachel. She was about to storm out of the house. I couldn't let her leave without making myself understood. There was enough animosity between us without creating more.

"Rachel, wait." I grabbed her wrist lightly, just enough to stop her from leaving.

When I touched her, she flinched, and that broke my heart. How did we get here? How was it that my touch made her flinch from me?

"Wait? Wait for what? When we should have been trying to work this out, you had nothing to say to me. You got what you wanted. There's nothing that Kiernon and I want, need, or expect from you except to leave us alone. You made your decision, and now you have to deal with it."

Tears sprang to Kiernon's eyes as her mother's voice rose. She flinched and buried her face in Rachel's neck, her cries muffled. Rachel turned away from me, but I knew if looks could kill, the daggers she shot at me before she did would have a brother laid out on the floor. Rachel bounced Kiernon gently, talking softly to her to soothe her.

"Rachel? Errick? What's going on?" My mom came in, looking back and forth between Rachel and me. She moved by me to pluck Kiernon from Rachel's arms, crooning softly to her as she rubbed her wet eyes.

Dad came in behind Mom, and it only took him a second to figure out there was something going on. "Son, go get the rest of the bags from the car for your mother."

I stood there a moment longer, sparks flying between Rachel and me with the stare down we had going on. Watching her eyes flash had me wanting to pull her in my arms and kiss her. The desire was almost overwhelming. I wanted to know if she was as immune to me as she appeared, but if I tried it at that moment, she would kill me with her bare hands.

"We'll finish this later," I told her before leaving her with my parents.

Chapter Forty-nine

Saxon

The terminal was crowded, people hurrying to meet family or friends picking them up or trying to make a connecting flight. The murmur of voices and laughter and the sounds of luggage and announcements over the PA system were loud as I made my way to the arrival pickup. The electric doors hummed open, and I was glad to see as I scanned the traffic that Rachel was parked in the fifteen-minute waiting area. My gaze ran over my wife when I spotted her. She had a hand shading her eyes as she looked for me in the crowd.

My blood raced, and I actually felt weak by how much I missed her. She was like a drug to me, and I needed my fix. I wanted to wrap myself in her softness, savor her sweet kisses, make love to her like it was our first time. She was leaning against the car. Her hair was pulled away from her face with a large white band, the white capris she wore hugged her full hips, and a black-and-white top flattered her. She looked soft and sexy.

Rachel smiled, waving when she spotted me, and my pulse raced. She was away from the car and in my arms in an instant. I held her, squeezing her tightly. She trembled, clinging to me. I held on even tighter.

"Hello, beautiful." I kissed the top of her head.

She didn't say anything. She just continued to hold on to me.

"Hey, what's going on? You okay?" I didn't know what it was, but there was something about Rachel that had me concerned.

She placed a kiss on my chest. "Hey, I just missed you."

"I missed you too." I kissed the corner of her mouth. Pulling away from the hug, I tucked her under my arm, and we went to her car. "Where's Kiernon?"

"She's with Anna. I want some alone time with my husband."

A low groan escaped me when she gave me a provocative smile. "Let's go."

I enjoyed the conference I attended. It was good to see some of the people I went to medical school with, but I missed my ladies. I touched Rachel continuously. I couldn't stop myself. I rubbed her shoulder and her thigh, played with her fingers, and brushed my fingers through her hair. I didn't know what it was. Maybe it was the fact that she loved me freely. Even after all the bullshit she went through with Errick, when she finally let me in, she never gave me anything less than her all.

At the house, we left my bags in the house, racing against each other as we started disrobing as soon as the door closed. We didn't even make it to the bedroom. At the top of the stairs we fell into each other's arms.

Later, I stroked Rachel's hot, silky flesh. Just having made love to my wife for the second time, I found that I still hadn't gotten enough. I wanted her again right away.

"Saxon?"

"Hmmm?" I replied absently. I was rubbing on her booty.

When she didn't answer right away, I rolled over. I could see in her face she was struggling with something. Propping up on my pillow—we made it to the bed after the second furious round—I pulled her up against my chest. "Hey, what is it?

"I saw Errick today."

My blood ran cold, but I forced my expression to remain neutral. "How did that go?"

I didn't want the answer, but I was here for Rachel. I always tried to hide the fact that I didn't want Errick in her or Kiernon's life. For the most part I didn't think about him, but since he'd popped up, I wasn't going to let him try to reclaim his place in Rachel's life. Or Kiernon's. As far as I was concerned, he didn't have a place.

"Not good."

I held her, just listening. I wished I could ease the pain I heard in her voice. It made me sad and angry to know that she was hurting behind this dude again. I wanted to put my hands around Errick's neck and squeeze the life out of him. Rachel didn't deserve to have to deal with this.

Wiping her eyes, she looked up at me with a smile. My stomach flipped at the sight of her tears. I ran my thumb under one of them. She laughed out of nowhere. That had me curious.

"I told him you are Kiernon's daddy. You are. You're always gonna be her daddy, you know that, right?"

My heart swelled. This was why I loved her. Saying I would always be Kiernon's daddy, telling Errick that I held that place in Kiernon's life, made me feel like my world was right. I loved this woman and the daughter we shared.

Chapter Fifty

Errick

Spending time at my parents' house over the next couple of weeks, I saw Kiernon several times. I found myself thinking about her a lot. Her bright eyes and infectious smile lingered in my thoughts. I wanted more and more to be a part of her life. I couldn't stop thinking about Rachel either. I hadn't seen her since the day she told me her husband was Kiernon's daddy. I wished she would drop by while I was here just so I could see her again, but she hadn't.

I was fascinated by Kiernon. She was already her own little person. I sat and watched her while she played or toddled around the house. She was inquisitive, smart, affectionate, and somewhat of a prima donna. She had my parents wrapped around her finger. My dad seemed much more laid-back when the little girl was around. It was nice to see.

I was sitting on my parents' back porch one afternoon watching Mom and Kiernon cutting flowers from the garden Mom planted every year. Mom had dressed her in a purple romper with a pink shirt and pink Chuck Taylors. She looked adorable. Mom was talking to her, pointing over in my direction. Kiernon looked at me, and they both waved. My heart melted, her smile touching my soul.

The ringing doorbell brought me to my feet. I made my way through the house to answer. When I saw Rachel through the peephole, my heart began to thump. She was dressed in cropped pants and a white top. Her hair was pulled up into a clip on the back of her head. When I opened the door, I saw the surprise on her face before it became quickly guarded.

"Hey." I opened the storm door for her.

"Hi, is Anna here?"

"Yeah, she and Kiernon are in the backyard."

Rachel started in that direction, but I stopped her. "Rachel, can I talk to you for a minute?"

"I'm really in a hurry," she said, trying to brush me off.

"It won't take long." I wasn't going to take no for an answer.

I watched as she rolled her eyes, but she stopped, turning to face me completely. I had never seen Rachel look so cool, so blasé, but she watched me with cold eyes. That hurt.

"I know there's not a lot I can say to make up for the way I hurt you," I began.

"Actually, there's nothing you can say."

Hanging my head, I looked away. Shame, hot and sharp, hit me because I knew she was right. "True, but I want you to know I'm sorry. I hurt you and that's unforgivable, but I do hope you will."

Eyes narrowing, she looked like she wanted to rip my head off. She pressed her lips together in a tight line, saying nothing.

"I want to talk to you about Kiernon."

"You know, Saxon and I wanted to talk to you about her as well."

"Really?" That caught me off guard.

Nodding, Rachel crossed her arms over her chest. "Yes, we've been talking for a while now about Saxon adopting

Kiernon. I'm going tomorrow to start the paperwork so that Saxon can sign her birth certificate and she can have our last name."

Anger hit me so hard I felt like I was suffocating. *Did Rachel just say that motherfucker is adopting my daughter?* She couldn't be serious, but the look on her face told me she was. Rachel wanted her husband to adopt Kiernon. My daughter. My expression changed. My face screwed up, and my temples were throbbing. "What?"

"Saxon is Kiernon's daddy. The only daddy she has ever known."

"I'm her father." I was heated, but I was trying to keep my cool.

"No, you made a conscious decision not to be her father. There's no discussion on this. I will send you the papers. All you have to do is sign them."

My heart ached. Glancing out the back door, I saw Kiernon with a white flower, holding it for my mother to smell. Her little face was shining with happiness.

"I can't do that." I shook my head. I couldn't. Seeing Kiernon, being around her for just this short time, I knew I couldn't just sign her away.

Rachel's voice was low, angry. "What do you mean you can't?"

"That's what I wanted to talk to you about. I want to get to know Kiernon. I want to have the opportunity to make up for all she's missed without me."

"That's where you have it wrong," Rachel said through clenched teeth. "Kiernon hasn't missed out on anything. How dare you? All the months that you've been gone, and now you think because you pop up that you have a right to know her? Where were you when Saxon paced the floor with her at three in the morning because she had a fever? What about when she was teething and he drove her around for hours to get her to sleep? What about when she took her first step? What about when he changed her first diaper? What about when I needed help and he was the only one concerned about me and my daughter? You weren't thinking about Kiernon when you were off living your life, doing whatever it was you were doing."

Her words hurt, but I couldn't let that stop me. "You're right. I know, but I'm here now, and I realize how much I've missed out on."

Rachel stopped me. "Do yourself a favor and sign the papers."

With that she turned and left me standing there watching as she moved through the house, then greeted Kiernon with a big hug and a smile.

"I can't just walk away again," I said aloud.

Kiernon wrapped her chubby arms around Rachel's neck, and my heart ached. What had I done? *What am I going to do?*

Chapter Fifty-one

Saxon

Rachel and Kiernon were in the kitchen, Rachel at the stove, Kiernon in her highchair. I moved over to kiss Kiernon's head. I loved to inhale her sweet baby smell. She was tearing up a roll, stuffing pieces in her mouth. Rachel turned to wrap her arms around me when I moved up behind her. I loved how her lush body felt against me.

"Hey, love, it smells good in here."

"Mmmm. Wash your hands. Dinner's ready," she said once she kissed my lips.

We sat down to meatloaf, turnip greens, and mashed potatoes. We talked about my day. I noticed that she was quiet, so I asked, "What about you? What did you get into today?"

Rachel smiled at me, but it didn't reach her eyes. "I picked up pretty from Anna's. They picked flowers today."

I followed where she pointed until my eyes landed on a vase full of colorful flowers. I glanced over at my daughter. She was trying to feed herself the mashed potatoes her mother put in a bowl in front of her. She missed her mouth most of the time, wiping the potatoes all over her face. My heart swelled with love for the pretty little girl.

"I also talked to Errick today."

A flash of anger rushed through me, but I kept it together. Laying my fork down on my plate, I crossed my arms on the table in front of me. "Really? What was that about?"

"He wants to get to know Kiernon. He wants to be a part of her life. I told him I'm going to start the paperwork for you to adopt her."

My heart filled with love. We talked about it before, but Rachel never felt like it was urgent to get the paperwork in motion. Now with Errick's return and this sudden revelation about wanting to get to know Kiernon, I was glad she was getting it taken care of.

"How'd he take that?" I couldn't imagine someone trying to take Kiernon away from me, but Errick didn't want her to begin with. I didn't understand why, all of a sudden, he wanted to be in Kiernon's life.

Rachel shrugged, trying to make it seem like it wasn't a big deal, but it was. I saw it in her eyes. "He doesn't want to hand over parental rights."

"What?" I exclaimed loudly.

Kiernon jumped in her seat, her eyes wide, her little mouth trembling as she looked at me.

Immediately, I reached over to rub her back. "I'm sorry, pretty. Daddy didn't mean to scare you." Once Kiernon was calm, I turned to Rachel. "What does that mean?"

"I don't know."

We finished dinner. I told Rachel I would clean the kitchen while she gave Kiernon her bath and put her to bed. I cleaned the dishes and wiped the stove and counters down. I couldn't stop thinking about Errick wanting to be a part of Kiernon's life. I had a feeling this sudden change in attitude had more to do with Rachel than Kiernon.

Going upstairs, I stopped outside Kiernon's door, watching Rachel get her settled in bed. Kiernon was tucked in, holding on to Timmy the Turtle, her favorite stuffed animal.

What are we going to do if Errick refuses to sign the papers? Would he really try to take my daughter away from me?

Rachel glanced over, and seeing me in the doorway, she gave me a smile. She crossed the floor, coming over so I could wrap my arms around her as she kissed my shoulder.

"It's going to be okay," she said softly.

I held her, placing a kiss on the tip of her nose. "I know. I don't want to ever lose you or Kiernon."

Reaching up on her tiptoes, she kissed me. "You won't have to. I love you. We are a family."

Chapter Fifty-two

Rachel

"I hate to feel like that, but I can't help it." I sighed before I took a long drink from my margarita.

"I understand where you're coming from, but it's not fair to Anna and Paul." Rosie hated to see me so down.

We were at our favorite Mexican restaurant having lunch. I just told my best friend that I had reservations about leaving Kiernon with Anna and Paul since my last conversation with Errick. Realistically I knew if Errick was around, he would see Kiernon over there, but I never thought he would want to get to know her. He was adamant about having nothing to do with either of us when he left. I didn't know what had changed, and I really didn't care. I just wished he would disappear and let me live my life.

"I know, that's why I feel so bad. They've been nothing but good to me, and they love Kiernon, and she loves them." I sighed heavily. "I'm not going to keep her away from them. I'm just venting."

"What are you going to do about Errick?"

That was the question. I was so angry at him that every time I saw him my stomach turned and I wanted to go into attack mode. The thing that stopped me was I didn't want him to know he affected me like that.

"I have no idea. I thought after selling the house I would never have to deal with him again."

For months I wanted to hear from Errick, to talk to him and figure things out. When Saxon came into my life, he made me see things differently. I fought my way out of depression and opened my heart to someone. Things between me and Saxon moved fast, but Errick walking away started a chain reaction of events that led me to the man of my dreams.

"Don't look now, but Errick just walked in," Rosie warned me.

He spotted us, because before I had a chance to look, he'd made his way to our table. "Hello, ladies."

"Hey, Errick," I spoke even though I didn't want to.

"Can I talk to you for a minute?"

Rosie excused herself for a minute. Errick took the chair next to me when she was gone.

"What's up?" I was curious.

"I just wanted to talk to you for a minute. I know you're out with your girl, but can we meet sometime in the next couple of days?"

I frowned at him. "Errick, I don't know what's going on with you or why you feel the need to talk to me all the sudden, but there's nothing to discuss. As I said the last time I saw you, the time for all that has passed."

"I don't feel the same." He scooted his chair closer to me. "I fucked up and I know it. I know you won't believe me, but I miss you, Rachel. Seeing you again made me realize how wrong I was to walk away from you."

Heat raced through me as the anger I tried to keep in check flared. My stomach churned as I fought to keep my composure. "You have a lot of nerve. What the hell do you gain from doing this?"

"I hurt you, and as much as I told myself it was your fault, I know I'm the one to blame. I love you, Rachel. I've never stopped."

"Too bad. Those days are over. I'm married and I'm happy."

Errick sat back in his seat with a smirk on his face. "You only married him because you're trying to get over me. You haven't even known him that long to be in love with him."

"Conceited much? When you left me, I started working on getting over you. You made it extremely clear you didn't want me or my baby. That was long before I met my husband, so he has nothing to do with how I feel about you. Even if he weren't in the picture, there is nothing you can do or say that would make me want to be with you again."

A flash of hurt crossed his face, but it was there and gone quickly.

"Is everything okay here?" Rosie asked as she came back to the table.

Standing, Errick nodded. "Yes, all's good. I'll talk to you soon, Rachel. You ladies have a good night."

A deep breath helped to ease my frustration. Rosie waited until he was gone before she asked what that was about. I waved the waitress over and ordered two shots of tequila. When she was gone, I told Rosie everything that was said.

"Are you okay, friend?"

"No, he made me mad. I don't get him. He didn't want me or Kiernon, and now all the sudden he realizes how much he loves me. Make it make sense."

"Errick was wrong. The guilt is probably tearing his ass up."

"I don't mean to sound petty, but good for him if it is. Enough about him. I'm not going to give him any more space in my thoughts." I changed the subject.

We stayed at the restaurant for a while, enjoying the food and drinks before going our separate ways.

Chapter Fifty-three

Errick

My office overlooked the parking lot between build-ings. There was a small courtyard where people who smoked congregated. I wasn't paying attention to my surroundings. Instead, I was thinking about how to approach Rachel and have a civil conversation with her. Swiveling in my chair, I picked up the business card from the blotter on my desk. I debated calling the number since I knew I wouldn't be received well.

Taking a deep breath, I picked up my desk phone and dialed the number. I gave my name to an assistant, and then a minute or two passed until the phone was picked up again.

"Why are you calling me?"

"Hello, Rosie. I know you're probably busy, but I was hoping that I could talk to you about Rachel and Kiernon."

"What?" The disbelief was evident in her voice. "What could you possibly want to talk about them with me for?"

"I wanted to ask if you would talk to Rachel. I think we need to sit down and have a conversation."

"Why do you think I would do that?" Rosie snapped.

"Because she's your friend and the two of us need to come to some kind of agreement."

Voice dripping with sarcasm, Rosie laughed. "When I spoke with Rachel the other day, she told me that all that needed to be said had been said."

"Unfortunately, it hasn't."

I could hear the irritated sigh she released. "Look, Errick, you know that I love Rachel. I hate what you did to her. You put her through a lot of bullshit, so I'm going to say this as kindly as I can. You're not all bad. You were good to my friend for a long time. I'm sure your family told you how devastated Rachel was when you walked out on her. You left her, no word, no contact. You weren't even man enough to tell her you were leaving. She was pregnant, scared, and alone. You didn't want to know. She was devastated, but she did exactly what you told her to do and managed to move on. It's not fair of you to come back now and decide all of a sudden that you want things different. It's not fair to Rachel, Kiernon, or Saxon."

I bristled when she said his name. "I love Rachel, and right now I don't give a damn about what's fair to Saxon."

"Well, you should, because he loves Rachel. Saxon loves the child you wanted nothing to do with. Kiernon is his daughter no matter how you feel about it now. He has never done anything but try to make them both happy. If you love Rachel, then you should want her to be happy. They are happy with Saxon. I have to go, Errick. Goodbye." Rosie hung up the phone.

I sat there for a long time, the receiver still clutched in my hand while her words played over in my head. Rachel and Kiernon were happy with another man. I didn't want to believe it, but I wondered if I really lost my little family.

Chapter Fifty-four

Rachel

The early evening weather was nice, the sun was low in the western sky, the temperature was in the low seventies, and a light breeze blew the leaves on the trees. We dropped Kiernon off with Ellen and Conner for the night. They were keeping the grandkids, so that gave us a free evening. We decided to go on a date night. I was more than excited to be spending some alone time with my husband.

We pulled up in front of the restaurant, Sinema. I waited for Saxon to open my door, then took his hand and walked to the door. It opened as we neared, and I was surprised to see Errick coming out of the building. I tried not to roll my eyes, but when Saxon nudged my shoulder playfully, I knew he'd seen me.

Errick seemed surprised to see us as well. He stared at me with a smirk. I didn't like it, but I didn't say anything.

"Hello." Errick gave his most charming smile.

I mumbled a greeting and went to move around him.

"Wait, Rachel, wait a minute. Can we talk?" Errick stopped me.

I ground my teeth. Saxon put a hand on my arm. His eyes met mine, gazing at me meaningfully. We had a conversation without a word being exchanged between us. I loved this man because he could calm me with just a gentle touch.

"What is it, Errick?" I wasn't in the mood for him. I just wanted to spend time with my husband, and he was holding us up from doing that.

Errick looked from me to Saxon before glancing off in the distance. When he looked back, I saw remorse in his features. "I haven't seen Kiernon at my parents' house lately. Mom said you haven't brought her over in a while."

"She's been spending time with her other grandparents," I said, referring to Ellen and Connor.

"Rachel, I don't deserve the chance to know Kiernon, but I can't stop thinking about her. Being able to spend time with her, getting to know her, that's what I want. Who is she? What does she like? What scares her, and what can I do to make it better?" Errick shook his head like he was struggling to get the words right. "She is my daughter."

Anger coursed through me. Errick had to be crazy. For weeks he told me to get rid of the problem. Once he left, he shut me out of his life completely and never looked back. When I tried to reach out about the house, he wouldn't even talk to me to handle business. *No contact for over almost two years, but now all of a sudden, I'm supposed to believe he wants to know the child he never wanted in the first place.*

"Why do we have to go through this? You had every opportunity, even if you didn't want to be with me, to be a part of Kiernon's life. You made the choice for both of us. Saxon is her father. He loved her even before she got here. Knowing that she wasn't his biologically didn't stop him from making room in his heart to love her. That's what a father does. Kiernon is Saxon's daughter, not yours. This is what it is."

I was struggling with the urge to punch him in his eye. Saxon's hand moved up and down my back, trying to calm me. I was on edge. All this with Errick and his sudden interest in Kiernon had my blood boiling.

"Rachel, I just want to get a chance to know Kiernon. I want her to know me."

It was like he ignored everything I said. *I don't understand why he can't just go on with his life just like he's been doing.* "Errick, Kiernon has a daddy." I wrapped my fingers through Saxon's and led the way into the restaurant.

We left Errick standing there. I could feel his eyes on me as I walked away. I wasn't going to deal with him anymore. Errick wasn't there for Kiernon when he should have been, so there was no need to try to step up now. She didn't need him or his regret.

Chapter Fifty-five

Saxon

It was late, and I was tired. Streetlights brushed away some of the shadows as I drove through a drizzle that was messy enough to make driving dangerous. The tension between my shoulder blades had settled into a dull ache. One of my patients had gone into premature labor, and we lost the baby. Seeing the devastation in the parents' eyes was a blow to the gut. After that fiasco, all I wanted to do was go home to see my wife, kiss my baby, and thank God that they were okay. I was sure Kiernon was asleep. I could imagine her looking so peaceful as she lay in her crib. Her mouth would be puckered, or her thumb would be firmly planted between her lips. Rachel would be relaxing on the sofa with a book or movie to keep her company until I got home. When we first got married, I came home to find her sleeping on the sofa. I tried to talk her into going to bed, but she insisted that she wouldn't sleep comfortably without knowing I made it home safely.

I drove through our familiar neighborhood, and a feeling of peace settled over me when I pulled into the drive. The porch light and the solar lights along the walk illuminated the night. It was a familiar sight, and I was glad to be home.

Inside I closed and locked the door, dropped my bag at the bottom of the stairs, then made my way down the hall.

Rachel decorated once I proposed, and everything was in place by the time she and Kiernon moved in. Rachel made my house a home, and I loved them being here.

All the rooms were painted in warm colors. The living room was a pale khaki green, and the furniture was beige and brown. Lots of green plants were scattered throughout the house. The kitchen was bright, sunny, and welcoming. The master bedroom was sexy and relaxing. Kiernon's room was a child's learning playland.

"Hey, I'm home," I called as I headed to the entertainment room.

My heart slammed in my chest and panic raced through me when I saw Rachel. She was sitting on the end of the sectional—balled into the cushions was more like it—tears streaming down her face.

In four long strides, I was at her side. My knees trembled as I knelt before her, pulling her into my arms. A sick feeling of dread filled my stomach as Rachel cried harder.

"What? What is it? Is Kiernon okay?" My voice was steadier than I expected because as much as I didn't want to be, I was scared.

Rachel struggled to catch her breath. Sobs shook her shoulders. She handed me a legal-sized envelope and some papers. I recognized the letterhead of a local attorney. The dread sank deeper into my bones. Reading the first few lines, I glanced over at Rachel. Her heart was breaking and mine was too.

Pain, anger, and a glimmer of fear were in her red, puffy eyes. Pulling her close, I kissed the top of her head, holding her while the tears continued to fall. Fury boiled in my gut, and my blood was steaming as I thought about what I read. Errick was suing Rachel for proof of paternity to establish visitation. I wanted to beat the shit out of him for what he was putting Rachel through. It wasn't enough that he'd walked out on her while she was pregnant and missed the first year of Kiernon's life. Now he was trying to barge his way in. Once again, this man's selfishness was tearing Rachel apart inside.

Waiting for her to calm down, I didn't want to add to her frustration by expressing mine. I had to be strong for her. The pain in Rachel's eyes made me want to kill Errick for hurting my wife, but I kept my anger in check.

Rachel and I talked for a long time, going over the situation and trying to come up with a solution that would be good for her and Kiernon.

"I know this is crazy, but why don't you do what he's asking? Set up a visiting schedule with him," I suggested.

Rachel looked like she wanted to punch me in my throat. "That's crazy."

"Love, I'm not happy about it either, but he's obviously not going to stop, and I don't want to see you upset like this." I kissed her forehead, running my fingers over the worry lines etched there, trying to smooth them out.

Rachel's features softened. Reaching up, she stroked my beard. "I love you."

I never got tired of her saying that. "I love you too."

It was true. I'd never loved a woman like I did Rachel. She and Kiernon were my everything.

"Let me think about it," Rachel told me once she'd given the thought a chance to settle in her mind. "Come on, let's go to bed."

Pulling her to her feet, entwining our fingers, I let her lead the way up the stairs. I held tightly to her hand. I needed that contact. We stopped in Kiernon's room to check on her. We found her just the way I expected: thumb tucked securely in her mouth, on her belly with her knees pulled up under her, her bottom in the air. I couldn't help laughing when she grunted and a small poot escaped her.

That little girl was my daughter, my baby. I couldn't love her more if she was my biological child. Now I would have to share her. *How do I deal with Errick being part of her life, him wanting to be her daddy?*

Glancing at Rachel, I saw her lips tremble a little while she watched our sleeping baby. I hugged her close to me, tucking her under my arm.

Fifteen minutes later I stepped from the shower, drying off vigorously. I wrapped the towel around my waist and returned to the bedroom, where I found Rachel undressed, waiting for me in bed.

"What do we have here?" I asked with a smirk.

"This." Rachel reached for me, pulling the towel from my waist.

Chapter Fifty-six

Rachel

"Oh, honey. That is wonderful news." Anna squeezed me in a tight hug. She was ecstatic about the news I shared with her. I was thankful, but this was another one of those times when I wished my own mother were here to share it with me.

"What wonderful news?" Errick came into the kitchen. His step faltered, and it was obvious from his expression he wasn't expecting to see me.

I looked him over when Anna and I came apart. He was still the same—tall, dark, and handsome—but I saw him in a different light now. I realized for the first time in a long time I wasn't as angry with him. I still resented the way he handled things, but I had to let it go. Our lives moved in different directions, and he'd done me a favor when he left. I got Kiernon and Saxon out of it, and I was grateful and needed to move on.

"Oh, sorry to interrupt," Errick said, and his eyes never left me.

"Hello," I greeted him pleasantly.

"Hi." He seemed unsure of himself, or maybe he was uncertain of my reaction to the papers he'd served me with.

"Can we talk?" I gave him my most dazzling smile. Even this conversation with Errick wouldn't ruin my day.

"Um, sure."

Moving by him, I didn't bother to look back to see if he followed. In the living room I waited, standing in front of the sofa. I took a deep breath, hoping Errick wouldn't make this harder than it had to be. Saxon and I talked about this for a week. He was right. I needed to talk to Errick and possibly set up some kind of visitation schedule.

Errick came into the room. I saw the curiosity in his eyes.

"I'm sure you know I received the paperwork from your attorney's office."

Errick started to say something, but I stopped him.

"Let me finish. We don't have to go to court. There's no need to establish paternity. We both know Kiernon is your biological child. I don't want to put her through tests and us fighting over her."

Errick's eyes lit up, and I almost believed he was happy with what I was saying.

"If you want to spend time with Kiernon, there will have to be some rules."

His smile slipped. "Rules?"

"Yes, rules. I'm sure you'll find I'm not going to be unreasonable, but there are some things I insist on. Your visits will be here, at your parents' house, and there must be someone from your family here at all times."

"Wait a minute," Errick snapped.

"No, you wait a minute. Kiernon doesn't know you. You're a stranger to her, and I will not have her being uncomfortable. You can agree now, or we can go to court, and I'll explain it to the judge."

Crossing my arms over my chest, I tried to keep my anger in check. I told myself this was going to be a civil conversation, and I wanted to make sure it was. I could see that Errick's feelings were hurt, but he backed down.

I really didn't care if they were hurt. This was about Kiernon. He went to take a seat on the sofa.

"As you know, Anna and Paul keep Kiernon often. You are welcome to visit her anytime. One thing must be clear." I knew Errick was going to lose his shit when I said this next part, but I didn't care. "Saxon is Kiernon's daddy. I will never lie to her about who you are, but Saxon is her daddy. I don't want you to say anything other than that to her."

"Who am I?" he sputtered. "Not lie about who I am? If he's playing daddy, then who am I?"

My brow creased, my shoulders tightened, and anger reared its head very quickly. "I think you have the roles reversed here. Saxon is not playing daddy. He is her daddy. You are her biological father, the man who helped create her, but that's it. Saxon is the man who loves her, the man who has loved her since before she was born. For now, you're Errick. As she gets older, we'll let her decide what to call you."

"Rachel, you're not giving me a chance. How am I supposed to establish a father-daughter relationship and not be her daddy? I know I messed up. I can't tell you how much I regret what I've done, that I hurt you, but when I saw her, I knew from that moment I would do everything, anything I could to make it up to her." Errick stood, moving closer to me. Reaching out, he ran a finger down my arm. "I want to make it up to you, too."

I took a step back, and my eyes flashed at his audacity. "That's just it. You can't make it up. And don't try to play with me. You know I'm married."

"I know." He looked as if he'd been slapped. "I will respect that even though it's hard for me. You have to understand I love you."

I give him the bitch face as I twisted my lips.

"I love you, Rachel. How did you fall out of love with me so quickly?"

"You didn't make it very hard," I snapped. Taking a deep breath, I was still trying to keep myself under control. "Errick, the past is the past. We've both gone on with our lives as you wanted. This is about Kiernon."

"Yeah, I know, I know. When I saw Kiernon that day, I've never felt anything like that. I realized that I need her in my life."

There was sincerity in his eyes. I didn't want Errick to come back into my life, but here he was. For my baby's sake, I was going to make this situation work.

"Kiernon usually spends the night with your parents on Fridays. You can spend the day with her Saturday. I'll pick her up around four. Does that work for you?" I suggested.

I could tell he wanted to say something, but he didn't. He just agreed. I nodded, picking up my bag from the sofa behind me.

"Rachel?"

I stopped, looking at him. The way he was studying me made me shiver.

"Thank you."

"It's for Kiernon."

Chapter Fifty-seven

Errick

Meeting David for a beer after work, I pulled up at Jonathan's Grille in Germantown. Finding parking took a little while. I had to park a couple streets over and walk back to the sports bar. The place was packed on a Friday evening. Most of the tables were full, and the bar had a line waiting for the bartenders to take drink orders. Looking around, I didn't see David, but I managed to find a table in a far corner. On my way to the table, something caught my attention. I had to do a double take when I saw Rachel's husband at a table with a woman who wasn't his wife.

I took a seat and kept my eye on him. He and the woman seemed caught up in their conversation. They weren't paying attention to their surroundings, but I paid attention to them. Taking out my phone, I snapped a few pictures when they laughed together. Their heads were close, and when the woman laughed, she touched his hand or shoulder. It seemed rather intimate, and it made me wonder if he was cheating on Rachel.

It wasn't long before David arrived. The waitress had just brought the round of beers I ordered when he walked up. We shook hands, and then he took a seat across from me.

"What's going on?" He took a long drink from his beer.

"You see dude over there?" I indicated the table where Saxon sat.

"Yeah."

"That's Rachel's husband."

"Husband? I didn't know she got married." David looked at the man again.

"Yeah, they been married a couple months."

"Wow. I saw her when she was still pregnant. She told me she wasn't sure if she was engaged because she hadn't given him an answer yet. I guess she finally decided."

I stared across the table at my boy. "You knew she was engaged and didn't say anything?"

"What was I going to say? You made it clear you didn't want to talk about Rachel."

David changed the subject, so I let it go. I couldn't help keeping an eye on Saxon. David and I caught up with each other. David was glad to hear I had moved back to Nashville.

An hour later, I excused myself to go to the men's room. I felt a little unsteady from the four shots I'd downed. The restroom was empty when I walked in. I headed to a urinal. The door opened and in walked Saxon.

I finished, zipped up, then went to wash my hands. I knew I shouldn't say anything to Saxon, but my petty side resented that he was with the woman I loved. I watched him through the mirror as he moved over to the sink to wash his hands as well.

"You know Rachel only married you to get over me."

Saxon made eye contact through the mirror. He smirked but didn't respond.

"What? You know it's the truth. If I hadn't walked away, you would have never stepped in to fill my shoes." Irritation ran through me at his lack of response.

"I don't walk in anyone's shoes but my own. I get it though. You fucked up, and now you're mad at me for stepping up." Saxon grabbed paper towels from the dispenser and wiped his hands.

"Don't get it twisted, white boy. You stepped up, but Rachel still loves me."

"Well, I'm mixed actually. Is that what bothers you? A mixed boy is married to the woman you can't have and daddy to the baby you didn't want?"

When he referred to himself as Kiernon's daddy, my temperature boiled. "That's my daughter."

"You didn't want her, remember? Yeah, I stepped up when you slunk away. You weren't even man enough to tell the woman you claim to love you were leaving. It's cool though. You did me and Rachel both a favor."

I didn't know if it was the liquor or what he said that pushed me over the edge, but I lost it. I swung on him, my fist connecting with his jaw. Saxon was caught off guard, but it only took a moment for him to shake it off. When he did, we squared up and were locked in on each other. He caught me on the chin with a right hook followed by a left to the head. I shook it off and came back with a left to the kidneys. We passed licks, tearing up the small bathroom. It didn't take long before people heard us and came running to see what was going on. Nothing fazed me. I blocked out the noise from the hall and concentrated on taking my anger out on Saxon. I had to give it to him, he hung in there with me. I felt someone grab me from behind just as Saxon swung and hit me in my mouth. I tasted blood. Infuriated, I tried to break free, but whoever had me fought to keep me away from him.

Someone grabbed Saxon and was pulling him out the door. Once I saw I couldn't get to him anymore, I calmed down, and whoever had me slowly let me go. When I turned around, I saw that it was David.

"What the hell?" He stared at me, waiting for an answer.

"Let's get out of here." I left the bathroom and went back to the table to drop enough money to cover our tab and a generous tip. People watched me as I moved through the crowd. The manager came over and told me I had to leave. The police would be called if I didn't. I did as he asked. I hadn't come to cause any trouble. I looked around but didn't see Saxon anywhere.

"What the hell happened?" David demanded when we got outside.

I didn't want to talk about it, but I couldn't do my boy like that. I told him that Saxon was talking shit. I left out the part where I started it. I ran my tongue over my lip. It was split on the inside. Saxon got a good hit off on me, but I would see him again.

Chapter Fifty-eight

Rachel

"Hey, babe," I said when I heard Saxon come into the room. I stayed home while he went out for drinks, and I fell asleep. Hearing him move around the room was what woke me up.

"Hey, love." Saxon didn't turn the light on, so I flipped on the lamp.

"How was your time out of the madhouse?" I teased, sitting up against the headboard. I noticed something immediately. "What's wrong with your face?"

I jumped out of bed and moved over to where he stood in the door to the bathroom. When he flipped on the light, I saw what looked like a bruise on his face. When I got closer, I saw that I was right. It was then I noticed that the shirt he had on was torn at the collar. "What happened?" I started to panic.

"Nothing. Calm down. I'm okay." Saxon rubbed my arms with his hands to soothe me.

"It doesn't look like nothing." Saxon wasn't telling me something. I knew him better than he thought I did.

"I'm good, love. Don't stress yourself."

"That's what we're doing now? When did we start keeping things from each other?"

Saxon knew I was serious. He told me to sit down. I did as he asked, then listened while he told me everything.

Fury boiled my blood as I thought about Errick doing something stupid like this. It made me angry that even though I was trying to get along, he was being disrespectful.

"I'm sorry, baby." I put my head down. Saxon had been nothing but good to me from the moment we met, and here my ex was attacking him.

Saxon sat down beside me. "Don't ever apologize for him. You didn't do anything. And don't worry. I'm good. He'll think before he tries me again."

"I love you." I kissed him softly. When we parted, I turned his head so I could see the bruise that was forming on his fair skin. His jaw was swollen, but other than that I couldn't tell he'd been in a fight.

"I'm gonna jump in the shower, and then you can show me how much you love me." He stood and pulled the shirt over his head.

I watched as my husband stretched, a smirk on my face. He didn't have to wait for his shower to be over. I followed him with the baby monitor and joined him under the hot spray.

Chapter Fifty-nine

Rachel

"I don't want to keep Kiernon away from you or Paul, but I refuse to let her be around Errick when he's pulling shit like this." I didn't mean to curse, but frustration hummed through me.

Anna didn't know about the fight between Saxon and Errick, and she said she hadn't seen him in a couple of days. "Rachel, you know we love Kiernon. I understand you're angry, but don't do anything rash. Talk to Errick. I don't want to be in the middle of what's going on. Believe me when I tell you he's going to hear about this from me. He never should have said anything to Saxon."

As far as I was concerned, there was nothing I needed to say to Errick. He was wrong for hitting Saxon. He shouldn't have said anything to him at all.

"I know you love Kiernon, and she loves you guys too. I'm not saying I would keep her from you. You're always welcome at our house or to take her out with you."

"That's not fair, Rachel. Kiernon loves being at our house."

"What do you want me to do?"

"Talk to Errick. You need to come to some type of arrangement for Kiernon's sake."

I didn't want to go back and forth with Anna. She didn't deserve my anger, and I was taking it out on her. "I'll talk to him."

We were at Anna's house. I brought Kiernon to see Ammah. I told her what happened the week before with Errick and Saxon. I had been busy with Kiernon and the house. Saxon's office was planning a retirement party for one of the doctors in the association, and I was helping with that, so I wasn't able to talk to Anna until now.

The conversation Anna wanted me to have with Errick must have been meant to be. Not twenty minutes later, we heard the front door open and him yell for her. Just thinking about what he did made me angry. Errick came into the living room where I was with Anna and Kiernon. She was toddling around the room, playing with the toys Anna pulled out for her.

"What's up, Ma?" Errick's steps faltered when he saw me sitting there with Anna. "Hey, Rachel." He turned to Kiernon and knelt to where she was. "Hey, beautiful. How's my girl today?"

Hearing him call Kiernon his girl set my teeth on edge, but I didn't say anything. I was angry at Errick, but as I watched him interact with Kiernon, I could see that he was trying. It was a few minutes later when he turned his attention back to Anna and me.

"Can I talk to you for a minute?" Errick asked before I could say anything.

"Yeah, we should talk," I agreed.

Anna gathered Kiernon, then left us alone. When she was gone, an awkward silence settled in the room. I waited to see what he was going to say.

"I'm sorry, Rachel."

"What are you sorry for?" I was skeptical.

"I'm sorry for the shit with ol' boy the other day. I saw him and let my jealousy take over. I was wrong, and I apologize for acting the way I did."

Errick's apology caught me off guard. I didn't know if I really believed him.

"Look, I don't know what's going on with you or why you felt the need to say anything to Saxon, but he's my husband. He loves me and Kiernon, and I don't appreciate you acting the way you did."

"I know I shouldn't have, but I love you. This shit is hard for me. I never expected to feel the way I do, but when I saw him that night, I just lost it."

"Don't do that. I don't want to hear how much you love me. This whole situation is hard for me too. I'm trying to work with you on getting to know Kiernon, but then you disrespect her daddy. I can't have someone around her who would do that."

Errick wanted to say something, but he didn't. Another surprise for me. "I do want to know Kiernon. I'll play by your rules. Just give me another chance."

Despite my apprehension, I nodded in agreement. I was doing this for Kiernon, so I would let it go this time.

Chapter Sixty

Saxon

Another late delivery brought me home long after the sun went down. I got home and was surprised when Rachel wasn't in her usual spot waiting for me. Taking the stairs two at a time, I stopped, out of habit, to check on Kiernon. Finding the room empty, I wondered if Rachel brought her in bed with her. We did that sometimes if she was fussy. It was then I remembered Kiernon was with Moira and Daniel tonight. It made me wonder what was going on with Rachel.

Standing at the door, I stopped to watch Rachel without her knowing. She lay across the bed, reading, dressed in my favorite red boy shorts and a white tank top. This woman was sexy to me no matter what she was wearing. She must have felt me watching her, because she looked up and gave me a slow, sexy smile. My body flushed under her smoldering gaze.

"Hey, baby." She crawled up on her knees to the edge of the bed as I moved to her.

She pressed her body against mine as I wrapped my arms around her waist. "Hi. How was your day?"

I didn't give her a chance to answer. I kissed her until we were both breathless, my hands reaching down to cup her bottom, pulling her hips closer to me.

"Wow, you missed me, huh?" she giggled when we came apart.

"I can show you how much."

Rachel's face flamed, and she glanced away shyly. I loved that she was bashful with me at times. My straightforward desire for her took her by surprise sometimes, but I didn't know why. I couldn't keep my hands off her.

"Go take a shower, and I'll show you how much I've missed you," she flirted back.

My body reacted immediately. I kicked off my shoes by the side of the bed, moving toward the bathroom, removing my clothes as I went. I felt Rachel's eyes on me. Stopping at the door, I winked at her. "Why don't you join me?"

"Go," she mock scolded.

Chuckling under my breath, I went into the bathroom. Something taped to the mirror caught my eye. I scanned it, and my heart raced and my head swam as excitement washed over me. I had to read it again before rushing back into the bedroom. Rachel was waiting for me. Her eyes were shining, but I could tell she was waiting for my reaction with uncertainty. My heart ached at the indecision in her eyes. I knew she was thinking about the past, but this situation was not the same.

"A baby?" I needed to hear her confirm it. She nodded, and I let out a yell and rushed to her. "We're having a baby?"

A tear ran down the side of her face when she told me we were. Jumping on the bed, I pulled her into my arms. Rolling around, I placed kisses all over her face while she laughed and cried at the same time.

I was the happiest man on earth at this moment. *I have my wife, my daughter, and now a new baby on the way.* Life was almost perfect.

Almost.

Chapter Sixty-one

Errick

After parking in front of my parents' house, I left the cool interior of the car, stepping into the heat of the early summer evening. I wiped my damp hands on my shorts as I stood there looking at the house like it was a strange place. The moisture on my hands wasn't from the summer temperature. It was from nervousness. I had to laugh at myself, shaking my head. I couldn't believe how edgy I was. Waving at my mother's neighbor when she spoke, I was glad she snapped me out of my thoughts. Taking a deep breath, I made my way up the walk.

"Hey, folks," I called as I opened the door.

Finding my parents and Kiernon in the family room, I saw that the sofa table had been pushed out of the middle of the floor. A blanket with pink and purple flowers on it was spread out and held several toys along with Kiernon and Dad. They were playing with a toy that you fit different shapes into, and they seemed to be having a good time.

Kissing my mom's cheek, I took the empty seat beside her on the sofa. I studied Kiernon and couldn't help noticing the similarities Kiernon had with me and Rachel. Her hair was thick and wavy. Rachel had it combed into several small ponytails with green barrettes on the ends to match the green denim shorts she wore with a pink and yellow top. Her pierced ears sported little sunflower earrings. She looked like a little doll. Her smile was mine, no doubt, and her nose was like mine and my mom's.

Watching as my dad fit one of the blocks in the toy, Kiernon laughed, clapping her pudgy hands gleefully. Crawling over to where Dad lay on the blanket, Kiernon patted his face and planted a sloppy kiss on his forehead. I chuckled at my dad's expression. He looked like a lovesick teenager at her display of affection.

Kiernon must have heard me laugh because she looked at me with big, dark eyes. My heart constricted, and I wondered what it was like to have her love. What was it like to be the one to receive her affection? To be the one to make her smile?

"Talk to her," Mom said softly. She was watching me. Leave it to her to know what I was thinking. I had been around Kiernon several times. I'd interacted with her, but I was still a little anxious around her.

"Kiernon, come here, sweetie," Mom called to her.

She toddled over to Mom's side, holding out her hands to be picked up. "Ammah, up." Those two words brought another smile to my face.

Mom picked her up, settling her on her lap close to me. Kiernon looked at me with wide eyes, studying me.

"Hi, Kiernon," I said, my heart melting a little more when she batted her long lashes at me with a shy smile.

For a moment I didn't think she was going to say anything, but then I heard very softly, "Hi."

Holding out my hands to take her, I said, "Will you come see me? Can I hold you?"

My stomach was in knots as I waited to see what she would do. Kiernon watched me, those eyes, Rachel's eyes, studying me for what seemed like forever. She looked up at my mother for reassurance. Mom smiled at her but didn't say anything. That smile seemed to settle things for Kiernon, and she climbed from Mom's lap into my arms.

I held my daughter for the first time, and a myriad of emotions washed over me. Elation, satisfaction, terror, uncertainty, sadness, fear—in the space of seconds these feelings overwhelmed me. It took my breath away. I had to fight the tears that threatened to spill. Kiernon was a little miracle, and I was lucky to have these moments.

Everything inside me screamed, *I'm your daddy,* but I didn't say it. I'd already done enough, so I would follow Rachel's rules. For now.

I spent the next two hours with Kiernon. I got down on the blanket to play with her toys, reading to her, just sitting, and watching her as she toddled around the room. Everything interested her. Mom and Dad left us alone once they were satisfied that Kiernon was comfortable, but I knew they peeped in on us from time to time. This was the best time I'd had in a long time. Every time she smiled at me, my heart ached because I missed so much time with her.

Around eight p.m., Kiernon had enough. She was getting cranky. She didn't want to play with me anymore. She began to whimper, looking at me with big, watery eyes. "Ammah?"

"Aww, you want Ammah, sweetie?" I picked her up and went to find my parents.

Mom and Dad were in their room. Dad was in front of the computer, and Mom was sitting in a recliner by the window, reading. As soon as Kiernon saw my parents, she wriggled frantically to free herself from my arms. She didn't bother trying to walk when I put her down. She fell on all fours and crawled to my mom's chair. Mom stood, picking her up, settling her on her hip. She stopped for Dad to give her a kiss, then went to give her a bath and get her ready for bed.

"You were good with her," Dad said once Mom and Kiernon were out of the room.

My dad's opinion was important to me. Since I'd been grown and learned to appreciate my father, I wanted to be the same type of man, the same type of father, he was. The time we'd been estranged was hard for me. I was relieved that we were on better terms.

"Thanks. You know, Dad, I want to say I'm sorry again for the way I treated you, and Mom, the whole family really, over the situation with Rachel. You and Mom were right. I know you tried to tell me, but I wouldn't listen. I've missed out on so much with Kiernon."

"I'm just glad Rachel decided to give you a chance to get to know Kiernon."

"She really didn't have a choice." The words were out of my mouth before I could stop them. Seeing my dad's expression, I knew I'd spoken too soon.

"What does that mean?" Dad asked.

I knew my dad wouldn't push the issue if I chose not to tell him, but I figured Rachel already told Mom. "I contacted an attorney and started the process of establishing paternity."

Dad's expression changed from stony to sad. Saying nothing, he shook his head. I saw the disappointment that settled in his features. I let him down again. When Mom returned with Kiernon dressed in purple pajamas, her eyes were droopy.

"Kiernon wants to give Poppy a kiss."

"Good night, Poppy's girl." Dad stood to take Kiernon from her. He looked at me one last time before he told us he was going to put her down. He told me to have a good night, then walked out of the room.

I was a 33-year-old man, but at that moment, I felt like a chastised teenager.

Chapter Sixty-two

Saxon

Rachel was on pins and needles as we waited for someone to answer the door. Taking her hand, I wrapped my fingers in hers, giving her a slight squeeze. I was just as tense as she was, but I didn't want her to know that.

Neither of us slept well the night before. I got up early this morning and made her breakfast in bed. We cleaned the house, then relaxed together, reading on the sofa. Now we were at Anna and Paul's, anxious to see Kiernon.

Aimee opened the door, and I let out a breath I didn't realize that I was holding. Errick's sister was the spitting image of Anna, with the same smooth complexion and thick hair, wide bright eyes, and quick smile. She and Rachel were cool. She'd been to the house many times, and I liked her.

"Come on in. We're out on the patio. Dad fired up the grill."

When we stepped on the deck, I saw Kiernon playing with her blocks. The tension that filled us both eased a little. I felt Rachel relax against me when she laid eyes on our daughter.

"Hey, pretty," Rachel said, catching Kiernon's attention.

Kiernon's face lit up when she saw us, and I fell in love all over again. Just her smile could make me feel like a million dollars. Kiernon's eyes sparkled, crinkling up at the corners as she laughed in excitement. She stood, toddling over, throwing her arms up to be picked up. "Mama. Mama."

I shook hands with Paul, kissed Anna's cheek, then dapped up with Jerome, Aimee's boyfriend. The whole time, Rachel smothered Kiernon's face with kisses.

Kiernon's giggles rang in the early afternoon. She wiggled and squealed as Rachel tickled her. "Dada. Dada."

My heart always swelled when she said that. I reached for her, and she almost leapt from Rachel's arms. Kiernon's grin was wide, showing off her eight teeth. Her little hands patted my face as she jabbered in her baby language. "How's Daddy's girl?" I blew a raspberry against her cheek, making Kiernon fall over with giggles.

"Dada. Dada. No, Daaadaa."

I turned, and my eyes met Errick's when he stepped out onto the deck. Anger hit me in the gut, but I kept my composure. He stared from me to Kiernon, and there was a flicker of envy in his eyes as he watched us. Tightening my grip on Kiernon, I held her close. I didn't care what he thought. Rachel and Kiernon were my family. I would never let him take them from me.

"Are you ready to go, pretty?" Rachel said to Kiernon. "Give Ammah and Poppy a kiss bye."

Kiernon was passed around for goodbye hugs and kisses. I felt Rachel tense when Kiernon was passed to Errick. Throwing an arm over her shoulder, I winked at her. Errick gave Kiernon a kiss on the cheek, but she was trying to push her way out of his arms. When he put her on her feet, she rushed back over to me.

"Dada. Go bye." She waved, making everyone laugh.

I saw the hurt in Errick's eyes as Kiernon rushed to get away from him, but I couldn't generate any sympathy for him. This was what Errick wanted, and now he was in his feelings about Kiernon not knowing him. I gathered my little family and left him standing there with his family.

Chapter Sixty-three

Rachel

The doorbell rang. I got up from where Kiernon and I sat playing with a large-piece puzzle. "Come on, pretty, let's see who's here."

Kiernon got up and followed me, chattering like she was saying, "Let's check." I answered her jabbering. We were having a conversation only she understood. *I swear I love this little girl.*

I was surprised when I opened the door for a florist who had a delivery for me. I accepted the huge bouquet of blood red roses. It was huge and heavy as I struggled to set the vase on the table in the living room. I stepped back and looked over the arrangement. Saxon really was the man of my dreams. He was always doing things like this just to put a smile on my face. I was about to reach for the card that was attached when the door opened.

"Dada," Kiernon yelled and took off. She was a little steadier and moving fast as she reached Saxon, who scooped her up in his arms.

Right behind her, I went to greet him too. He wrapped his free arm around my waist as I puckered up for a kiss. We both laughed when Kiernon mimicked me and puckered her little lips. Saxon gave her a kiss before placing another one on my lips.

"I was just about to read the card," I informed him.

"What card?" He looked confused.

We went into the living room, and he saw the flowers on the table. He glanced at me before walking over to where they sat. "Who sent flowers?"

It was my turn to be confused. "I thought you did."

He pulled the card from the flowers and handed it to me. Saxon took a seat, settling Kiernon on his lap. I opened the card. When I read what was written, anger burned in my chest.

"Who are they from?" Saxon asked as Kiernon climbed down so she could walk around.

"Errick." I handed him the card and took a seat beside him.

> *Rachel,*
> *These flowers are just a small token of the way I feel about you. I can't stop thinking about you and our daughter. I just want a chance to make things right. Give me a chance to show you what you mean to me.*
> *Love, Errick*

"This clown." Saxon chuckled when he handed the card back to me.

"I'm sorry, baby. I don't know why he keeps doing this."

Since the fight with Saxon, Errick hadn't been outright disrespectful to his face, but he kept doing little things like sending these flowers, trying to get me to talk to him. He professed his love, but I didn't want to hear it. Every time I ran into him at Anna's, he tried pleading his case. He called and sent text messages, and each time I deleted the messages and ended the call if it didn't have to do with Kiernon. I was trying to keep things civil for the baby's sake, but Errick was making it hard.

"We talked about this before. Don't apologize for him. You didn't do anything wrong. I get it though."

"You get what?"

"I get why he's doing all this. I wouldn't be stupid enough to walk away from you, but if I lost you for any reason, I would do everything I could to get you back too." He kissed my temple.

Heat warmed my face as I blushed. He always knew what to say to make me feel better about the situation.

I had to find a way to get Errick to stop the nonsense. I hated to get Anna involved, but he obviously wasn't listening to me. Putting Errick out of my mind, I spent the rest of the day with my family.

Chapter Sixty-four

Rachel

Centennial Park was crowded as I sat in the shade of a large tree on the warm summer afternoon. We kept a close eye on Samarra as she ran around the playground with the other kids. Kiernon and Dathan were in the portable playpen we set up under the tree with us. The day was beautiful. The sky was a washed-out blue from the brightly shining sun, and there were a few clouds drifting lazily along on a light breeze. I was glad it wasn't as hot as it had been the last week or so. It had been in the high nineties for days. Since the temperature was bearable, Moira and I decided to take the kids to the park. Rosie joined us once she found out we were going to hang out for a while.

Sharp pops made me jump. Looking in the direction of the noise, I saw a group of kids setting off fireworks. The Fourth of July was right around the corner, and the smell of gunpowder lingered in the air.

"Mother and Daddy are so excited. They have some surprises planned but won't tell us what they are. You're coming, aren't you, Rosie?" Moira questioned.

"Are there going to be any sexy single men there? All you married people are starting to disturb me," Rosie teased. I noticed a change in Rosie lately. She seemed a little more relaxed. Her face was free of makeup, which was unusual for her, and her long hair was pulled back in a simple ponytail. She looked five years younger.

Moira laughed, tossing a balled-up napkin at her. "Mother invited just about everyone on her block. Anna and Paul are coming with some of their family, and along with Jamie and Errick's single friends, Daniel has some fine coworkers and cousins."

I heard nothing other than Ellen inviting Errick as I gazed absently off in the distance. I didn't want to spend the day with him around, but that was Anna's son. As much as I didn't want to be around him, Ellen and Anna had become fast friends. They bonded over Kiernon while I was still pregnant. Ellen accepted Anna's children just as she accepted me.

It was almost a month since Errick had been spending time with Kiernon at Anna and Paul's, and that was more than enough time I had to deal with him in my opinion. I gave him credit though. From what I saw and what Anna told me, Errick was doing very well getting to know Kiernon.

A Hispanic man slowly pushed an old-fashioned hot dog cart by us, and the smell wafting over immediately turned my stomach. A sweat broke out over me, coating my entire body under the loose sundress I wore. My churning stomach brought me to my feet as I frantically searched around. A wave of dizziness hit me, and I stumbled. Panic raced through me. I knew I was going to be sick, violently. Hurrying on my rubbery legs, I found the closest trash can and heaved until only dry retching clenched my stomach. The sounds of Moira and Rosie's voices were far away, as if they were talking to me from the end of a long tunnel. Clinging to the rim of the trash-can, I heard children's laughter and smelled honeysuckle before everything went dark and I blacked out.

Chapter Sixty-five

Saxon

The faces were blurs as I rushed by people in the corridors of the hospital. My breath was burning in my chest. I felt as if I ran a marathon at top speed, and my blood was pumping with adrenalin. I tried to wrestle down the panic that threatened to overcome me, but I was only slightly successful. Fear clung to me, chilling me despite the sweat that ran down my forehead.

The phone call from Moira terrified me. I listened, sick, while she told me what happened at the park. The thought of losing Rachel was almost too much to think about. I made arrangements with one of my colleagues to see my patients already in the office and the nurses to reschedule all they could for the next day as well.

Rushing from my office across town to Centennial Women's Center, so many things were tumbling around in my mind, good and bad thoughts. Memories played over each other randomly: Rachel lying in my arms, her eyes heavy lidded with sleep after making love, a couple of days before when we argued over something irrelevant, her irritating habit of leaving wet towels on the bathroom floor, the way her head tilted to the right when she laughed, and the love in her smile when she looked at Kiernon.

I stopped the first doctor I saw. I flashed my credentials and explained what I needed. Breathing an exhale of relief, I followed the man as he led me to the emergency room, leaving me outside the room Rachel was in.

Wiping my face on my sleeve, I tried to slow the racing of my heart. I didn't want Rachel to know how scared I was. Moira and Rosie sat on either side of Rachel, but my attention was focused on my wife. Moving to her bedside, I saw that her usual caramel complexion was sallow and a little gray. A deep smudge of blue bruised the skin under her closed eyes, and her face was drawn.

Moira stood, moving toward me. I saw the fear in her eyes, and my stomach dropped. I hoped what I saw wasn't an indication that something was wrong. Before I could ask, a petite Asian woman dressed in lilac scrubs entered the room. Her name tag read "Dr. Toshi." Picking up Rachel's chart, she studied it for a moment, then checked the machines that monitored her.

"Dr. Toshi, I'm Saxon Carmichael. How's my wife?"

Dr. Toshi looked at me with deep brown eyes. "Your wife is dehydrated. I've called her obstetrician, but it appears the baby might be in a little distress. Don't worry, we're monitoring her. I'm sure Dr. Charles will be here soon. For right now she needs to be still and rest."

Swallowing the lump that formed in my throat, I heard one of the women gasp when Dr. Toshi mentioned the baby. Glancing at the machines, I saw that the fetal heartbeat was strong, and I felt a momentary relief. Dr. Toshi laid a hand on my arm, a comforting gesture, and then she left us.

"Baby?" Moira stepped up beside me, looking into my eyes. "You're having a baby?"

My eyes watered a little as I met my sister's gray gaze. Struggling a little, I nodded. "Yeah, we found out a few weeks ago."

Laying a hand on my shoulder, Moira said a soft congratulations before out of nowhere she hit me on my arm. "Asshole."

I flinched, laughing, pulling my sister into a hug. "We were going to tell everyone on the Fourth of July."

Rosie came around the bed to hug me, and then she threatened to hit me as well.

"Hey, no beating up on my husband."

We turned at the sound of the soft voice. Rachel was looking at us with tired eyes. My heart actually felt like it relaxed a little when I saw she was awake. Moving closer to her, I bent, placing a kiss on her lips.

"Hey." I expected my voice to crack with relief, but it didn't. Just to see her looking at me, to see the trust she had for me in her eyes, made me feel better.

"Where's Kiernon?" She looked around the room.

Moira spoke up. "Don't worry, she's with Daniel and the kids. He'll watch them until I get home."

"The baby?" Her eyes clouded with concern.

"John will be here anytime. Everything is okay, but he wants to check you out to make sure. You want anything?"

Rachel shook her head no, and her eyes slipped closed again. I was relieved that she was okay, but I was still concerned about the baby.

John Charles arrived shortly after and gave Rachel a thorough checkup. He admitted her overnight to make sure that she got plenty of fluids. Rosie and Moira stayed with me until Rachel was comfortably settled into a room. Moira promised to keep Kiernon overnight.

Hours later, Rachel slept soundly, but I was still awake. I sat at her bedside, watching her. I was worried about her even though John assured me the baby was fine. There was a slight problem with the baby's heartbeat. He told me it was from Rachel being dehydrated, and once she was better, everything would regulate, but I still worried. I couldn't take it if something happened.

Chapter Sixty-six

Errick

The sun was setting, casting deep shadows in the corners of the room. We were watching the baseball game. The Braves were playing. It was a regular thing for me, Dad, Jamie, and David to get together when they were playing.

I was working harder than ever. My new position was demanding. I thrived on challenges, and I was getting the work done. Other than that, I was spending most of my time getting to know Kiernon. Just thinking about her made me smile. She was a good baby, very inquisitive and so much like her mother, even at the age of 1. She was stubborn and independent but also loving and sometimes shy.

The relationship between me and my parents was better. They were disappointed with the choices I'd made dealing with Rachel, but they didn't say much. They were just glad I stepped up where Kiernon was concerned.

The phone interrupted our cheers as the Braves made a triple play. Dad snatched the phone from the table, saying a quick hello.

"What? What hospital?" Dad's face creased with worry, his words and expression catching our attention.

"What happened? Baby? Is the baby okay?"

My heart thumped painfully. *Baby?* Was he talking about Kiernon? I wanted to snatch the phone from him, but I held myself together, waiting until he finished the call.

"All right, son, give us a call if you need anything." Dad finally hung up.

"What happened?" Jamie asked before I could.

"Rachel was rushed to the hospital this afternoon." Dad told us the little he knew from Saxon's call.

Time seemed to stand still when Dad said that Rachel was pregnant. The words didn't seem to sink in. *Déjà vu?* This was the same feeling I had when Rachel told me she was pregnant with Kiernon. The difference was that this time I wished the baby were mine. Rachel was having a baby with another man. She was married to another man, creating a family with him. I was still having trouble accepting that she was married to someone else.

Shit, man, this is what you want, my subconscious pricked at me.

Shut the fuck up, my irrational side yelled back.

Offering to grab fresh beers, I stood and went to the kitchen. I needed a minute to take in the news Dad just dropped on me. As I leaned against the counter, staring out the window over the sink that gave a view of the backyard, my thoughts were spinning. *I have to get a grip on the fact that Rachel is pregnant.*

Hearing a fumbling at the back door, I moved to grab the beers from the fridge. Mom opened the door, her hands filled with bags. Setting the beer down, I took the bags from her and placed them on the counter next to the fridge.

"Hey, son." She kissed my cheek, then set her purse down on the counter next to the bags. She glanced at the bottles. "A beer run, huh?"

"Yeah, I need it."

It was obvious she could see the stress in my face. "You okay?"

I knew Dad would tell her, but I couldn't stop myself. I saw a moment of panic flash across her features. I reassured her that Rachel and Kiernon were okay.

"Pop said Rachel's being admitted for observation. She's pregnant."

"Is the baby okay?"

I noticed that she didn't seem surprised by the news as we were. "They think so. You knew Rachel was pregnant?"

"Yes, she told me the same day she talked to you about Kiernon," Mom said casually as she began to put away her groceries.

I remembered walking in on their conversation that day. Mom was saying she was pleased with the news Rachel shared with her. I assumed she meant Rachel letting me see Kiernon. "You knew she was pregnant and didn't say anything?"

Mom stopped and looked at me, rolling her eyes. "It wasn't my place to say anything. When Saxon and Rachel are ready, they will let people know."

She shut me down, and I had no argument. Grabbing the beer from the counter, I kissed her cheek. "You're right, Ma." I didn't have any right to feel the way I did, but fuck that. I was selfish. Rachel moving on didn't sit right with me.

Chapter Sixty-seven

Errick

After tapping on the door, I waited a minute before I pushed it open and entered. Rachel was coming from the restroom when I did. She was shocked to see me. Mom mentioned what hospital she was in, so I took a chance to come to see her.

"What are you doing here?" She climbed in bed and got comfortable.

"I wanted to check on you. I was there when Dad got the call about you being here." I moved over to stand next to her bed.

"Errick, you shouldn't be here. I don't know why you are so insistent on talking to me or thinking that we might have a chance to reconcile, but it's not happening. I love Saxon. I married him, and he's the man I plan to grow old with."

"I hear what you're saying, but I just can't believe that after the years we were together and all the love we shared, you can tell me you don't feel anything for me anymore."

She studied me for a long time. I thought I was getting through to her until she hit me with her response. "Errick, I don't know what you expected. How can I feel anything for you but resentment? Disgust? Anger? I have worked on containing those feelings because I want to keep the peace for Kiernon. She doesn't deserve to be pulled in two directions, and I don't want her to resent me when she gets older. She's the only reason I say anything to you."

My heart ached because I could tell that Rachel meant what she said. She didn't love me anymore. I broke her, and when she built herself back up, she wanted nothing to do with me.

"I don't know how to let you go." I took her hand in mine.

She jerked away from me, a frown on her face. "I've tried to keep it civil, but you're being disrespectful as hell right now. You've already assaulted my husband, and we let it go. You've sent flowers and love notes trying to make him think something is going on when we both know it's not. Errick, please, stop this."

I heard what she was saying, and the ache in my chest grew stronger.

The door to the room opened. Rachel's husband stepped in. He stopped when he saw me, his eyes going from me to Rachel and back. He crossed the room to the other side of the bed. "Hey, baby, are you okay?" He kissed her. My stomach turned.

"Yes, I'm good. Errick was just leaving."

I watched as he took her hand. They both looked at me, waiting.

"Yeah, I'm gone. You take care, Rachel." I left even though I wanted to plead my case some more. *She made it clear she's made her choice, and I'm not it.*

Now I just had to get my heart and my head on the same page.

Chapter Sixty-eight

Rachel

The sun was beating down from a faded blue sky, and midsummer had settled in with a constant ninety-degree heat wave. The grass was browning, and everyone was wishing for a few days of rain. Saxon was washing the car as I sat on a blanket spread in the shade under a tree with Kiernon. My husband was sexy dressed in blue basketball shorts, a gray T-shirt, and shower shoes. He was still the sexiest man I'd ever seen. I watched his muscles flex and move under his taut skin. It made me want to touch him.

Feeling my eyes on him, Saxon looked over and winked. My pulse raced, and I had to glance away to keep from jumping on him. I couldn't believe after all this time Saxon still made me feel weak with something as simple as a wink.

Kiernon started fussing. She was over this heat. I scooped her up in my arms, then walked over to the edge of the drive where Saxon was. I let him know we were going inside.

"I think I know what might help."

"What?" I was curious.

Saxon turned the hose on us, chasing us as Kiernon and I shrieked from the shock of the cold water. I took off running, trying to get away from him. I couldn't run too fast with her in my arms, so in no time Kiernon and

I were soaked. Saxon didn't get away with it though, because he was just as wet as we were by the time we were done.

"No fair. Look at my hair." I pouted when we stopped to catch our breath. Kiernon was laughing and clapping in my arms as she jabbered at Saxon.

"You're still sexy." Saxon pulled me into his arms, nuzzling my neck.

We separated when I heard a car door close. I frowned when I saw Errick coming up the drive. I glanced at Saxon, wondering what he was doing at our house.

"Sorry to stop by unannounced, but Ma called me. She had a flat, and Dad went to fix it, so she asked if I would pick up Kiernon. She called, but there was no answer." Errick smiled pleasantly.

"We lost track of time," I informed him.

"Yeah, I see." Errick chuckled. He looked at me and Kiernon, and I had to fight not to roll my eyes. Glancing at Saxon, I saw the smile he wore. He knew what I was thinking.

"Hey, pretty girl." Errick reached out, tickling Kiernon's neck. She ducked away from him, giggling.

"Give me a few minutes to get her changed. Her bag is by the front door." Turning on my heel, I headed inside, leaving Errick and Saxon outside.

I got Kiernon changed, putting a dry diaper on her, then dressing her in a pale purple jumper with her purple and pink Chuck Taylors. I wasn't crazy about the idea of Errick picking Kiernon up, but she was used to him now. Over the last few weeks since my release from the hospital, Errick stepped up. He would have Anna or Paul get Kiernon, then meet them at their house by five thirty to spend a little time with her before one of them would drop her off on the nights they weren't keeping her.

Once she was ready, I held her hand as we came down the hall. She was walking like a pro now and always on the move. When we neared the front door, I couldn't help overhearing the conversation going on outside.

"I'm just trying to get to know my daughter. I want to do right by Kiernon."

"Have you ever thought that the right thing to do is to step out of the picture? I understand where you're coming from, but you were the one who walked away. You can't expect Rachel to be all in when just a few short months ago you didn't want anything to do with her or our daughter."

There was a long pause before Errick continued, "Kiernon is my daughter. Is Rachel gonna punish me forever?"

Putting Kiernon in the pack and play in the living room, I tried to keep my anger in check as I hurried to the door. I snatched it open and found Saxon and Errick standing at the bottom of the stairs. My adrenalin was pumping as I thought about what he said.

"Punish you? Do you think that's what this is? I'm mad at you, so I'm trying to punish you?" My voice started to rise.

Saxon came to where I stood and laid a hand on my arm, but I jerked away.

"No. This needs to be said. I haven't asked you for anything since you left. This halfhearted attempt at playing daddy is all on you. Kiernon and I have been doing fine since the minute you walked out of our lives, and we still are. You're the one who came back pressuring me, talking about you want to get to know her. Kiernon has a daddy. Saxon is, and always has been, her daddy. You don't seem to realize that I have no reason to punish you. Saxon stepped up when you refused to, so if you're feeling some kind of way because I'm not doing backflips in excitement that you now want to be a part of her life, that's on you."

Errick glared at me, his jaw clenching. He wanted to say something, but he didn't. We stared at each other for several long moments until he spoke.

"Rachel, I fucked up, I know I did and there's nothing I can do to change that. I appreciate you letting Kiernon get to know me. I haven't always done the right thing because I was too stupid to realize how much I need her in my life."

Kiernon's cry pulled me back into the house. She was standing at the side of her pack and play, tears rolling over her fat cheeks.

"Oh, pretty girl, Mommy didn't mean to leave you alone for so long." I picked her up, kissing her tears away.

Getting the rest of her things together, I carried the bag and Kiernon outside.

"Errick, the three of us must get along for Kiernon's sake. Please don't make this any harder than it already is." I was tired of having the same conversation with him. I prayed that he would get it this time and we could move on. I had a feeling that was just wishful thinking on my part.

Chapter Sixty-nine

Rachel

"Come on, pretty, are you ready to go?" I strapped Kiernon in her seat. We were leaving the Opry Mills Mall after spending the morning shopping with Rosie.

"I'll call you later." Rosie kissed Kiernon, gave me a hug, then went in search of her car.

Climbing behind the wheel, I strapped myself in and checked my phone for messages before I turned on the audiobook I listened to in the car. The day was overcast. It had rained while we were shopping but stopped before we came out. I was glad because I hated dealing with Kiernon in bad weather. Traffic was heavy leaving the mall. We moved slowly toward Briley Parkway. By the time we got onto the thoroughfare, the rain had returned, and it was coming down steadily. Glancing in the rearview mirror, I saw Kiernon watching her tablet, but her eyes were getting low. She would be knocked out soon. Traffic thinned as we left the area of the mall, and it began to flow smoothly.

A bolt of lightning struck a tree on the side of the road. The flash was so bright it blinded me momentarily. My heart jumped in fear, a brief afterimage burned against my vision. The lightning strike was followed immediately by a clap of thunder so loud it made Kiernon shriek and burst into tears.

"It's okay, baby." I pressed on the brake softly to slow down.

I spoke too soon. I saw what happened next like a movie that had been slowed down. The tree the lightning struck fell into the street at the same time a car flew by me, speeding even though rain fell steadily. The car tried to swerve around it, but the driver lost control and careened across the four lanes, hit the concrete median, then spun back into traffic, directly at me. There was nothing I could do except brace for contact.

My gaze jumped to the rearview mirror, where I saw my baby crying at the top of her lungs. My heart broke to see her so distraught, and I couldn't do anything to comfort her.

Boom.

The car hit me in the front end on the driver's side. The sound of contact was loud, and my car was whipped over into the next lane. Pain radiated through me immediately, and my whole left side flared as I was jerked against the seat belt. *My baby.* I wanted to put my hands on my stomach, but that wouldn't help. My car smashed into one beside me, and my head slammed against the window. We bounced off and ricocheted back in the direction of the car that started the collision.

Kiernon and I were both crying. I tried my best to tell her things were going to be okay, but I didn't know if that was true. Her cries shredded my heart. I said prayer after prayer to keep Kiernon and the baby safe. I would deal with whatever injuries as long as they were good.

The last thing I saw before I blacked out was the same car that caused the collision overturned on its side.

Chapter Seventy

Saxon

The sound of the phone was loud in the quiet of the room. Jumping out of my sleep, I fumbled around for my cell phone on the nightstand, answering with a mumbled hello.

"I'm trying to reach Saxon Carmichael."

There was something in the strange voice that shook me fully awake from the nap I was taking. Rubbing sleep from my eyes, I glanced at the clock on the wall. It was after five p.m.

"This is he."

"Mr. Carmichael, I'm calling from Vanderbilt University Medical Center."

That shook any last remnants of sleep away immediately. "Yes? What's wrong?"

"Your wife was brought into the emergency room after a car accident."

My heart jumped, and my stomach clenched as I listened. "What about my daughter?"

"You should—"

"I'm on my way."

Still on the phone, I was already up and moving through the house. I wasted no time going to the bathroom to hit the bottle of mouthwash before I slid on a pair of sneakers and grabbed my wallet, keys, and credentials before I rushed out to my car. I listened as the woman told me where to go when I reached the hospital, and then we ended the call.

Thirty minutes later, I was parking in the emergency lot at the hospital and rushing through the electric doors that opened with a hiss. I rushed over to the counter and told the woman behind it who I was there for. She asked me to have a seat and said she would get someone for me. She hung up the phone and let me know someone would be out as soon as possible.

A police officer heard me introduce myself. He and his partner came over to where I waited. He had the receptionist open the double doors that led to triage and multiple bays that held patients. We went into a small office. He invited me to have a seat, then closed the door.

"What happened to my wife and daughter?" I didn't give him a chance to speak before I was asking questions.

My stomach churned as I listened to him tell me what they knew about the accident. It grew even worse when he told me that Rachel had to be cut out of the car. They asked me questions and gave me their cards before they took me back to the waiting room.

I paced the waiting room, my heart aching the whole time. I didn't know how Rachel, Kiernon, or our baby were doing. My whole family was laid up in the hospital, and there was nothing I could do. After walking back and forth for about ten minutes, I took a seat in the corner of the lobby. I pulled out my phone to call my parents. I hadn't thought of it before, but looking around me, I saw several family members of patients. My dad answered, and after I gave a brief rundown of what was going on, he told me they would be here as soon as possible. I knew I should call Rosie and Anna and Paul, but I wanted to wait until I knew what was going on. They would have questions, and I wanted to have answers for them.

My head was in my hands when I heard my name called. I didn't know how long I'd been sitting there, but when I looked up, an older white man in a pair of navy scrubs was looking around the room. I stood and quickly moved over to where he was. I introduced myself and showed him my credentials.

He took me back to the same office I spoke to the officers in.

"How are my wife and daughter?"

"Your wife was rushed to surgery. Your daughter is in PICU."

I wanted to break down when he told me that Rachel was in surgery. She broke her leg in three places, and they were going to have to put a metal rod in it. The baby she carried seemed to be fine at this point, but they were monitoring her pregnancy, too. Kiernon was unconscious when she arrived and had not awakened since. They were running tests and keeping an eye on her vitals. I had to sit there for a minute after he delivered the news. I felt lost, scared, and a whole bunch of other emotions I couldn't name at that exact minute. Shaking it off, I thanked the doctor and then returned to the lobby. It was going to be a long wait.

Chapter Seventy-one

Saxon

The time passed slowly. It was after seven, and I was still waiting to hear something. I had gotten on the nerves of the woman behind the counter, going up to ask for an update every thirty minutes. My parents got here about an hour after I called them. Moira followed a short time later. I called Anna and Paul to let them know what was going on, and they were on their way to the hospital. At this point I was numb. In a state of limbo, I wanted someone to come tell me something before I lost my mind.

Anna and Paul hurried in with Errick on their heels. I was immediately irritated to see him. I was sick of his shit, and if he said anything out of the way, I was going to lay him out.

"We got here as quickly as we could. What happened?" Anna took a seat in the chair across from me.

It was easy to see she'd been crying. They all had a look of terror in their eyes. I knew it well because I'd seen the same in mine when I went to the restroom and saw my reflection in the mirror. Exhaling a deep breath, I told them what I knew. I saw Errick brush away a few tears, and for the first time since I met him, I could relate to him. He actually seemed as worried about Kiernon as the rest of us.

We sat there for another twenty minutes before a doctor came out and called for the family of Rachel Carmichael. We all stood and waited for him to come over. This was a different doctor from the one I'd spoken to earlier, so we did a brief introduction. I let him know it was okay to speak freely. He told us that the surgery to set Rachel's leg was a success, but she suffered a concussion, and she would have to be in the hospital a few days. The baby was okay, but they would continue to monitor her while she was there. I wanted to know about Kiernon. The tears I managed to keep under control burst free when he said that she was going to be transferred to Monroe Carell Jr. Children's Hospital. She was being prepared to move, and one person would be able to travel with her. He shook my hand and told us he would let us know when Kiernon was ready to go.

Once he was gone, I took a seat in the chair I'd been in since I got there and let the tears flow. I wasn't embarrassed to be crying. My whole world had been turned upside down, and I wanted to see both my girls so I would know they were okay.

"I'll go with Kiernon," Anna assured me. "I know you want to stay here until you can see Rachel."

"Me and Pop will go with her," Errick stepped up.

For a minute I just stared at him. I didn't want him around my daughter, but I had to be realistic. With Rachel and Kiernon being in different hospitals, I was going to need all the help I could get.

"That's cool, thanks," I told him. What I didn't say was that as soon as I could check on Rachel, I would be there to do the same for Kiernon.

A short time later, the doctor came to tell us Kiernon was ready to be moved. We explained the situation to him, and then Anna and I followed him to the PICU. I just had to see her before she left. We got there to find

Kiernon on a gurney. She was strapped down with an IV in her arm. She had a knot on the side of her head and a few scratches across her pretty face. I kissed her cheeks softly before they took her away. I went with them as far as I could, then returned to the lobby with my heart in my throat.

Chapter Seventy-two

Errick

When Mom told me that Kiernon and Rachel had been rushed to the hospital, I had never been so scared in my life. I had stopped by my parents' place after work and ended up having dinner with them. We watched the news and saw the coverage of the wreck, but I would have never guessed they were involved.

Dad and I followed the ambulance to the children's hospital. By the time we parked and made it inside, we had to call Mom to see where she was. It took about forty-five minutes before we were able to see Kiernon. When we did, tears fell from my eyes in a steady stream. She looked so small in the big bed. There were wires and tubes coming from her little body. She appeared to be sleeping, but I knew better. I went to the far side of the bed and took her hand in mine. Her skin was warm and her face was relaxed, but it was then that I noticed the bruises on her arms. Mom must have noticed me looking, because she gently lifted her shirt, and there were marks from the safety strap of her seat from where she'd been tossed around. My heart broke even more to see that when she was so helpless.

I took a seat in the chair next to the bed while Mom and Dad settled on the small love seat that was in the room. Lost in my head, I thought over the last two years.

Things in my life had changed so much since Rachel told me she was pregnant. When I went to Phoenix, I just knew I had a fresh start. I loved my job and the people I met. I pushed Rachel out of my mind as best I could. It wasn't until I lived there for several months that I realized I missed Nashville, my family and how close we were before I pushed them away, and the life I had before Phoenix. When I decided to transfer back to the Nashville office, I didn't tell anyone until I was sure it was going to happen. For the last few months of my stay, Rachel and her baby crossed my mind more often than I wanted to admit. Anytime I did think of her, I remembered her as she was or the way she looked in the pictures my parents sent at Thanksgiving. I began to wonder what sex the baby was, who he or she looked like, what it would be like to hold my child for the first time. I was still in denial for the most part, but the thoughts lingered. When Rachel walked into my parents' house that day, I couldn't see anyone else. Rachel was the love of my life, and I pushed her away. The moment I laid eyes on Kiernon, I fell in love. It hit me like a ton of bricks. I walked away from my child and the woman I loved all because of a stupid plan that I was too stubborn to see could be modified. I thought about all the time lost, all the memories and love that I missed out on being an asshole. My heart hurt as I watched another man be daddy for my child. When Kiernon smiled at the other man, went to him for kisses or to share something with him, I realized how badly I messed up with Rachel and Kiernon both. Seeing Rachel with someone else didn't help my mood. I stayed off to the side all day and felt like a complete fool.

There was a knock on the door, and the doctor came in with two nurses. They checked her vitals, then gave us an update before they left us alone again.

"Do you guys want anything from the cafeteria? I think I'm gonna get some coffee." I stood up and stretched. I took their requests, then went to catch the elevator.

After I grabbed the stuff I wanted, I ran into Saxon on my way back to the elevator.

"How's Rachel?" I hated to have to ask this man for information on the woman I loved, but I swallowed my pride and checked on her.

"She's good," was his brief reply.

I wanted to ask more, but I didn't. The ride up on the elevator was filled with awkward silence. I glanced at Saxon out of the corner of my eye. Worry was all over his face.

We got to Kiernon's room. He went straight to the bed, where he kissed her face several times. He talked to her quietly, telling her that her daddy loved her and he couldn't wait for her to wake up. That almost brought tears to my eyes. For the first time since I returned, I could see that Saxon really loved Rachel and Kiernon. The question was, how would I deal with it?

Chapter Seventy-three

Rachel

Beeping, loud and constant, brought me out of what felt like a deep sleep. My eyes squinted in the light that shined directly over the bed. When I tried to reach to turn it off, pain flared through my body. I didn't realize it at first, but my leg was suspended above the bed on a pulley and covered in a cast to my hip. The memory of the accident flashed through my mind, causing me to yell out.

"Hey, baby, you're okay."

I immediately relaxed when I heard Saxon's voice. Tears filled my eyes when he stepped into view and brushed a few strands of hair from my face. It only lasted a moment as my thoughts went to Kiernon and the baby I was carrying. I sat up so quickly I was dizzy.

"Where's Kiernon? How's the baby?" My hand flew to my stomach. A little bit of relief hit me when I felt the firmness of my bump, but that didn't tell me about Kiernon.

"Calm down, Rachel. You're going to hurt yourself." Saxon pressed me back into the pillows that were propped behind me.

"Where's Kiernon? Please tell me she's okay." Tears spilled from my eyes as panic gripped me.

"Baby, you have to calm down." Saxon pressed the button for the nurse. "The baby is okay, but if you keep on worrying, your blood pressure will go up, and that could cause problems."

Saxon was right. I had to calm down. Taking several deep breaths, I closed my eyes and concentrated on relaxing. My eyes opened when the nurse came in.

"It's good to see you awake, Mrs. Carmichael. How are you feeling?"

I wanted to tell her I was scared, but I just told her I was okay. She checked my vitals and the machine that showed the baby's information. She turned it up a little so we could hear the heartbeat. It was strong, and that made me relax a little more.

Once the nurse was gone, Saxon sat on the side of the bed and took my hand. "Tell me what happened."

The memory of the wreck had me shook. I told him everything that happened, and then I asked about Kiernon again. I had calmed down and tried not to let the worry overwhelm me while I waited for him to tell me what was going on with my daughter.

"She's been moved to the children's hospital. She was unconscious when she was brought in. They are scheduled to do an MRI to make sure there's no brain damage. Rachel, she hasn't woken up yet."

"How long have I been here?" I wiped my eyes with the Kleenex he handed me.

"Since yesterday. You were out of it for a while. You came around but then went right back out."

"Who's with Kiernon?"

"Errick stayed the night with her last night. Anna came back this morning so he could go to work."

That news was unexpected. Errick was getting to know Kiernon, but I didn't expect to hear that he'd volunteered to stay with her.

"When am I getting out of here? I need to check on my baby."

"Slow down. You're not going anywhere for a couple of days. I've already worked out a schedule with Anna and the others. Rosie has been here too, and you know she's ready to help any way she can."

It hurt my heart to know I couldn't be with my baby, but I was thankful for my tribe. They had my back and would make sure she was okay.

Chapter Seventy-four

Errick

Taking a deep breath, I knocked on the door. It had been two long days since the accident, and Kiernon still hadn't awakened. The doctors were optimistic, and her brain function was normal with no swelling, so they said she should wake up on her own anytime.

I pushed the door open when I heard her say, "Come in." Sticking my head in, I was glad to find Rachel alone.

"Hey, how are you feeling?" I went to the side of her bed and set the vase of flowers on the bedside stand.

"Um, I'm okay. Just ready to get out of here so I can go check on my baby."

The mention of Kiernon brought a lump to my throat. Just seeing her lie there so still, knowing she was so full of energy, was awful. "She's a fighter."

An awkward silence fell between us. I studied her. The lump on her head had gone down, and the bruise that was on the side of her face was a painful-looking dark blue. Other than that, she was the same beautiful woman.

"What are you doing here, Errick?"

"I just wanted to stop by and check on you before I go back to sit with Kiernon." I could see the surprise on her face. Things between us weren't the best, and that was my fault.

"I appreciate you helping out with Kiernon since I can't be there. I don't want to intrude on your life though."

"Don't do that, Rachel. I'm trying. Getting to know Kiernon has been one of the greatest times of my life."

She looked like she wanted to say something, but she bit her tongue.

"Have they said when you'll be released?"

"Not yet. They still want to monitor the baby and my leg to make sure infection doesn't set in."

I stayed with Rachel for another ten minutes. It was strange having a civil conversation with her. I missed this, just talking to her about nothing.

"Hey, boo." The door opened. Rosie breezed in. She stopped when she saw me, then came in and moved to the other side of the bed. She hugged Rachel, then asked how she was feeling. She didn't speak to me.

"Hello, Rosie."

"Errick." She nodded curtly.

"Well, I'm gonna get out of here. If you need anything, give me a call," I told Rachel before I left the room. I could hear Rosie asking why I was there as the door closed behind me.

The trip to the children's hospital was quick. I'd been gone for several hours, so I couldn't wait to see her. Pushing open the door of her room, I found Ellen and Moira there instead of my mom. That surprised me because she came every day and was here for hours.

"Hello, ladies," I said, greeting them before moving to Kiernon's side. "How is she doing?"

Moira spoke first. "The doctor said he's optimistic that she'll wake anytime."

That couldn't happen soon enough for me. I leaned over and kissed her forehead. "You got to wake up, pretty girl. We miss you," I spoke softly by her ear.

Saxon came in with food for his mom and sister. He nodded in my direction before checking on Kiernon.

It was awkward being here with Saxon and his family, so I told him I would let him spend time with her and I would return later.

Saxon stepped out into the hall after me. "Errick."

"What's up?"

"I appreciate you, man." He held out his hand for me to shake.

Looking at his hand for a second, I didn't know how to react. Then I reached for it, we shook, and he went back in the room.

The early evening sky was clear as I went to my car. I left the hospital property and just drove around aimlessly for a while. When my phone rang, I thought it was Saxon, but it was David. He called to meet up for a beer. I agreed. I needed to do something to pass the time.

Chapter Seventy-five

Saxon

Mom and Moira left shortly after Errick. I got to spend some time with Kiernon before I went back to Rachel's room. I read her favorite book to her, talked to her, then turned on her favorite kids' program. I was ready for my baby to wake up. Seeing her like this was hard. I was exhausted and ready to get my girls home.

Errick came back around seven thirty. He surprised me when he handed me a cup of coffee, but I appreciated it. He stopped me when I got up to leave. "Thanks for letting me help out with Kiernon."

"Rachel and I appreciate you being willing."

"I know you don't believe me, but Kiernon coming into my life—"

The door burst open. Two nurses rushed in. I was confused for a minute before I saw the red lights flashing above Kiernon's bed. My eyes immediately went to her. Her little chest was heaving as she panted, and she looked clammy with a thin sheen of sweat covering her. One of the nurses checked the machines while the other took her vitals. I wanted to jump in to help as much as I could, but I stayed out of their way. Kiernon's body started to shake.

"She's having a seizure," one nurse called while she pressed the button to alert others.

"We need you to step outside." The other nurse ushered us out of the room.

The doctor in me wanted to protest, but I didn't. It was critical for them to have the space they needed to do their jobs. My interference wouldn't be good for Kiernon.

"What happened? What's going on, man?"

When I looked at Errick, he was scared. I could see it in his face. I probably held the same expression because no matter my training, that was my daughter in there.

The anxiety increased when the doctor and another nurse rushed by us and went into the room. Someone had turned up the sound of the machines, because the beeping could be heard once the door opened. My chest tightened, a lump settled in my throat, and it took everything in me not to go back into the room. To keep myself sane, I turned to Errick to answer his questions.

"She had a seizure. I'm sure they'll let us know what's going on as soon as they can," I said, stating the obvious.

After what felt like an eternity but was only ten minutes, the door opened, and one of the nurses waved us in.

I stepped in first. I needed to lay eyes on Kiernon to see that she was okay. My heart pumped painfully. Anxiety constricted my breathing. One of the other nurses was in the way, fixing the blanket or something inconsequential. She moved, and tears blurred the vision in front of me.

"Dada." Kiernon's voice was soft, but her eyes were the same bright ones I was used to seeing.

I moved to the side of the bed with tears running down my face. I reached down to hug my baby, dropping kisses all over her face while repeating, "I love you," over and over.

"We're going to take her down for tests shortly. Someone can go with her."

"I'll go, but I have to call her mother first."

Rachel is going to be so excited to see Kiernon awake. She'd been talking about discharging herself so she could come be with her. The only reasons she hadn't were that she couldn't get around on her leg by herself and because of the monitors on the baby.

The minute the doctor and nurses left the room, I pulled out my phone to call Rachel.

Chapter Seventy-six

Errick

My heart felt like it was going to beat out of my chest when the nurses rushed into the room and started checking on Kiernon. I felt sick when her little body began violently shaking and they called out that she was having a seizure. When they pushed us into the hall, I didn't know what to think and tried not to go crazy.

Those few minutes in that hall were some of the longest of my life. I wasn't a man who prayed a lot, but I sent up a few that Kiernon would be okay. Flashes of the time we spent together hit me. I kept seeing her smile, the way her eyes sparkled when she was happy. She was a sweet baby, and I was a fool to miss out on so much of her life.

The nurse opened the door and waved us in. Saxon rushed in before me, but I was right on his heels. When I realized that Kiernon was awake, I could have leapt with happiness. That light was dimmed when she called out, "Dada," for Saxon. Even though I was elated that she was awake, there was pain that came along with watching the other man when he hurried to the bed and kissed all over her face. Her little arms wrapped around his neck as he cried and told her he loved her.

The doctor and nurses left the room, and he called Rachel on FaceTime. It never really hit me how much of an outsider I was until I stood there watching Saxon and Kiernon interact with Rachel over the phone. It was obvious they were a family unit.

Stepping out of the room to give them a minute, I also needed a minute to myself. Going to the nurses' station, I asked for what I needed, and they pointed me in the right direction. Pushing the door open, I stepped inside the midsize room and took a seat on the second row of chairs. There was one other person in the chapel, but that didn't bother me. Closing my eyes, I sent up a prayer of thanks. Thanks that I was able to meet and get to know Kiernon, that she had awakened, that Rachel and her unborn child were okay, and as much as I didn't want to face it at first, thanks for Saxon being in their lives. The other man had stepped up and stepped in where I failed. I loved Rachel and would have loved another chance with her, but the love she had for her husband was something I couldn't compete with, and I wasn't going to try any longer.

After sitting in the chapel for a few minutes, I left to call my parents and let them know their granddaughter was awake.

Chapter Seventy-seven

Rachel

A week had passed since Kiernon and I were released from the hospital. I got out the day after Kiernon woke up. The first place I insisted on going was to see my daughter. It took a lot of maneuvering to get me in Saxon's SUV with the cast on my leg and this big belly, but we managed. When Kiernon saw me, her whole face lit up. I cried for an hour while I held her and talked to her. She was feeling better, because she wanted to get down and walk around even though she couldn't with the IV in her arm. When we had to leave, it was the hardest thing I'd ever done. Now we were home and trying to get back into a routine. We turned the downstairs guest room into our room since I couldn't maneuver on the stairs. Kiernon slept in her pack and play in the room with us. I wasn't ready for her to be upstairs away from me.

It was Saturday, and the grandparents came to take over the house. I didn't mind because I appreciated all they'd done for us. I was surprised when Errick showed up with Anna and Paul, but I had to give him credit. He'd really stepped up to help out with Kiernon. He called every day to see if we needed anything, brought food, or stopped by just to spend time with her. He was a totally different man from the one who walked out on me a couple of years ago.

I was in the family room on the sofa with my leg propped on the ottoman. Kiernon was stretched out on her blanket, watching one of her kid shows on her tablet. Paul and Connor were on the grill, Anna and Ellen were in the kitchen, and Moira took Samarra to the backyard to play while Saxon and Daniel went to the store to grab some things Ellen asked for.

"Hey." Errick came in and took a seat in the chair next to the sofa. "How are you feeling? You need anything?"

"No, I'm good."

We sat there for a minute, my attention on the TV while he watched Kiernon.

"I'm sorry, Rachel."

There was sincerity in his eyes. It was time for me to get over the hurt and anger I had for Errick. I was happily in love with my husband, and if Errick hadn't hurt me the way he had, I would never have been blessed with Saxon and the baby we were now having. "I appreciate that."

Errick and I ended up talking, really talking, for the first time in a long time. He admitted that when I told him about the pregnancy with Kiernon, he froze. He was scared, and the thought of having a baby at that time had him feeling unprepared. It was the first time I felt like I could move forward and not hold the resentment I had against him. Errick's cruel dismissal of me and the baby had nothing to do with me. It was his own issues that caused him to act that way.

"I was so stupid. I was selfish. You tried over and over to tell me, and I wouldn't listen. I can't believe I almost lost her. Seeing Kiernon in that bed like that, not knowing when she would wake up, it felt like I couldn't breathe."

I understood exactly what he meant. Not being able to be with her while she was going through that was devastating. Hearing him express his pain at the thought of losing Kiernon also made me realize that the more people Kiernon had in her life to love and care about her, the more well-rounded her life would be. I still had to think about how I would explain to Kiernon her relationship with Errick, but it was time to let him fully be a part of her life.

"Hey, babe, I brought you your favorite ice cream." Saxon's smile faded slowly when he came into the family room and saw Errick and me sitting together. He looked a little confused and hurt.

"Thanks, babe. Errick and I were just talking." I reached out a hand to him.

Saxon crossed the room to hand me the sundae he brought me. Errick stood up and faced him.

"I want to apologize for the last several months. I overstepped and I know it. I appreciate you for the way you stepped up for Rachel and Kiernon both. And for letting me be a part of her life." He held out his hand for Saxon to shake.

Saxon looked from Errick to me before taking his hand and shaking it. All the hard feelings wouldn't go away immediately, but this was a step in the right direction.

Chapter Seventy-eight

Rachel

Putting the finishing touches on the tree, I stepped back and admired the decorations and twinkling lights. My lower back was aching, so I placed my hands in the small of my back and stretched.

"You okay?"

Feeling my husband's arms around my waist and settling on my belly, I leaned back into him with a smile. Closing my eyes, I relished feeling him so close to me. As soon as I settled against him, the baby kicked.

"I'm just fine," I assured him.

It had been a long few months, but I finally got the cast off my leg and was now in a boot. I went through physical therapy. It wasn't easy while being pregnant and caring for a toddler. The limp in my gait wasn't as pronounced. Once the boot was removed, I would be walking with no problems.

"Daddy."

I glanced down and smiled. Kiernon had come over and thrown her arms around Saxon's legs, holding up her sippy cup for something to drink.

"Hey, my pretty girl. What do you want?" He released me and picked her up, settling her against his side.

"Juice," she told him.

"Okay, give Daddy a minute. Mommy wants to show you something." Saxon kissed her cheek.

I picked up the remote to turn on the lights for the tree. As soon as they were on, Kiernon squealed with delight. She clapped her hands as she jabbered in excitement. Just seeing her smile after all we'd been through made my heart sing.

Saxon put Kiernon on the floor, then took me in his embrace. I wrapped my arms around Saxon's neck. He bent to accept the kiss I placed on his lips. What started out as a gentle brushing of my lips against his intensified when Saxon pulled me closer and slipped his tongue in my mouth, deepening the kiss.

"Get a room."

I jumped, trying to pull away from Saxon, but he held me tightly. He kissed me again for good measure. "We will, just as soon as you leave," Saxon teased Moira.

Releasing me, Saxon reached for Kiernon's hand, then led her to the kitchen to get her juice. I followed them, stopping in the dining room. The table was filled with mouthwatering dishes. There were plates of ham, turkey and dressing, fried and baked chicken, sweet potatoes, greens, mac and cheese, sausage plait, and so much more, more food than we could possibly eat, but the house was full, so I was sure we would try.

"Time to say thanks," Paul announced as we assembled around the table.

"Let me."

I was surprised to hear Errick volunteer to lead the prayer to bless the food. He was there along with Jamie and his date. Aimee had gone with her boyfriend to visit her family. Moira and her family, Rosie and her date, Ellen, Connor, and a few other friends and family were there too.

"Father, thank you for the blessings that we have, our families, our friends, our homes, and jobs. But most of all, Father, thank you for getting us through the last few months. We are so grateful that we're all together. Thank you for forgiveness and healing. I also want to say thank you to Kiernon's parents, her mother, Rachel, and her daddy, Saxon, for sharing the blessing of her with all of us. I pray that our blended family will continue to be blessed. Amen."

My head rose, my eyes popping open to find Errick looking at me. He nodded, then took his seat.

I was touched by Errick's prayer. In the months since our accident, my dislike for him eased. I fell in love with Saxon more each day when he took the step to get to know Errick. It was slow going, but they were civil and at times even cordial. I thought Errick realized that Saxon loved Kiernon unconditionally, enough to share her with another man.

Ellen and Anna had the kids seated by them. They always took over when we had family functions. Anna fed Kiernon while Ellen took over with Dathan. Dinner was filled with laughter, good conversation, and great vibes. I hadn't been this happy in a long time. I sat with Saxon at my side, my daughter was healthy, and the baby was growing. I was thankful for these moments.

Later that afternoon, after almost everyone left, Saxon and I walked Errick to the door. He'd stayed around awhile playing with Kiernon and the other kids. At the door he told us he'd be right back. He ran out to his car, then returned, pushing a little baby pram. He brought it inside and called Kiernon over. When she saw the stroller and baby doll inside, she screamed with happiness. Errick took the doll from the stroller to give to her. When I saw the baby, tears stung my eyes. The baby was an exact replica of Kiernon.

"Baby." Kiernon took the doll, squeezing her tightly.

"Yes, that's baby, Kiernon," Errick told her.

Our eyes met, and for the first time in a long time, I saw the considerate man I used to know.

"Thank you. This is gorgeous," I told him with a friendly hug. When we parted, I saw he had tears in his eyes as well.

"I ordered this before the accident. I'm just so glad she's here to have it," he said, and my heart ached for him.

"Thanks, man. I'm sure this will be one of her favorite things."

It appeared that way, because Kiernon was already walking around, carrying the baby with one arm. The three of us watched her for a few minutes in companionable silence.

We'd come a long way.

Chapter Seventy-nine

Rachel & Saxon

Rachel

"Come on baby, push," Saxon encouraged me.

Taking a deep breath, I pushed. I was so thankful for the epidural. I'd been in labor for fourteen hours and was more than ready for the baby to make an appearance.

"All right, mom, one more push and your baby will be here."

Bracing myself, I pushed again, tears blurring my vision as sweat stung my eyes. I heard the sharp wail of my baby as the doctor cleaned out the mouth and nose passages with a syringe. Saxon kissed me, his eyes filled with unshed tears.

"Mom, dad, you have a beautiful little girl," Dr. Charles announced.

A daughter. Another beautiful girl for our family. Kiernon was going to be so excited to be a big sister to a little girl. At least I hoped so.

"I love you," Saxon whispered, wiping my damp forehead with a towel.

He cut the cord. I watched as he took the baby in his arms for the first time. I was filled with love as he brought our daughter to me. He laid the baby on my chest, and I cried as I kissed her little fist. I was so thankful that the baby was healthy. I was thankful that the delivery was relatively easy. But I was most thankful that I had Saxon here with me sharing the birth of our second baby girl.

After the nurses gave her a quick wipe down, I counted fingers and toes. She cried as she stretched her little body out, her face scrunched up and her wails loud. After the scare with the accident, her cries were music to my ears.

Saxon

Watching with pride as my wife checked over our daughter, my heart was full right now. Seeing my daughter born made me realize how blessed my little family was. Rachel, Kiernon, and this baby were my entire world. I couldn't wait for Rachel and the baby to be released so I could have all my girls at home with me.

Rachel had the glow of contentment. She was beautiful as she studied our daughter, her eyes filled with love and amazement. I loved that about her. She always made me feel like the most loved, cherished man in the world. Our family was the most important thing to her, and I knew she would always make our lives as good as she could.

Placing a soft kiss on her lips after the nurses took the baby to be cleaned up, I couldn't stop staring at her. She was the perfect woman for me, and I was so glad she gave me the opportunity to love her and let me be a daddy to our girls.

Chapter Eighty

Saxon & Errick

Saxon

Bursting into the waiting room, I looked around at all the expectant faces. Mom and Dad, Anna and Paul, Moira and Daniel, Rosie, and Errick were there, waiting for news of the birth.

Dad and Paul were pacing like they were expectant fathers. Mom and Anna were laughing at them, teasing them. When they realized it was me, they turned with expectant looks on their faces.

"It's a girl," I announced.

The waiting room erupted with laughter, shouts of happiness and thanks, chatter, and congratulations. I was passed from one set of arms to the next as I tried to hug everyone. There were slaps on the backs, there were kisses, there were tears, but most importantly, there was joy.

I stopped in front of Errick. He held Kiernon in his arms.

Errick

"Congratulations, man." I shook Saxon's hand. "How is Rachel?"

"Thanks, man. She's fine."

Over the last several weeks, Saxon and I spent time together, mostly taking Kiernon and his niece and nephew to the park or to some other kid-friendly places. It was something I never saw coming, but we seemed to be becoming friends. I wanted him to know that, despite our past, I wasn't trying to cause problems between him and Rachel. He was a good dude, and he loved Rachel and Kiernon without a doubt.

"Daddy." Kiernon reached for him.

It didn't hurt as much now when I heard her call him Daddy. I was thankful for the place I had in her life.

"Thanks for letting me be here."

"No problem, man. I wanted to talk to you about something."

I left Kiernon with my mom, then followed him out into the hall away from the others. I waited to see what he was going to say.

"Rachel and I have been talking."

"Okay?" I wasn't sure where he was going with this.

"We would like you to be the baby's godfather. That is, if you'd like."

I was speechless. Was he serious? *They want me to be their baby's godfather.* My heart wrenched in my chest. I didn't know how to feel, but I couldn't believe it.

"Are you serious? Rachel wants this too?"

"Yes, we both want it," Saxon assured me.

My heart lightened. Knowing that Rachel wanted to include me in this made me want to cry. "I'd be honored. Thank you."

Chapter Eighty-one

Rachel & Errick

Rachel

The door opened. Errick stuck his head in when I called for whoever it was to come in. I was propped up in the bed, the baby wrapped up in my arms. I felt peaceful and content. I knew it showed on my face.

"Hey. How are you?"

"Hey, I'm good."

"You look good. How's the baby?"

Smiling at the compliment, I shook my head. "Bullshit, but thank you. She's good. You want to hold her?"

"Really?"

There was a little uncertainty in his gaze. I held her out for him to take. His expression as he looked down at her was one of amazement. I felt the same way.

Errick bounced her gently in his arms. "She's beautiful."

"She is."

Errick

Rachel's baby was gorgeous. She was light brown, the color of chocolate milk, with a head full of dark brown hair. Her eyes were closed, and her little hands were balled up into fists. She was sleeping with her little mouth open. She was perfect just like her big sister.

"What's her name?" Saxon never told me.

"Ashton. Ashton Kyleigh Carmichael."

"Ashton," I repeated softly. "Hello, Ashton."

The baby's eyes fluttered open, and she blinked, trying to focus on me. I chuckled as a quizzical expression crossed her face.

"I talked to Saxon. He told me you want me to be god-father?" I looked over at Rachel, and she looked peaceful.

Rachel studied me for a long time. There was a lot of water under the bridge, and I would have never imagined us here when I proposed to her. She was married, having a family with another man.

"Yes," Rachel said, breaking the silence. She smiled, and her eyes sparkled. "Yes, Saxon and I want you to be her godfather."

The little bundle in my arms squirmed, letting out a tiny squeak, getting our attention only to release a small grunt and pass gas. Our eyes meeting, we laughed at Ashton as she settled back to sleep.

"Thank you, Rachel. Thank you for everything."

Chapter Eighty-two

Rachel

"'Happy birthday to you.'" The chorus of voices ended on a high note before there were cheers and clapping.

Candles were blown out, the cake was cut, and I was ready to open presents and finish out the day. We were celebrating Kiernon's fifth birthday. I still couldn't believe my big girl was 5. The last several years had been good. Saxon and I just celebrated our fourth wedding anniversary with a trip to Antigua. He still had his practice with the association where I met him, but his patient roster had increased. He worked four days a week, twelve hours a day, so we could spend the weekends with the kids. I was still a stay-at-home mom, but I started writing children's books. I hooked up with a publisher, and my first book became a bestseller. I'd written seven books and was working on my eighth.

Anna and Paul were living their best lives. They were now the grandparents of four. Along with Kiernon, they had twin grandsons from Aimee and her husband and a granddaughter from Jamie. They loved having all the kids, including mine, anytime they could get them. Ellen and Connor were still spoiling all their grandbabies, too. Moira and Daniel now had three children. They had a daughter a year ago, and they said they were done. Rosie had settled down and was in a long-term relationship with a man she met at the bank. At the time she met him she didn't realize he was the chief financial officer and a millionaire. You would never be able to tell. He was down-to-earth, and he didn't carry himself like he was rich.

"Here, babe. He wants you."

Taking my 7-month-old son, Slade, from him, I kissed his fat cheeks. Saxon and I had four kids. We had our daughter Rowan eighteen months after Ashton, and then Slade came along.

"You having fun?" Saxon took the seat next to me.

"I always have fun when I'm with you and the kids."

Errick came over with an envelope in his hand. "This is for Kiernon's college fund."

I knew it was money. He gave me money for each of the kids' birthdays to put toward their education. There were times I looked back over the past several years and still couldn't believe everything I'd been through. When Errick left me all those years ago, I was devastated and couldn't imagine how I could get over the pain. Saxon came into my life and swept me off my feet. He loved me through the ups and downs, and he stuck around even when I tried to shut him out. I would have never thought I would marry him and have four kids with him.

The best thing I'd ever done in my life was allowing myself to be loved by him. Saxon showed me that love was unconditional, and I tried every day to do the same for him and our little family.